MW00528157

Sweet Thing

Sweet Thing

A Novel

David Swinson

MULHOLLAND BOOKS

LITTLE, BROWN AND COMPANY

NEW YORK   BOSTON   LONDON

Copyright © 2023 by David Swinson

Hachette Book Group supports the right to free expression and the value of copyright. The purpose of copyright is to encourage writers and artists to produce the creative works that enrich our culture.

The scanning, uploading, and distribution of this book without permission is a theft of the author's intellectual property. If you would like permission to use material from the book (other than for review purposes), please contact permissions@hbgusa.com. Thank you for your support of the author's rights.

Mulholland Books / Little, Brown and Company
Hachette Book Group
1290 Avenue of the Americas, New York, NY 10104
mulhollandbooks.com

First Edition: November 2023

Mulholland Books is an imprint of Little, Brown and Company, a division of Hachette Book Group, Inc. The Mulholland Books name and logo are trademarks of Hachette Book Group, Inc.

The publisher is not responsible for websites (or their content) that are not owned by the publisher.

The Hachette Speakers Bureau provides a wide range of authors for speaking events. To find out more, go to hachettespeakersbureau.com or email hachettespeakers@hbgusa.com.

Little, Brown and Company books may be purchased in bulk for business, educational, or promotional use. For information, please contact your local bookseller or the Hachette Book Group Special Markets Department at special.markets@hbgusa.com.

Library of Congress Control Number: 2023936414
ISBN 9780316528610

Printing 1, 2023

LSC-C

Printed in the United States of America

For Jennifer Leigh Fries

Let's pray that the human race never escapes
from Earth to spread its iniquity elsewhere.
—C. S. Lewis

What is terrible in what I did? Don't we forgive
everything of a lover? We forgive selfishness,
desire, guile. As long as we are the motive for it.
—Michael Ondaatje, *The English Patient*

Sweet Thing

There is a hell, but it's not what you think.

It's worse.

An infinite darkness, but in the distance, a tiny pinhole of light. The light doesn't seep into the darkness. And there's a kingdom through the pinhole—what I know is some kinda heaven. Comfort. But it's a place I'll never get to, for my darkness will be an eternity of suffering. There's no sense of time. I am aware of everything but have no physical body. I am everywhere and nowhere.

I kissed her on the corner of her mouth, reached for the pack of cigs on the nightstand and offered one. I lit hers first and then mine. Grabbed the ashtray and set it on the bed between us. She blew a perfect smoke ring. I watched it as it lingered for a bit and frittered away. She grabbed the bottle of vodka off the nightstand on her side of the bed, took a hefty swig, passed it over to me. I did the same and handed it back and after another healthy swallow she set it back on the nightstand.

She snuffed her cigarette out and said, "I have to pee," and slipped out of bed.

She walked like she was moving to a song in her head. Made love the same way. Always at the end her back would arch and she moaned like the gentle release of breath held, finally letting go. That's what I liked most. The sound, the visual—how she lived at that moment. It was intoxicating. Addicting.

Her death was like that too.

1

The redbrick row house was located in a quiet, well-maintained neighborhood off 18th in Northwest DC. Last time my partner, Kelly Ryan, and I were called to this area it was for a suicide. That was about a year ago. Couple of blocks north of here. Hoped that's what this was. A murder at this location would draw attention. Surprised the news reporters weren't already on the scene. Last thing we both wanted was something high profile, and another dramatic conclusion to a story we had to piece together with a resolution we could only hope for.

Three marked cruisers and an unmarked detective cruiser were double-parked in front of the house. It was on a narrow one-way road lined with ginkgo trees. Late fall and the duck-feet-shaped leaves were beginning to turn yellow. A beautiful sight, but the fruit from most of the trees would soon fall to the sidewalk and leave the worst kind of smell, like ripened shit. A body was like fallen fruit too. Everything falls. That was the world we lived in. The world I was reminded of every time I was about to walk into a crime scene.

In my job, OCD was your best friend. I was trained to be enslaved by routine. Procedure was our ally. Procedure was my obsession. General orders were like Leviticus.

Everything was defined. I was defined by this.

Two of the marked cruisers belonged to Third District patrol, the other one to the district watch commander. Too many feet trampling on a crime scene, is what I thought. And that was usually the case, because they all wanted to see a dead body. The best I could hope for was a good Crime Scene Search officer to keep the scene contained, but they hadn't arrived yet. I was one of those types back in the day: rushed to the scene for a shooting, stabbing, or an unconscious male or female, hoping to find a dead body. I remembered my first. Stayed with you like the first girl you had sex with. I have devout memories of both.

Still hoped for a suicide at this location.

No curbside parking, so we pulled in front of the detective cruiser. Concerned neighbors standing on their front porches and sidewalks looking on. We stepped out of the car. Two uniformed officers were on the stoop at the front door. One of them I recognized. A master patrol officer who'd been on for a bit. I didn't recognize the younger one. Made our way up, shot the MPO an upward nod.

"What's up, boys," he said.

"Just another day," Kelly replied.

The young officer looked at our name tags and wrote in his notebook. He stepped aside to let us enter as we put latex gloves on.

The familiar stench of a dead body that had been there for a few days lingered heavily inside. Not so bad as other scenes.

The watch commander, a tall, thin older man, was in the living room talking on his Nextel. All the command and most of the detectives, especially in Homicide, were issued Nextel cell phones. Pain in the ass, really, because they could always get in touch with us. Not as easy to ignore as a pager.

He glanced at us sideways and said over the phone, "The Homicide detectives arrived. I'll call you back. Yes, sir."

"Blum. Ryan," he said, pronouncing my name like Bloom. Most people did. I got tired of correcting them.

"Lieutenant," I acknowledged.

Two officers entered from another room.

"I'm assuming they were the first on the scene?" Ryan asked.

"They were."

Ryan pulled her notebook from her rear pants pocket. I noticed that she wrote down the date and the LT's name as being on the scene. The officers stepped up.

"The body's in the dining room," the overweight one advised. "Crime Scene's on the way."

"How was the body discovered?" I asked.

"Out-of-state sister called 911 to check on the welfare of her brother after she hadn't heard from him in days, and he never returned her messages. We responded. The front door was slightly opened. We could smell the stench of the dead body, so we entered, announced ourselves, but got no response. Found the body where it lay. Called for Homicide and the Fireboard. EMTs left just before you guys got here. Declared him dead on the scene."

"You have the sister's information then?"

"Yes."

Ryan flipped a page in her notebook. The officer took out his, flipped through.

"Robin Doyle," he said, and then provided a phone number and address.

Ryan wrote it in her notebook.

"Brother's name?"

"Chris Doyle."

"All right then," Ryan said. "You can release the scene to us, Lieutenant. We got it from here."

The LT glared at Ryan like he didn't like taking orders from a woman or he deserved a more respectful tone. "You heard the big boys," he told his officers, and they followed him toward the door.

Ryan smiled, like she knew he was mocking her with "big boys." I knew she didn't give a shit.

"Appreciate if you keep the two other officers at the door, LT," I said politely.

He nodded and walked out.

"It ain't pretty," the older, overweight officer's partner told us before exiting.

Wasn't like we hadn't heard that before. We walked toward the dining room.

2

The odor was sharper. Stung the nostrils.

Detective Bobby Butner was in the dining room, standing a few feet from the body, which was on the tiled floor flat on its back. Blood everywhere.

Butner was a good detective, made a name for himself working robberies at the district level. Always was a good source of information when it came to corner thug-boy shootings in 3D.

"What's going on?" he said.

"Don't want to be here, that's for sure," Ryan said bluntly.

I shot Butner a nod.

We scanned the room for a few seconds, then moved to the decedent. Dried blood was thick on the tiled floor around the head and upper body. Looked like you could ice-skate on it. Nose and left eye were swollen and bruised. Nose had to be broken. Blood from both nostrils, now dried and purplish in color, painted over the upper lip and left corner of the mouth. The collar and chest area of the blue long-sleeved dress shirt was also covered in blood. Looked like he took a couple, maybe more, of small-caliber rounds in the chest.

"Anyone disturb the body?"

"Not our people," Butner replied. "EMT did a quick check but didn't move the body."

"Need to confirm this is Chris Doyle," Ryan said.

"What's your story?" I whispered to the dead man.

"His story is maybe he got himself into a bad fight with someone he knew. Looks like he was a lover boy to me. Probably let the suspect in. Place doesn't look ransacked. Suspect left in a hurry and didn't close the door. Domestic is what I think," Butner said.

"Nose looks broken so obviously a fight. Like I said, probably domestic," Kelly said.

"That'd be too easy. Don't think we can get that lucky."

I turned to notice two Crime Scene Search officers entering.

"Good to see it's you two," Kelly told them.

Like Butner, Troy and Kimble were two workers. Couple of boys you could depend on. They were both old-timers, having spent most of their years at Crime Scene Search. We let them have the scene to do their thing. Didn't have to say much. They knew what to do. Kelly and I broke up to search the rooms.

"Maybe he doesn't have a mobile phone, but hopefully a wallet with identification somewhere," I told Kelly. "Maybe in one of his pockets. Wait for the ME first."

"I'll take the kitchen for now," she said. "Maybe get lucky and find something in the trash."

"I'll start here."

"And I'm outta here unless you guys need me. We're shorthanded and I'm the only one on call."

"See you around," I said, as Butner walked out.

Based on the nice wooden furniture, and fine art and numbered prints on the wall, it appeared that the decedent was well off. Place looked nice. Well kept. Furniture appeared to be recently polished. *Suspect do that?* Maybe it was an attempt to wipe it clean of possible prints? I opened the humidor on the bookshelf. It was filled with nice cigars.

"Aside from the body on the floor, it's too damn clean in here," I told Troy and Kimble.

"I like a nice clean crime scene," Kimble said.

"Yeah, makes your job easier, huh? But not ours."

"Got that right."

Not much was in the dining room. Decided I'd get back to the body when they finished with photos. I walked back into the living room.

Kelly entered.

"Searched the trash and didn't find anything useful. I did find a scale, cutting agents for heroin or coke, and several baggies and a ton of clear little zips that would hold tens and twenties."

"He was probably dealing then?"

"Looks that way."

"I'm gonna go find his bedroom," I advised.

"I'll be up in a minute."

"All right."

A narrow staircase led to the second floor. I walked up, careful not to touch the banister. The hallway was also narrow. Three doors. One to each side of the hallway, and another in the middle across from the banister. The bedroom doors at each end were open. Middle door opened into a bathroom. Looked over the sink, then opened the shower curtain. Everything spotless.

The door to the left of the bathroom led to the master bedroom. I stepped in. The king-size bed was unmade. There were two other doors, with one that led into a walk-in closet and the other the master bathroom. Large painting on the wall above the headboard. To me it looked like a nude in abstract, but that's just the way my mind works. Probably nothing but splotches of paint, like a Rorschach test. Other smaller pieces on the other walls.

No computer was here either, but maybe he kept that at an office somewhere. A Nokia cell phone, wallet, and a Rolex were on the nightstand. I checked the wallet. It contained a couple of credit cards and a DC driver's license, but no cash. The name and photo on the license confirmed that the body was Christopher Doyle. Someone would have stolen the cards and that Rolex, even the cell. I was surprised they were still there. No telling how long that front door was left open. Lot of burglaries in this area. Maybe there was an attempt, but after seeing the dead body in the dining room the burglar decided to get the hell outta there.

The cell phone would be going with us.

I opened the nightstand drawer. Looked like an "everything drawer," filled with change, papers, couple of rings, and a flash-light. After Crime Scene took photos, I'd go through everything. I looked under the bed, found a shoebox. Pulled it out. It was filled with photos, including a stack of Polaroids. I picked up those first. Several taken of nude women, posing in all sorts of ways and smiling like they were high. Most of them looked nice, not like crackheads. Looked to have been taken on the king-size bed. One photo, though. Fuck. It was the decedent arm and arm with Arthur Holland. Son of a bitch. *Arthur.* My fucking confidential informant from when I was assigned to the narcotics branch before I got to Homicide. What are the odds of that? I looked over my shoulder. It was clear. I slipped the photo into the inner pocket of my suit jacket. Decided I was gonna keep this to myself for now. Probably not the best decision, but I've been known to make a few bad ones in my time.

3

I searched the other room but didn't find anything worth taking. Crime Scene dusted the paraphernalia that Kelly found. Got a couple of good prints. Latent prints were also recovered throughout the house. Kelly and I took a few items that might prove useful, like the cell phone, the decedent's wallet and keys to the house, and the shoebox containing the photos, minus the Polaroid of Arthur, of course. The cell phone was good. Kelly was probably right, and the decedent knew the suspect and the numbers on the cell might lead us to who it was. I was hoping that Arthur would not be that person. He made some great cases for me back in the day, but other than that, he was nothing but a piece of shit. Would have had nothing to do with him if he hadn't been such a great informant. I got close to him back then, so I had to look into him myself. I trusted Kelly with my life, but because of my history with Arthur, I had to keep this one from her. For now, anyway.

When we got back to the office I told Kelly I had some personal shit to take care of and asked if she'd cover for me. I'd done it for her several times when it came to her kid.

"I'll take care of the write-up," she advised.

"Shouldn't be more than a couple of hours."

"No worries. Do what you have to."

As soon as I'd left her at the office and rounded the corner in our car, I grabbed my cell from my suit and scrolled until I found Arthur's number. Tapped to call. It went to an automated voice mail. I didn't leave a message. I headed toward Rhode Island Avenue, NE, where I hoped Arthur still lived. He had a three-story brick row house that he'd inherited from his deceased mother. Mortgage paid. Last time I was there, the place looked like shit. He lived with a young girl. Celeste. They never maintained the home. A drug lifestyle and all that shit. The house stood on the corner of Rhode Island Ave, like so many of the other deteriorating homes. But when I arrived, it was a far cry from that, like it had a face-lift. The yard on the sides of the steps that led to the patio had mums of different colors planted, along with other seasonal perennials. The red brick was now a soft blue. I wondered if he had sold it.

I found a parking spot around the corner. The neighborhood was still a bit rough. Couple of boys who were standing on the corner at the next street a block from Rhode Island had made me. They spit on the sidewalk and slunk away. I looked up to the windows at the side of his house. Blinds were closed, but there was a dim light through the slits. That was where the dining room was. I admired the yard as I walked up the few steps to the patio. A couple of wicker patio chairs were to the right of the door. I rang the doorbell. Waited a second and tapped on the cast-iron security door. The metal rattled a bit. Heard movement, like light steps along a creaky wooden floor. There was a pause and I assumed whoever was on the other side of the door was checking me out through the peephole.

"Can I help you?" asked a female voice. It was a delicate tone. Sounded young. Like Celeste.

"I was looking for Arthur. Didn't know if he still lived here. My name is Alexander. I'm an old friend of his."

The door opened. It was Celeste. Few years older, but still beautiful as ever. Maybe even more beautiful. Like she had cleaned up, except for the bruises on her arms. I was pretty sure what that was from. Fucking Arthur. I didn't see any tracks. Her hair was a wavy light brown and shoulder length. She was stunning. It took me a second to compose myself. Hoped she didn't realize. Women's intuition, though. Much stronger than a detective's, so I'm sure she knew and was also probably used to it.

"Detective Blum."

I loved how she said my last name. She said it right. Didn't forget.

"Hi, Celeste. I'm glad you remember me."

"How could I forget."

"The place looks great. You two made some nice changes. You look good too."

"Thanks. Lot of work on my part, but yes. I got tired of living like a squatter. Arthur isn't here right now. In fact, I don't know where he is. Why are you here?"

"Just needed to get with him about something."

"Get with him about something? I know he's still involved with that kinda work but didn't think it was with you anymore."

"It's not. I'm with Homicide now and I think he can help me with something."

"Homicide? What would Artie know about anything having to do with that?"

"I don't know if he does, but I still need to get with him, 'cause you never know. He's not in any trouble, though. He didn't answer his cell, so I thought I'd drop by. Do you know when he'll be home?"

"He hasn't been home for two days."

"Do you know where he is?"

17

"No. You know how he disappears sometimes. It's usually because of what he does with cops he works with. I don't question it. Never did."

"Do you know who he's working with now?"

"No. Like I said, I don't question anything anymore. It's safer that way."

I knew what she meant.

I smiled like I wanted to show comfort and said, "I need to talk to him. Can you get in touch with him?"

"I tried and left a message. Do you have a card? If I hear from him I'll have him call you."

"Yes."

I pulled out a card from a leather card case in my front pants pocket and handed it to her. She looked it over.

"Yes, it says Homicide. You're moving up, Detective Blum."

"I don't know if I'd say that."

"I'll pass it along to him when I see him."

"Thanks. You doing okay, by the way?"

That seemed to confuse her, like why would I be asking that.

"I'm doing just fine."

I had to wonder how the hell someone like Arthur ever hooked up with someone like her. I know back in the day it was all about drugs, but he was at least fifteen years older, and last time I saw him, a bit disheveled in appearance.

"All right then. I appreciate your time. Please be sure to tell him it's important that I speak to him."

"I will, and like I said, I'll pass this on to him when I see him."

"Appreciate it."

"Detective Alexander Blum," she read off the card one more time, like it was supposed to mean something. "Been a long time since I heard that name."

And I liked hearing her say it.

She closed the door before I could respond. I stood there for a second, taken by surprise.

As I walked along the side of the house, I noticed her peeking through the blinds, checking me out. The boys at the corner were gone. I drove around the block and back to Rhode Island, where I found an illegal parking spot with a good vantage of Arthur's house, and far enough back that I wouldn't be made. I'd give it an hour, see if he showed. Don't want to stay out too long and leave Kelly to do all the work.

It was chilly out, a nice breeze. I cracked the window to allow a little fresh air in, get rid of some of that cigarette stench that remained from Kelly's occasional smoking and mine. After forty-five minutes of surveillance, I made my way back to the office. There *was* a dead body that needed some attention, and for some reason I could only think about Celeste.

4

I worry about things. Sometimes I worry about having nothing to worry about.

Like now.

I don't worry about death, just the means of death. I was allowed back once before, but the road back wasn't fun. I got stabbed way back when I was a rookie in uniform. Routine patrol. A domestic violence situation and I didn't wait for my backup. If it had ended that night, all I would have realized was a fearful, hopefully temporary discomfort.

I'm one of the few who survived. And it is *few*. If you were to consider all the deaths resulting from crime in this country alone, and then all the victims and survivors like me, you'd realize we are a select few.

What I feared most in life now were things like sudden blindness, dementia, getting caught up in a bad shooting, maybe going bald. That was by no means a comprehensive list. I'm sure I could come up with more, but I didn't want to think about it, or it'd stay in my head for the day.

I was hoping to get through the remainder of this tour without another call. We had a full squad, but if it was something like a multiple then we'd all have to go.

A lot of people were being moved around in the department. The result of a new mayor taking office at the beginning of the year. A city councilman made mayor. Had the backing that came from a powerful community, a confederation of loud voices and old money. But our new mayor also had the talent to not only convince those who were less fortunate in life that he could make a difference but unite them around the idea. Those were the people in this city who could provide a candidate the winning numbers.

The new mayor named a new chief during the transition. He was the reason for all the movement around here. Months of preparation and only a couple of days to shake the whole department up.

Change was inevitable in this line of work. You could depend on it, like the changing of seasons, but you could never accurately predict what would come with it. There were those who've tried. All they got at the end was a reputation for having looked stupid. The best thing to do during times like this was to keep your head down, do your job, and wait for the teletype. Cry later if you had to, but only in the privacy of your own home.

You choose your position in life. The ones that choose rank damn well better make sure they also chose the right side. Members like me—the lowly working homicide detectives—didn't have sides, just jobs. Fortunately, we didn't have to worry much. We had too many cases to handle.

The cell phone we recovered still had some of the fingerprint dust on it. I wore my latex gloves anyway and scrolled through the numbers. Some with saved names that I wrote down along with the number. Kelly was in a cubicle behind me, on the phone with the jurisdiction in Philly where the sister lived, coordinating to get a supervisor to go to her residence and advise her of her brother's death. We'd have to talk to her after the notification was made, though. Kelly was better at that sort of thing. She had a way with connecting with family members.

I found Arthur's name in the cell phone. Checked the info on it and found that it was the same number I had for him. Looked like they talked a couple of days ago. That would be about the same time as the homicide, but I wouldn't know the time frame for the death for sure until we received an autopsy report from the ME. Worried me, though. Actually, more than worried me. Didn't know if I could keep this from my partner. Gonna end up fucking myself at the end if it turned bad. I heard Kelly behind me, still talking on the phone. I used the decedent's cell to call Arthur, see if he'd pick up. It rang a few times and went straight to the automated message again.

Damn.

Cell battery looked healthy. There were several other incoming and outgoing calls on his cell. Several of the incoming calls were made yesterday and even today. Seems our boy was popular. We'd have to identify all the numbers and who they came back to.

Kelly must've read my mind, because she asked behind me, "You going to check the book for the numbers that might be a landline see if they come back to anyone?"

"Yeah, was just about to record the numbers and do that."

I knew Arthur's would not come back to him because it was a cell. It's not always a guarantee, but our thick-as-hell book we had did have addresses for most hardline numbers. If that failed then we'd do it the old-fashioned way and make cold calls, being careful not to reveal that it was about a homicide. Kelly was good at that, too. She could easily play whoever was at the other end of the call. If we found someone to be uncooperative, then we'd subpoena the carrier for the phone number to find out who it came back to.

It took a while to go through the directory. I was able to get listings for several of the numbers, but not even close to all of them. I was taken by surprise to find one of the numbers coming back to Arthur's address. It was his hardline, a number I didn't have. I realized it was something I could no longer keep to myself.

5

E nded up working a double. By the time I got home it was close to midnight and all I wanted to do was go to bed. My landline was blinking red. I hesitated to check the messages because I already knew it would more than likely be my mother. I picked up the phone despite my reluctant side advising me otherwise.

Four messages.

The first one:

What have I done for all of you to treat me like this? Nobody, nobody talks to me. Nobody answers the phone. Why don't you, Alex? Why won't you answer? What about Abigail? Have you heard from her? Do you know where she is?

I knew the next one would be her too, but still, I listened.

Why don't you answer my calls, bubbeleh? You avoid me. I'm your mother and I feel like I don't have a son...

She was calling me bubbeleh a lot lately, like the dementia was taking her back in time to experience her Ashkenazi Jewish heritage. She was born in Brooklyn, but my grandparents, who I never knew, were Jews from Ukraine. She could speak the Yiddish fluently. I always struggled. She was now in Richmond. I put her up in a Jewish assisted living facility there. It's about an hour and a half from me, but it is made affordable with her insurance, and we have a couple of cousins there too who would look in on her. She was not so far gone that she needed full care, but the disease was progressing. There were good days and very bad days. This was a bad day. It was painful, and I have been negligent.

The next one was her too. Same kind of message but said with more anger. She'd sometimes forget that I talked to her. Talked to her almost every day. Her brain was dying a slow death. I felt guilt and anger at the same time. No reason for the guilt. At least I tried to convince myself of that, but still, there it was. I was going to call her. Tomorrow morning, though.

I did often wonder where my sister Abigail was. I followed her from Brooklyn to DC long before my mother was losing her mind. Abigail was five years older than me, and left New York to live with a musician here. We were always close. I moved a couple of years later, joined the department. Always entertained the idea of becoming a cop. Having a pension was great too. Eight months later, when I graduated from the academy, Abigail broke up with her boyfriend and without a word packed up and left DC. Last I heard, she was in California. Probably another musician, or maybe one herself. She was a talented singer. She was tough, fearless. That's why I never worried about her. I often wondered, though, because I missed her.

I went to the bedroom and undressed. Put my badge, pager, leather pouch that held two magazines, my Glock 17, and handcuffs on the dresser across from my bed. I folded my suit jacket and pants over an armchair. Tossed my shirt in the dry-cleaning hamper in my closet. Last I set my cell down on the nightstand and fell on top of the covers in nothing but my T-shirt, boxer shorts, and socks. Tried to find sleep, tried to find peace, but the case we just caught, Arthur's possible involvement, and the mournful sound of my mother's voice stayed with me. For some reason the image of Celeste popped into my head. Such a beautiful creature. Oddly enough, that made me feel better. Don't know why.

An anxiety dream woke me up at six thirty. It involved another shootout where my gun fell apart in my hands so I couldn't get any rounds off. I couldn't fall back asleep, though, so I got out of bed, dragged myself to the bathroom to take a piss and then to the kitchen to brew a strong pot of coffee. Poured myself a cup and sat on the leather recliner to watch the morning news. According to a reporter, the world was expected to shut down when the clock struck midnight on January 1, 2000. A fucking apocalypse. That was a little over two months away and the way I was feeling, it didn't sound so bad. Let the world shut off. Bring on the chaos. Maybe that's what we needed, darkness and a global fucking reboot. Then there came a report on the murder we caught "in a quiet neighborhood of Northwest, DC," where, of course, something like that was not expected to happen. My cell phone rang shortly after the report. Kelly's number on the display. I hesitated to flip it open and answer, but then thought at least it wasn't the commander so how bad could it be.

"I saw it," I told her.

"Didn't think you'd be up. LT woke me up after he saw it on the news. You ready for some overtime? Ching ching, baby."

"Fuck that shit. I haven't even got through my first cup of coffee."

"That's what 7-Eleven's for. I'll be at the office in about an hour."

"Damn news. I'll see you there."

"Like you have a choice, fuckwad."

"Fuck you." And I flip the cell closed, hanging up on her.

No amount of coffee was gonna help me. What I was experiencing was beyond fatigue. Not even close to fifty and my body ached like I was in my eighties. My brain even worse. I would never admit stress, though. That was a dirty word in the department, but I damn well was suffering from it. I knew that much, and it wasn't all about the job. I couldn't shake my mother from my head. It had happened so quick, one day she was there and the next she was losing it. Only a matter of time before it took her away.

I stopped at the 7-Eleven on Connecticut Avenue despite knowing the coffee wouldn't help anyway. When I got to the office I realized I didn't call my mother. I'd find the time later in the day. I hoped.

Kelly was at her cubicle going through the photos in the shoebox, specifically the Polaroids of the naked women. Sean Caine, one of the detectives from the squad on daywork, was hunched over Kelly's shoulder, looking hard at one of the photos.

"Damn," he said. "Your decedent was into some nasty shit. Couple of them not so bad, though."

Caine turned to see me, shot me a nod. I sent one back, set my coffee on my desk, dropped my shoulder pack, and sat down. Wanted to cradle my head in my folded arms and close my eyes for a while, but doing something like that on daywork was difficult. Midnights it was easier to get away with. Most of the time on midnights, if nothing was going on, we'd turn all the lights off in the office, except for the one or two cubicle lamps that a working detective kept on, and we'd catch up on our sleep before court. There was only Caine and his partner, Jacoby, there for daywork. Everyone else was in court or on the street.

"Let me see that one again?" I heard Caine ask.

"Get off my back already. I can smell your breath. It's foul."

"You actually think you're going to get any of these women identified?" Caine asked.

"Of course not."

"One of them he fucked was probably married. Husband found out and that was that," he said.

"You wanna take this case from us? Seems like you got a lot of interest."

"Hell no, Kell. I got my own shit to deal with."

"Then why the hell don't you go deal with it."

"Give him a break," I said. "See if he's good enough to get anyone in the photos identified."

"Oh, you know I might be good enough, but I don't want to steal your glory. You caught yourself a high-profile one here, and it's all you."

With that he walked away and said, "Gonna go get myself some breakfast. You coming, Jac?"

"Yeah," Jacoby replied from a cubicle on the other side of the office.

"You want to follow up on some of those names from the directory sometime today?" I asked.

"Yeah, that'd be good."

Thought to myself again that it'd probably be a good time to advise Kelly about Arthur. Even give up the photo I pocketed. She'd give me some shit but nothing more. I trusted her enough that she wouldn't take it further than that. Arthur was the only lead we had. I didn't want to believe he had anything to do with the murder, despite the piece of shit he used to be and how he abused Celeste. Still kicking myself for never doing anything about that. I felt terrible about it then. Still do. Despite her lifestyle, she was an innocent. Arthur was the kind of guy who kept his ear to the curb and knew what was going on. He was great and that's why I left it alone. Maybe he'd be good for that kind of info again and could identify some of the people in the photographs. Yeah, I couldn't keep it from my partner, but in order to keep the language that would spew out of her mouth in my direction a little more private, I decided to wait until we got in the car.

Smelled like snow when we stepped out. Comforting.

I stepped into the passenger side.

"Have something I need to tell you before we go."

She started the car to get it warmed up.

"Sounds serious. You finally meet a girl?" she joked.

For some reason, Celeste popped into my head again. Why the fuck did that keep happening?

I took the photo of Arthur and the decedent out of the inner pocket of my suit jacket. Looked at it for a second and handed it over to Kelly.

After looking at it briefly she turned to me and asked, "What the hell is this?"

"Something I picked up at the scene and decided to keep to myself for a bit."

Kelly looked confused but said nothing.

"The dude with the decedent is a former CI of mine when I was at the branch. He made some big cases for me. I called him Superman. I owe him a lot."

"Okay, that's significant. Important shit, so explain why you thought to keep it to yourself?"

"I don't really have an answer 'cept my first thought was to protect my CI, look into it for myself first. I was gonna turn it in."

"That's bullshit and you know it. Fuck, he's a possible suspect. You were thinking you'd protect him? You pocketed fucking evidence. You owe him your pension?"

"Don't act like you're so clean, Kell."

"I wouldn't keep something like this from you, fuckhead." She looked at the photo again. "So you talk to him without me?"

"No. I think he's in the wind. Won't get back to me."

"Shit, Alexander. In the wind? We lost more than a day on this. I don't know what you were thinking."

"I went to his house yesterday and talked to his girl. She hadn't seen or heard from him in a couple of days."

"We need to go back there. Now. If we don't find him, then get a BOLO out right away."

"Yeah, I know."

"Shit. Give me the fucking address."

6

K elly was harder on her than I would have been. Made it sound like she didn't have a choice. Hindering an investigation and all that shit. We were inside the house within a couple of minutes. I noticed that the tennis trophies were still on the buffet table in the dining room. Always wondered about them, but never asked Arthur.

I kept thinking how the hell could someone like her be with someone like Arthur? Probably because she was still using. But then, I looked the place over. Did he finally get his act together, quit heroin, and clean up? Get himself looking better in the process. Start taking showers? Celeste was wearing a light gray long-sleeved sweatshirt and tight faded blue jeans with thick socks. Her teeth looked clean, and she didn't have that sweet foul smell most addicts carried with them. Like I said before, more than once—she was beautiful. A natural beauty. Didn't need makeup. Didn't have any on, either. I had to stop my mind from going there, but there was something about her other than her appearance that I was still deeply attracted to.

I rarely met Arthur here when he was my CI, but sometimes I

had to show up to check up on him. I was very careful about that. We usually met at a location far removed from where we did our business. When I did show up at his home, though, I would never want to sit. The dilapidated furniture, like Arthur, was nasty. Now there was new stuff, and the place was clean. Had a different touch. I knew it was all her.

Kelly and I sat on the sofa, she on one end and I on the other. Celeste sat on a purple armchair near Kelly. I allowed Kelly to take over the questioning. Not even allowed, really. It was a given because I fucked up so bad.

"How long have you known Arthur?"

"I don't even remember. A few years. Detective Blum said this involved a homicide investigation, but you won't tell me if Arthur's involved somehow. Is he?"

Kelly takes the photo of Arthur and the decedent. She shows it to her but doesn't let her take it.

"Can you identify the two men in this photo?" she asked.

Without hesitation she said, "The one on the left is Arthur. I don't know the other man."

"You've never seen this other man before?"

"Never."

Kelly slipped the photo back in the inner pocket of her suit jacket.

"Do you know anyone named Chris Doyle?"

"No. Is that the man in the photo with Arthur?"

"Arthur never mentioned anyone by the name of Chris?"

"I said no. And you didn't answer my question."

"It is the man in the photo," I said.

"How long did you say Arthur has been missing?"

"I didn't say he was missing. I just said he hasn't come home yet."

"When was he last home?"

"Three days ago."

"And he didn't tell you where he was going?"

"No."

"Did you ask where he was going?"

"No."

"Why?"

"Because he goes away sometimes for days. Does his own things. Detective Blum knows. I don't want to know what he's up to as long as he pays the bills. I'm not working right now."

"I'm sorry, Celeste, but I find that very odd. Difficult to believe."

"Believe what you want. We don't have your *typical* relationship."

"Do you have a cell phone?"

"Of course."

"I'd like you to try to call him on it."

Her lips tightened and she shook her head like we were nothing but a disruption.

She looked at me as if it was my fault. She stood from the chair.

"It's in the other room." And she left to retrieve it.

Kelly looked at me, rolled her eyes. I nodded like I knew what she was thinking and agreed.

Celeste returned after a few seconds with her cell, sat down again and flipped it open. Scrolled down to find the number.

"Can I see what number you have for him?" I asked.

She showed me the phone's display. It was the same number I had.

"Give him a call," Kelly told her.

She tapped the number. I could hear the muffled sound of it ringing.

A moment later she closed the phone and said, "It just went to his voice mail."

"Call again and leave a message for him to call you. Tell him it's important, but don't say anything about us," Kelly told her.

Again with her tight lips, but she made the call.

When it went to voice mail she said, "Call me. I need to talk to you. It's important."

She hung up.

"Thank you," I said. "And he's not in trouble. Like I told you yesterday, he might be able to help us with this homicide. I don't believe he had anything to do with it, but it's obvious he knew the man."

She nodded, briefly made eye contact with me again, but it was different that time. Softer.

I don't know if she believed what I said but I had to say it. I didn't want her to tell Arthur he might be in trouble, because that could turn on us. He'd really be in the wind. At this point, he was all we had.

"How often does Arthur disappear like this?" Kelly asked.

"Not a lot. And I don't worry when he does. He always comes home."

"Is he still using?" I asked.

She gave me the kind of look like that's none of my business. Couldn't help but think she was very expressive without having to say a word.

"He goes off on a binge sometimes."

"Give us the name or names of who he might be with," Kelly said, like it was an order.

"I don't have any names of who he might hang with," Celeste said without hesitation, and then turned to me. "You used to work with him. Why can't you just make a call and see who he's working with now, if he even is?"

"We will."

I thought Kelly was pushing too hard and wanted her to ease up a bit.

She didn't.

"You telling me you don't know any of the people he hangs with?"

"That's his business and he keeps it to himself. He knows I don't want to know about that side of his life."

"So you don't know any of his friends or anyone else?"

"I didn't say that."

"Well, yeah, you did."

"I meant that I don't know any of the people he goes out and binges with."

"Then give us the names of those people he doesn't use with. Just his friends or your mutual friends."

"I don't want to get any of my friends involved in this."

I jumped in and said, "Celeste, for all you know, Arthur could be in danger. This is a homicide investigation. If you care for him then you want to do what you can to help. Right?"

"Of course." After a brief moment: "We only have three friends in common."

Kelly turned to a blank page in her notebook, handed it to her with her pen.

"Can you write the names down with an address and phone number?"

"I just have cell numbers."

"That'll work," Kelly said.

She wrote the names down along with the numbers, handed the pen and notebook back. Kelly looked them over for a second.

"Thank you," she said sincerely, tone changed a bit.

Kelly pulled out the photos of the naked women from her inner pocket. Yellow sticky notes concealed their nakedness and only revealed headshots. She handed them over to her.

"Do you recognize any of these women?"

"I'm guessing they're all naked."

"You'd be right," she said.

She flipped through them, looking them over carefully, handed the photos back to Kelly.

"I don't recognize any of these women. Are they dead?"

"We don't have that information."

She put them back in her pocket, closed her notebook and looked at me.

"You got anything you wanna ask?" she said to me.

"Only thing is, Celeste, you make sure Arthur calls me when you hear from him or see him. I also want you to call me just in case he doesn't."

"Okay."

I felt uncomfortable with her eye contact. It was like she was looking right through me. It made me wonder if Kelly picked up on it too. Was Celeste mad at me because of all that happened in the past and probably still was happening? That I did nothing about it. I could have easily stopped the abuse, had him arrested.

After we got in the car, Kelly handed over her notes turned to the page where the names were written down along with the cells.

"We should run those names, along with the other ones we have through WALES before we make any cold calls," she said.

"I can get on that. So, you really believe she's not in contact with Arthur?"

"I don't believe a fucking word she said."

Kelly got a call as we were driving back to the office. I could hear what sounded like a woman at the other end.

"Okay," she said, lips pursed like she was angry.

When she got off I asked, "Everything okay?"

"We need to make a stop before hitting the office."

7

We pulled the car into the driveway of her house in Takoma Park. Not so far outside DC. It was a nice cottage-style home with a large porch and a well-maintained front yard. She took it over from her parents a few years ago after they moved to North Carolina. Kelly was still visibly angry. It was an all-too-familiar thing in her life with her daughter. Can't count how many times we had to take a detour so she could come to the house or the high school.

I'd gone in with her on a couple of occasions, but today she asked if I could wait in the car.

"No problem."

She stepped out and went into the house. I could hear the door slam.

I rolled the window down a bit and lit a smoke. Not even a few seconds and I heard yelling, mostly from Kelly. I couldn't make out what the argument was about, but it was a potent one.

A few minutes and two cigarettes later, she came out. Didn't slam the door that time but double-checked to make sure it was locked.

"Fucking fourteen-year-olds," she said, and pulled out her pack of cigarettes before driving.

"What happened this time?"

"She didn't answer the door when the tutor showed up. Said she was in the bathroom and didn't hear, but that's bullshit. I know she was playing fucking video games."

"Better than using drugs."

She shot me a glare, put the car in reverse and almost skidded out.

Back at the office and before I went to run the names, I stepped into the conference room and called my mother on her room number. I used the landline and blocked the number. If she had my cell or the phone number here, she'd blow it up with calls. She didn't answer. Probably in the rec room watching television.

It went to voice mail.

"It's me. Sorry I haven't called. Got crazy at work. I've been thinking about you. I'll try to call you later. I love you."

I disconnected. Left the room to go run the names through our system. The only hit I got was on Raymond Wakeling, had a warrant for an FTA. He was arrested in 1998 for possession with intent to distribute but didn't show up to court. I'm guessing heroin since that was Arthur's drug of choice. I printed it out.

I typed the PDID number into the live scan and his photo popped up. He didn't look like a junkie. He was clean-shaven with short black hair. Lost his smile for the photograph. Certainly didn't look happy. I printed it out.

I dropped the WALES printout and the photo in front of Kelly on her desk.

"This is all I got from those names. Gonna have to cold-call the other two."

She picked up the live scan photo, quickly looked it over, and said, "It's something." Handed it back to me.

She was still pissed.

I grabbed the WALES and slipped them both into the working case jacket, which was on Kelly's cluttered desk. I called the narcotics branch and asked to speak to an old friend of mine there, Frank Marr. See if he knew anything about Arthur and who he might be working with. I didn't trust speaking with anyone else. The officer who picked up said that Marr was not available, and probably wouldn't be for a few days. Didn't say why. I checked my cell for his name. He had a departmental cell phone. Found it and tapped the number in.

"Hello," said a female voice.

"I'm sorry, I thought this was Frank's cell."

"Who is this?"

"Detective Alexander Blum with Homicide. Needed to get with him about something."

"The phone was passed on to me over a year ago. I'm with Intel and I'm sure he has one of those new ones."

"Do you have a cell number for him?"

"No, I don't. I don't even know who he is."

"All right, thanks."

I disconnected before I got a response.

"I'm hungry," I told Kelly. "You up for going to Polly's for lunch?"

"Yeah. I could eat something."

"Maybe check out the address for Wakeling after. See if we get lucky."

"Sounds good to me."

Polly's Café was located on the thirteen hundred block of U Street NW. We sat at the bar drinking coffee. We knew one of the owners. He wasn't there that day. Polly's had a great jukebox—Iggy Pop, Velvet Underground, Social Distortion, and some great blues and jazz, too. I had slipped a couple of quarters in when we first got there. Velvet Underground's "I'm Waiting for the Man" was playing. I thought that was apropos. The bartender was cute. Her dark wavy hair had blue streaks in it and she had a little gold hoop nose piercing and several tattoos. She served us our burgers and thick-cut fries.

"There you go," she said with a smile.

I always had a crush on her but never worked up the courage to do anything about it. Told Kelly about it once. She told me she was probably too dangerous for me. I was always shy around women, especially if there was an attraction. Kept me alone most of the time. I had a couple of girls I could call in times of need. They were not the kind of girls you'd want to get into a relationship with, though. They had no motivation in life. Probably their age. They were younger than me. Decent girls, though. Maybe I'd get my nerve up one day with the bartender here. Despite what Kelly thought, I was attracted to her and the possibility of getting into trouble didn't matter. In fact, it made me want her even more. Kelly had a teenage daughter and was a workaholic, so she didn't have a life outside of that. She didn't date. At least that I knew of. I respected her for that. Wish I had her strength.

After lunch and before we made our way to Wakeling's address, we called Milloff at the Fifth District. He worked plainclothes with his partner, Leonard. We worked with them in the past and figured two guys in suits knocking on a wanted guy's door probably wouldn't work out so well. They were good at doing what we called an okey-doke, a way to con someone into thinking you were there for something different from what you were. Hard to do when someone knows they're wanted, but I've done it in the past and I knew these boys were more than capable.

We met them at a McDonald's lot a couple of blocks from the address. Milloff was a burly guy with a crewcut and unshaven face. He walked to the driver's-side window. Kelly handed him a copy of the live scan photo.

"He's wanted on an FTA for PWID, but if you manage to pick him up don't tell him that."

"He probably knows," Milloff said.

"Yeah, but we'll want him transported to VCU and that'll make him think otherwise. His name came up in a homicide we caught so we want to talk to him."

"And we get the stat, right?"

"Of course. You think we need to worry about those kinda stats and waste our time papering it?"

"Naw, you're the big leagues."

"Let's get to his address and sit on it for a bit before you do your thing. Switch your radio over to 5D surveillance."

"Copy that, sweetie."

"Don't fucking call me that," she snapped back.

I know he did it to piss her off. He liked to do that shit, not just to women. Pretty much everyone. He had a way with getting under your skin, but both Kelly and I liked him despite his abrasive character.

He walked back to the old beat-up gray Honda Civic they were driving. Piece of shit car, but that's what they had to work with.

The address belonged to a small run-down two-story white-brick row house set between two larger homes. We found a parking spot along the curb across the street, near a liquor store. An old homeless man sat on a plastic crate turned upside down, panhandling. Four younger men were gathered at the corner, pacing around like they were in need of something. Looked like crackheads. One of them had a small brown paper bag that probably contained a forty or hard liquor. They quickly made us but didn't scatter, so they probably weren't waiting for drugs or holding. The man with the paper bag took a hefty swig from whatever was concealed in the bag, like he was mocking us. Didn't give a shit. Most of them didn't. I was used to it, and it was something that bothered me when I was a rookie, like spitting on the ground toward me. That was worse. Got me into trouble once or twice, because I had some anger issues back then.

"We're in front of the location," Leonard transmitted over the radio.

"We see ya," I said over my radio, keeping it low and near my crotch.

They were parked across the street a few homes down from Wakeling's. No one near the liquor store noticed them. They hunkered down in their vehicle.

The curtains were drawn in Wakeling's home. Hard to tell if there were any lights on. Don't know if he even lived there anymore.

The corner cleared after about thirty minutes, but the old panhandler was still there. He looked our way occasionally. A ghostly figure of a man, like someone who shouldn't be alive. Face riddled with deep, filthy lines. Eyes dark and lifeless, but without that milky glazed-over stare you see in death.

After about twenty minutes, I noticed a man walking from the sidewalk at the other side of the liquor store and to the corner where the others had been standing. Fit the description. Kelly noticed too.

I got on the radio and said, "This might be our boy. Northwest corner at the liquor store. Getting ready to cross the street."

"Got him," Leonard said.

They casually stepped out of their car, walked toward the corner that our possible boy would hit once he crossed. They blended in well. Couldn't tell they were the police.

He waited for the walk sign and crossed.

Milloff and Leonard stood near the corner a couple of houses up from his. They were talking. Leonard lit a cigarette. Acted like they belonged. Our possible boy didn't pay them much attention. He began to pass them, but they stopped him.

Didn't take long for him to break away, turn, and bolt.

"Shit," I said.

Leonard and Milloff quickly chased after him, but he was fast.

I grabbed the bubble light from the center console and stuck it to the Velcro on the dash, plugged it in the lighter just as Kelly pulled away from the curb, nearly hitting two oncoming vehicles. Horns honked. I flipped the trigger switch under the radio and activated the siren. The old panhandler almost fell from his crate. We sped toward the light. It was red.

They had already turned the corner, heading south, Wakeling almost a quarter of a block ahead of them.

I looked left then said, "Clear."

Kelly busted through the red light and made a right.

We caught up to Milloff and Leonard. Leonard was on the radio, probably 5D channel, calling out for other units.

Wakeling cut into a narrow alley rear of his home.

"Slow down. You're not gonna make that turn."

"I got it."

We got to the alley ahead of the boys. Wakeling was just ahead.

"Stay left. Stay left," I told Kelly. "Give me room on my side."

"I don't have that much room, fuckwad."

She tried anyway.

Wakeling looked over his shoulder and ran toward the right, closer to the fence. Probably was going to jump a fence into another backyard to get off the alley.

"Get up to him."

Kelly got right on him. I swung the door open when he was close enough. It smacked Wakeling on the backside, sent him a few feet and to the ground. We weren't going fast enough to bust him up, though. We passed him a couple of feet and blocked the alley as best we could with the car. Wakeling was just beginning to stand. Apparently didn't get badly injured.

I jumped out of the car. Milloff and Leonard tackled Wakeling before I got to him, slamming him back to the pavement face-first.

Wakeling had his hands cuffed behind his back.

Sirens close by. A marked cruiser sped toward us and stopped. Two uniformed officers jumped out to join us.

"You hit me with your fucking car. I'm gonna sue your ass and the whole department."

"Shut the fuck up," Milloff told him.

"I'm hurt bad. I need an ambulance."

I grabbed him under his arm and pulled him up to a sitting position like he was nothing. Couldn't have weighed more than a buck thirty. Fast motherfucker, though.

"Ow, ow!" he screamed. "What you arresting me for? I didn't do nothin'."

"We'll explain everything to you. You guys a transport?" I asked the two uniformed officers.

More sirens nearby. Another marked cruiser pulled up.

"He's got to go to VCU," Kelly added.

Leonard got back on the radio and advised that the suspect was apprehended and to call off the other units.

"I need to go to the hospital," Wakeling cried.

The palms of his hands had little scrapes, but nothing serious. No apparent injuries anywhere else.

"You'll be fine," I told him calmly.

"I'm suing your ass. And what the fuck is VCU?"

"We'll meet you boys there," I told Milloff.

Milloff put on some latex gloves, patted Wakeling down.

"You got anything in your pockets that'll poke me?" Milloff asked him.

"No, I don't got anything. What are you arresting me for—I got a right to know."

Milloff searched his pocket, pulled out a wallet, pack of cigarettes, keys, and a Ziploc bag that had several smaller green zips containing a light tan powdery substance.

"Shit," Wakeling said. "You got no cause."

8

Wakeling was in the interview room, sitting on a metal chair without rollers. The door was closed. He waived his rights and agreed to talk. Kelly had a way of explaining the reality to a defendant without taking advantage or breaking the rules. I did too for that matter. It was rare for either of us to have someone lawyer up. A learned talent. It wasn't always like that, though. It was about getting them to understand that their story was important. It was all about their story, or their version of the story. It was our job to eliminate the fiction and determine the truth.

I watched him briefly through the small plexiglass window on the door. He had a handcuff on his left wrist with a long chain that was bolted to the floor. He was resting his forehead in the palm of his right hand. There was a small table in front of him and two other chairs with rollers on the other side of the table.

Kelly was in the video room setting up the recorder with a CD. Milloff and Leonard were at a vacant cubicle doing the arrest paperwork and putting the drugs and his personal property on the book. I advised Milloff not to put his cell phone on the book. We'd do that ourselves later. We would use the cell for the interview. It had evidence that he'd called Doyle several times. The powder also tested positive, and there were enough little zips that Wakeling could be charged with possession with intent to distribute heroin. That on top of his FTA would get him held and gave us a lot to work with when we were ready to get in there and talk to him.

I went to the vending machine to get him a Coke, and then the machine next to that one for a Snickers. Stepped into the video room after. Kelly had everything ready.

"You wanna take the lead?" she asked.

"Sure."

"Good, you're better with the drug shit."

She picked up a case jacket that was thicker than it should be. Had a lot of paperwork in there that had nothing to do with Wakeling, but he wouldn't know. The case jacket did have the Polaroids of the naked women, the one with Arthur and Doyle, and a crime scene photo of Doyle's body. I grabbed the unsealed evidence bag that contained Wakeling's cell phone.

One thing we were lucky to get was the coroner's report. According to it, Doyle's cause of death was from the gunshots he sustained to the chest from a .22 caliber. One of the rounds into his heart. All that other shit was probably nothing more than a physical fight beforehand. The report also indicated that older hypodermic needle puncture marks were found on his forearm and a newer one on his neck, just under the left ear. It was deep and part of the needle had broken off in his neck. Not something a user would commonly do to themselves. Suspect wanted to make sure he was more than down by shooting him with a lethal dose of heroin, or maybe it was a statement.

Wakeling was sitting up when we walked into the room. Looked tired, eyes glassed and a sullen expression like he was in need. Kelly sat down. I set the Coke and the Snickers on the table before him and the evidence bag with his cell phone at the other side of the table near my chair. He looked at the bag but didn't seem worried.

"Thanks," he said politely. His demeanor had changed. I've seen it before. He accepted his fate. Probably even looked forward to getting in jail and cleaning up. Funny how most of them thought that way. Though usually not the younger ones who haven't been using for years.

I sat down. Kelly set the case jacket on the table between us. Wakeling looked at it briefly, opened the can of soda, took a hefty swig. Burped after.

"Excuse me."

Kelly shook her head with half a smile. I had to smile too.

"Can I save the Snickers till later?"

"As long as you eat it here," I told him. "You can't take it with you to the cell."

"I will."

"Do you know why you're here?" I asked.

"Figure the court no-show and you guys work some fugitive thing or something, 'cause I'm not at the regular station. I don't really have some big story to tell ya, like you asked before, and I sure as hell ain't a snitch."

"The extra charge you caught with the heroin on top of the court no-show will probably get you held."

"That shit's personal use. I don't deal."

"We think you can help us out with some stuff we're working. We can't make any promises, but if you do, we will talk to the prosecutor to let them know you were very cooperative. That's always helpful. Can go a long way."

"I've heard that before and like I said, I ain't a snitch."

"Yeah, based on your record, it looks like you've been through the court system a few times so I can understand your skepticism. You're in a different house now. Our word goes a long way."

"How many times I gotta keep saying the same thing?"

"Not asking you to give anyone up. We're looking for certain information about someone we know you know. Doesn't have to do with drugs."

"Who you think I know?"

"Chris Doyle."

He didn't give the reaction I expected. Just looked at me with dead eyes. Stone cold or he doesn't know Doyle is dead.

"I don't know anyone by that name."

"There you go. Already lying. You want to be very careful about that, Raymond, because we already have evidence that says otherwise."

"Evidence? Evidence of what?"

"Just what I said."

He looked at me like he didn't understand.

I decided to go for it 'cause sometimes you have to go with your gut.

"Raymond, I gotta be straight with you. My partner, Detective Ryan here, and I could care less about your court no-show or whether that heroin you had in your possession was for dealing or personal use. We work Homicide."

He quickly set his Coke on the table. I could hear the remaining soda fizzing in the can. He looked at me directly. Seemed genuinely confused, not so stone cold and with dead eyes.

"What the fuck you want to talk to me for?"

"Well, obviously about a murder."

"Murder? You sayin' that that Chris dude got himself killed? I sure as shit don't know anything about something like that."

"So you do know him?"

"I never said that."

"Raymond, cut the shit. It's not going well for you here. You're looking more and more like someone we should be looking closer at. Someone of interest."

"I ain't no murderer."

"Then tell us the truth. We know you know him."

I pull his cell out of the bag, flip it open.

"You need me to show you how many times you called him?"

He took another hefty swig, finished the soda. Burped again, but we didn't smile that time.

"Three of those times you talked were around the time of his death. We have Chris Doyle's cell phone too. Shows your name as a contact and how many times you talked."

Before he could respond, I took the case jacket, opened it so he couldn't see what was inside. I grabbed the death photo and set it before him.

He looked at it for a second and quickly turned away.

"Damn. Shit, I don't need to see that. What the hell you thinkin'?"

"Look at it," Kelly demanded.

He looked at Kelly as if he didn't realize she was there, appeared reluctant but looked down at the photo again. A bit longer this time.

He turned away from the photo and said, "Yeah, I know him."

9

H e get himself shot?"

"Did Chris get his dope from you?" Kelly asked.

"Fuck no. I told you I don't deal the shit."

"How do you know him?" I asked.

"I met him a while back through someone else."

"Give me a name."

"I just know him as Artie."

I knew who he was talking about but had to confirm it. I grabbed the photo of Doyle with Arthur and set it down before him.

He tapped on the image of Arthur with the index finger of his right hand and said, "That there is Artie."

I took the photo and put it back in the folder, closed it.

"How long you known Artie?"

"I've known him for a bit."

"How long is a bit?"

"Three or more years."

"Does Artie supply you?"

He went quiet again. Shook his head like he didn't want to say.

"Like I said, we could care less if Artie is a dealer."

"We just use together sometimes is all. He ain't no dealer."

"What's his affiliation with Doyle?"

"Guess it don't matter me sayin' that since Chris is dead."

He fiddles with the Snickers bar like he wants to open it.

"Go on."

"Chris is the one we got our shit from most of the time."

"Chris Doyle sold you and Artie heroin?"

"That's what I said. Can I eat my Snickers?"

"In a minute," Kelly told him.

Wakeling took his hand away from the bar, seemed disappointed.

"How long you been getting dope from him?" I asked.

"Since the time I known him, when Artie first introduced us."

"How often?" Kelly asked.

"Shit, once a week. Sometimes more."

"What about Artie?"

"About the same. He has the car. I don't so he drives there."

"When was the last time you were there?" I asked.

"Four days ago."

"You had a lot of zips on you for having bought four days ago. Seems like you use often."

"Like I said, we get from him on occasion. He didn't answer his phone, I guess 'cause he got himself killed, so I got that shit from someone else. And don't ask me to tell you who 'cause I won't."

"Just tell me if the person you bought that shit from knows Chris or knows that you also get heroin from him?"

"No, he don't. He just a corner hustler."

"When did you last see Artie?" Kelly asked.

"'Bout two days ago."

"Did he go with you to buy from the corner hustler too?"

"Naw, he was good."

"Do you know where Artie is now?"

"Fuck, man, c'mon."

"You help us out here, Raymond, and we'll make you look good with the prosecutor and the judge."

"He's no killer either."

"Still have to talk to him. He might know other people we'll need to talk to."

"All we want to do is talk," Kelly told him.

"You have a number for him on your cell here?"

"So you know I do since I known him for so long."

"You know where he lives?"

"Shit."

"Just tell me if he only stays at one place?"

"Yeah, he does."

"For now just give me a street."

He thought hard about it.

"Rhode Island."

"Northwest, Northeast?

"Northwest."

I wasn't going to press him for more yet.

I take his cell phone out of the bag and hand it to him.

"Call him. Tell him you need to get yourself some dope."

"C'mon now."

"Do it, Raymond," Kelly said firmly.

"Sheeeit. You gonna really help me."

"We're gonna make you look good," Kelly said.

He flipped the phone open, scrolled a bit until he found the number. Tapped it. We could hear it ring several times, but it went to voice mail.

"It went to message," Wakeling said.

He tapped the off button, closed the cell.

"Try again and leave him a message," I directed him.

He did and when it went to voice mail he said, "Yo, call me. Need to talk."

Pressed the off button again and set the phone down. I left it there just in case he got a call back.

I took the photos of the women out of the folder, set them on the table in front of Wakeling.

"I want you to tell us if you know any of these women."

"Why you got these sticky pads on them?" He picked one up, lifted the edge of one of the Post-its. We let him. "Oh damn, I see." He smiled.

"Don't do that again," Kelly said. "Just look at the faces."

He studied each photo carefully, almost like he thought if he looked at them hard enough he'd see through the sticky notes.

After looking at the last one he said, "Naw, I don't know these girls. They hookers?"

I took the photos from him and put them back in the folder.

"Where did you and Artie go after you bought the dope from Chris?" I asked.

"My place. We got high together."

"How long was Artie there for?"

"Few hours. I don't know. It was dark when he left."

"Anyone else there?" Kelly asked.

"Naw."

"Where were you the next day?"

He had to think on it.

"I was high for a couple of days. Stayed home all day and night."

"No one else came to visit you?"

He hesitated.

"Give us a name so we can rule you out as a suspect," Kelly said.

"Just some girl I get with sometimes."

"Name?" I asked.

"Fuck. I just know her as Maria."

"You got her number in your cell?"

"I just hook up with her sometimes. Get high with her."

"You wanna be ruled out as a suspect, we gotta talk to her," Kelly said.

"Yeah, I got her number."

I gave him the cell and he showed us the number. Kelly wrote it down in her notebook.

"You have an address for her too?"

"No. I don't know her like that. She always came to me."

"If we call her and ask if she was with you, what do you think she'll say?"

"Damn, I sure as hell hope she'll tell you she was with me."

"Is there anyone else you know that also knows Chris?" I asked.

"Just Artie. That's all."

"No one else you know that also buys from him?"

"I told you no."

"What about any other people that Artie hangs out with?"

"I just know his girl. Celeste."

"Where does she live?"

"She stay with him."

We went at him for about another hour but got nothing useful. We let him eat his Snickers and then the boys took him down to the cell block to get processed. Kelly called the number for Maria. Had to work her for a bit, even threatened to have her subpoenaed, and she finally admitted she was with him that day and through the night. She told her to save us the trouble of also getting a subpoena for her number in order to get her address, so she gave that up too. Kelly thanked her and advised that we'd have to meet in person soon. She agreed. We put it on our to-do list for the next day.

I called the morgue to check if any possible ODs showed up. I gave them Arthur's name and description. Fortunately, it was negative. After that I called Howard Hospital and MedStar, which were the closest hospitals to his neighborhood, also with negative results. I stretched it out to GW and Georgetown and a couple of other hospitals too. Nothing. A few John Does, but they didn't meet his description.

When we were at our cubicle writing everything up and organizing the case jacket, I got a call on my cell. I didn't recognize the number. I answered anyway.

"Hello."

"Detective Blum?" a familiar female voice asked.

I knew it was Celeste but didn't say her name. Don't know why.

"Yes."

"This is Celeste."

"I know."

"I'm worried about Arthur now. I know I said he disappears, but never this long. He's also not returning my calls. Can we meet this evening and talk? Just you, though. I don't like your partner."

I looked behind me. Kelly was plugging away on the computer's keypad.

"Yes. What time and where?"

The sarge let me take the last two because Kelly was still working the case. I got off at eight p.m. Told both Kelly and the sarge that I had to take care of some issues concerning my mother and I couldn't do it from the office because I needed to reference medical documents I had at home. I lied, of course. Fact is, I didn't want to wait until ten thirty to see Celeste. I didn't know why she needed to see me, only that she was worried about Arthur. Something like that could've been discussed over the phone.

I met Arthur after about a year on with the narcotics branch. I arrested him for PWID heroin. He had backup time, so he got held. I talked to the assistant U.S. attorney who picked up the case and asked her to get with his defense and see if we could debrief him, maybe work out a plea deal if Arthur was willing to cooperate. He was willing, and he gave me his world. I got him out to work for me as an informant and he got me into his everything.

Proved himself to be one of the best informants in my squad. Made a name for myself because of him. Kicked in a lot of doors. Got some real weight—cocaine, crack, and heroin. Rolled a lot of defendants, too.

Arthur had to piss weekly. Couple times he pissed dirty and got stepped back. Got him back out, though. Had a good judge who acknowledged the value of the work he did but warned Arthur that he would not tolerate it happening again. Arthur cleaned up after I got him into a good program. Well, he cleaned up long enough for me to ram through a few more doors. It wasn't even six months before he pissed dirty again and then my best and only man was gone. I never knew or even tried to know what happened to Celeste. I wanted to check in on her several times, but never did. Again, there was such innocence despite the habit and the company she kept. I thought about her often, though. I put in for Homicide shortly thereafter and good ol' Arthur was nothing more than a CI who made for good conversation with Kelly and other drinking buddies. "Some of the shit we got into. Fuck," I would say. It took some time, but I eventually forgot about Celeste, and my guilt went with her.

10

Celeste answered the door right away and invited me in. She was wearing tight blue jeans, an overly large V-neck T-shirt that could have belonged to Arthur, and thick gray socks. I followed her to the living room.

She turned to me while walking.

"Do you want something to drink? I have vodka and Irish whiskey."

"No, I'm good. Thanks."

"You sure?"

I wasn't sure. Did feel like a drink, but still said, "No, thank you."

She sat at the end of the sofa.

"You going to sit down?"

I smiled awkwardly and sat on the armchair at the other side of the sofa. A dark wood coffee table was in front of the sofa and between us. There was a glass tumbler with ice and filled halfway with what I assumed was vodka. She picked it up, took a sip, and scooted herself to the other side of the sofa and closer to me. She drank a bit more and set the glass down on the end table to my right. The move she made while placing the glass down revealed just enough to show off her small, beautiful left breast. She stretched out her legs, feet closer to mine. I wondered if that was intentional.

I jumped right into it and asked, "So you haven't heard from Arthur?"

"No, and now I'm getting worried. More so because of the murder."

"Why did you need me to come over? This is a conversation we could have had over the phone."

"Because I like my conversations in person." She smiled.

It felt strange to me the way she smiled, like she wasn't really concerned for Arthur.

"Well, here I am, and I want to assure you we're doing everything we can to locate him. Did you have anything you want to share that might help us?"

"I've called him several times and left messages. Do you think he might have OD'd?"

"I'm not going to lie to you. That's a possibility. I did check the morgue and hospitals, though, and there was nothing. You honestly don't know any people that he might get high with, or places he would go?"

"No. I know you know that we have a strange relationship. I don't know his friends, nor do I want to know his friends. It's all a matter of convenience."

I hesitated to ask but still did.

"Does he still hurt you?"

She looked down. That was my answer.

"I have no work, no savings, and nowhere to go."

"So you allow him to do what he does as a matter of convenience."

She looked angry. Stared at me directly and said, "I'm not weak. It's not as bad as it was."

"Do you love him?" I don't know why I asked.

"I don't think so." She said this without hesitation.

"We'll just leave it at that then."

"Probably best to."

"There's things I might know, Celeste, so are you sure you don't know anyone he uses with?"

"I don't."

"So you don't know Raymond Wakeling? Because he sure as hell knows you."

She gave a different kind of smile, almost like a child who just got caught would.

"Yes, I guess I know him. I just didn't want to get him in trouble is all."

"Don't hold things back from me again."

"I'm sorry. I won't."

"When was the last time you saw him?"

"A few days ago, before Arthur disappeared."

"So how do I know you're not holding back on anyone else?"

"I guess you don't, but I'm not."

"I hope I don't find out otherwise."

"Would that be like hindering an investigation or something?"

"Something like that. You get that from experience?"

"No. TV. I like watching crime shows."

"Do you still use?"

She took a bigger swig from the glass, maybe to give herself a bit of time to think.

"I do sometimes, but I prefer to smoke it now."

"How often do you use?"

"Why is that important?"

"Just wondering if you need a little something now and if Arthur is the only one who you get it from."

"I don't use all the time. Not like I did before. I do like to drink and smoke weed. I'm a casual user. Are you going to search the house now?"

I knew she was being sarcastic, but I said, "I could care less about drugs, unless there is someone else you get them from who may or may not be connected to Arthur and the homicide victim." She didn't respond fast enough, so I asked, "So is there?"

"No," she said confidently.

"When was the last time you tried to call Arthur?"

"Earlier this afternoon, just before I called you."

"I was under the impression that you might have something more and that's why you wanted to see me. I sensed urgency."

"I'm just worried and was hoping you might have something too."

"I wish I did, but we don't. I'm confident we'll find him, though."

She finished what remained in her glass.

"I'm getting a refill. Are you sure you don't want a drink, or is it the whole *drinking on duty* thing?"

"I'm off-duty, so I do think I'll take you up on it now."

"I'm drinking vodka soda, on ice."

"That's good for me."

She got up, walked to the dining room. I watched her backside and damned myself for what I was thinking.

I was nursing my second drink. Celeste was on her third. I knew I shouldn't have been there, and yet there I was. Feeling alone in life is a bitch. There was something about it that made you desperate. Not the best thing when it came to something like judgment, but I wasn't about to make a move or even show interest. I still had some restraint, a little common sense left. I knew Celeste didn't have what would be defined as a healthy relationship with Arthur. Hell, based on some of what I heard, I didn't even know if they slept in the same bed. *Matter of convenience.* That stuck with me. It could mean so many different things. I'm sure all bad.

We got off-topic for a bit. She asked personal questions about me. I tried to be professional and was vague with my answers. Obviously there was something about her I couldn't quite trust. She was living with a junkie abuser and suspect in a homicide. She was more than likely a junkie too, despite what she said. And there I was having drinks with her, chatting it up like none of that mattered. Part of me was hoping that Arthur would show up and break up the party that was about to happen in my head.

After I finished my drink, I managed to pull out what little moral fiber I had left and said, "I need to go. I have an early day tomorrow."

She looked genuinely disappointed. Made me almost want to change my mind.

"Stay for one more."

"I really need to go."

I wanted to ask why she needed me to stay, but I was afraid of the answer.

I pulled myself up from the armchair.

"Will you call me, though? If you learn anything. Anything at all."

"Of course."

She walked me to the door. She put her hand on the doorknob to open it for me, but then took it off and turned to me. I thought she was going to say something, but she slipped her hands under my arms, wrapped her arms around me, and hugged me. I was uncomfortable for a second, but then hugged her back. It felt nice.

"Thank you," she said it softly and then broke away.

"I'm afraid of him coming home," she said.

"If he comes home and you're afraid you're in danger, you call 911 and then you call me right after. Okay?"

"Okay."

"I mean it."

"I will."

"You'll be okay."

"Thank you."

"Bye."

I left.

I was tired as hell when I got home, but had to call Kelly. My cell rang before I could. I didn't recognize the number, but I answered.

"Hello."

"It's me," said the all-too-familiar voice at the other end.

11

Arthur agreed to meet me at a quieter part of what we referred to as P Street Beach. It was late enough so there would not be so much action there.

I parked on 23rd, about a quarter block past P Street, walked back and across the stretch of grass toward the creek. Lamppost from the street and the nearby apartment building provided enough light so I didn't need my flashlight. I got to the wooded section just before an incline that led down to the creek and on the other side Rock Creek Parkway. There was a certain safe spot along the creek where I would meet with Arthur.

I looked around to make sure no one else was hanging out in the area. It looked clear. I saw someone who appeared to be Arthur near the creek, leaning against a tree. The ember from a cigarette illuminated a portion of his face. It was darker down in that area. I made noise as I carefully made my way down the incline.

"Blum?" Arthur asked before I got all the way down.

"Yeah."

He looked the same, which I thought odd because of all the shit he put into his body. I walked up to him. It was like he wanted to hug me, but stopped. The creek was babbling through the trees.

"Let's go down to the creek."

"Okay," he said.

I took out my stream light and lit up the area in front of us. There was better light on the other side of the creek because of the parkway up a steeper incline. The creek was narrow at that section. Large rocks, like they were placed there intentionally, led to the other side.

"The other side," I told him.

"You kiddin' me."

"Easy peasy, brother."

I stepped across first, gave him some light along the rocks to make it easier for him. There was a grassy area a couple of feet up. We walked there. I turned to face him as he lit another cigarette.

"Where the fuck have you been?"

"Man, it's all gone crazy, Blum. I had to get away. Think things out."

"Tell me what's going on."

"I need your help—"

"I'm here to help, but why me?"

"Because the both of us, you and me I mean, go way back. I know you always been there for me."

"Talk to me."

"You know how much I've done for you, right? I put my life on the line to get you what you want."

"I know. And I'm gonna try to protect you."

"I know you been to Celeste's. I seen you go in there from my car."

"Then you know we're looking for you."

"Yes, but not sure why. I got a feeling, though, because I got myself in a situation."

"I know you did. I know all about Chris Doyle."

"Shit. That wasn't me, man. You have to believe me."

"Convince me. I will help you. I've helped you out of bad situations before. I will again."

"Man…"

"Go on, Arthur. I already know more than you think."

"I don't want to see Celeste take a hit on this one."

"Celeste? What does she have to do with any of this?"

"Blum, she's the one that killed him."

That took me by complete surprise. Cars were rolling by on the parkway, so I turned off the stream light.

"I did something bad to her," Arthur began. "I brought her to Chris 'cause he was my guy. I needed a fix real bad and had no money."

"What did you do?"

"He liked her, and…" He hesitated to go on.

"And?"

"He got her high and I let him take her."

"Take her how?" Like I didn't know.

"In exchange for heroin. He started to rape her. I fucking let it happen but changed my mind and tried to break it up. We fought. You were always there for me, Blum. I gotta trust that you're gonna help. I got no one else. You know how much I've done for you."

"I'm here for you, Arthur, but I got to know everything."

"I had a pistol in my waist. It dropped out when we were scuffling. He saw it and backed off. Celeste…It was like she didn't even think about it. She was so fucked up. Naked. Shit. She picked it up and shot him. I don't know how many times. He fell. I freaked out bad, tried to get her dressed, but she stood over him like she wanted to keep shooting. I got the gun away from her."

"Then what?"

"I finally talked her down and we got out of there."

"No. Something else happened. You have to tell me everything, remember?"

He thinks about it for a moment.

"Yeah. Shit. She got the syringe, the one he made for himself. Next thing I know she stuck it in his neck and shot it in. I didn't even ask why. I figured she was so fucking messed up. I finally got her out of there."

"Place was clean. All we got was a bit of paraphernalia. No drugs. You take his shit?"

"Yeah. I did. She can't go to jail, Blum. She wouldn't survive. You're going to help her, right? Help me?"

Of course I would.

"Do you still have the gun?"

"Yes."

He reached into his coat pocket. I instinctively grabbed the grip of my weapon.

"Take it out slowly, Arthur."

"What do you think I'm gonna do? And what the fuck are you doing?"

"I don't want you to accidently shoot yourself, or for that matter, me."

He shook his head.

"You think I'm stupid?"

"And don't fucking laser me."

"Shit, man."

He handed it to me grip-first. I took it by the top of the grip between two fingers and slid it into my right coat pocket.

"I'll keep all this from my partner for now, until we can figure something out. I don't know what yet, but we will."

"Thank you. Thank you, man. I knew I could depend on you."

"Need to get you somewhere safe, 'cause the whole department is looking for you."

"Okay."

I looked at him. Couldn't stand the sight of him anymore.

"You're no good for Celeste."

"What the hell? She loves me, all right? So?"

Didn't know what to say to that. Didn't know why I even said what I said. Fuck.

"Damn." He looked panicked. "You supposed to protect me, Blum, protect her."

"Okay, okay," was all I could mutter. I was dizzy.

"Please, man."

I turned away from him.

"Okay," I quietly said.

12

H ome was always a comfort.
　　Not tonight, though.

I had to figure this thing out with Arthur. Kelly had to be left out of it, though. That was one thing I knew for sure. It would come to me after I get some sleep, even if it was only gonna be a couple of hours.

I went to the kitchen and poured myself a double scotch, almost downed it all at once.

I couldn't get Celeste out of my head. What she must have gone through. What she had to do. Getting numb with whiskey would help, though. For now. I took a steaming-hot shower after and hit the sack.

It didn't take long.

I was torn out of sleep by the landline ringing. Felt like minutes. I rolled over, checked the time. It was early, but about time to get up anyway. I looked at the phone. The Caller ID showed it was my mother. I shook myself out of what sleep was left and answered.

"Hi, Mom."

"Hello, my son," she said like her brain was normal.

"It's early. Are you getting ready for breakfast there?"

"I just ate breakfast, but not a big breakfast. This sweet man I met is taking me out for lunch later."

What the fuck?

"What man? Someone who lives there too?"

"No. Oh my God, no. I could never be interested in any of the men who live here."

"What are you talking about?"

"This nice young man comes to visit. Helps me out and brings me those cookies I like. From a Russian store here."

"Young man? You mean a volunteer or something?"

"Oh no, no. He works for one of those drug distributors. I met him in the garden a while ago. I can't remember when. Must have been some time ago, though."

My Spidey sense was tingling.

"Did they put you on new medication? You sound different."

"No, sweetheart. Don't be so silly. I'm just happy."

"How does he help you out?"

"Just good advice, you know, about dealing with orderlies here, about my insurance, about keeping myself safe, investments."

"Investments?"

"Well, yes, that's why I wanted to talk to you. I can't find my account information anywhere. I know you have my bank information. Could you give me the account number again?"

"Why do you need that?"

"First of all, Alexander, because it's mine, and secondly, like I told you, because Richard is going to help me out. Stop being such a detective."

"I don't mean to. I'm just interested. Tell me more about this man. What's his name?"

"Richard."

"Richard who? What's his last name?"

"It sounds like you're interrogating me."

"Of course not. I'm just interested in this new man in your life."

"I just call him Richard."

"You don't know his last name?"

"Now you are interrogating me. I don't like it." She sounded angry.

"I'm sorry, Mom. I'm just interested in what's going on in your life. That's all."

"Don't be concerned, Alexander. Richard is a good, very helpful young man. He loves me. He's going to help me with some good investments. That's all."

"Okay. That's nice," I lied. "I don't have your account information handy. I'm at work, but it's never a good idea giving that kind of information to someone."

"It's my account and I would like to have it, Alexander."

I was going to set her off if I continued and then who knows what would happen. I thought it best to play along.

"Okay, I'll dig it up when I get home. You said he's taking you out to lunch today?"

"Yes. A late lunch because he has to work."

"A late lunch? You should eat something in between then. You know you need to eat with your medication. What time is he picking you up?"

"Two o'clock. I'll have a little snack before then. Don't worry."

"Well, I'm happy for you," I lied again. "You do sound so much better."

"And how are you, Alexander? Is there a good woman in your life yet? We hardly talk anymore."

I wanted to remind her we spoke recently but thought it better to keep the conversation moving in another direction.

"Yes, there's someone in my life. Someone I'm interested in."

"You need to tell me more."

"I can't now, Mom. I have to work. I'll call you when I get home, see how your lunch with Richard went."

"Okay, sweetie. Take time for yourself, though, and this new woman. You work too much."

"I will. I promise. I have to go now. I love you."

"I love you too, Alexander. Say hello to Abigail for me. I can never get ahold of her."

"I will. Goodbye."

"Goodbye, my love."

"Goodbye."

I disconnected. Yes, she was only partly there. Bringing up Abigail was a definite indication. Abigail has been in the wind for a while. It's only been me, and now I have to do something about this guy—Richard.

Nothing good could come of this. It was like my childhood again—one love after another, one failed relationship after another. Except back then her brain was mostly intact and she could only be taken advantage of emotionally, not financially. For all I knew, this creep already got ahold of her credit card. I was the only one who had the bank account information. Something had to be done. It couldn't wait. I've been on the job long enough to know that this just ain't right.

Fucking no-last-name Richard.

13

The early-morning air had a bite. According to the morning news we could be in for a rough winter. That was all right with me. Whatever it took to shut this city down, even for a little while. Give us a fucking break.

I called Kelly when I got to the car.

"Yeah," she said like I woke her up.

"You still in bed?"

"No, I'm in the fucking office."

"Damn, already? Well, I'm heading in. You sound out of it."

"Went out for drinks with a couple of friends."

"Can't handle it anymore, huh?"

"You try raising a teenage girl."

"Don't see that in the cards anytime soon."

"I got the BOLOs for Arthur out the other day. Delivered them to headquarters, and most of the districts except for the Second and Third. Gave a stack to Intel. They'll distribute them to surrounding jurisdictions. Still have a stack on my desk if you want to get on the other districts. We also need to go interview Wakeling's girl Maria when you get in."

"Let's talk when I get in" was all I said. Didn't want to get into what I needed to ask of her over the phone.

"See you soon."

Kelly had been overworking herself. A lot going on with her daughter, too.

Seemed like the temperature dropped a couple of more degrees when I stepped out of the cruiser. Kelly was at her desk.

"Meant to ask if you call the sister yet?"

"No. Was waiting for you," she said.

I slipped my coat off, wrapped it around the back of the chair at my desk, took my suit jacket off and put it on a hanger then I hung it on a wooden coatrack that we kept near the wall.

"I'm going to give her a call," Kelly advised me.

I was still early enough that I had time to do what I had decided to do about my mother and this Richard creep. I would bring it up after she called the sister. I rolled up my chair beside her cubicle. I had my notebook ready. She used the landline to call and put it on speaker.

After a couple of rings, "Hello," said a delicate female voice.

"Is this Ms. Doyle?" Kelly asked warmly.

"Yes."

"Hi, this is Detective Kelly Ryan with the DC Police. You're on speaker and I'm sitting with my partner, Detective Alexander Blum."

"Hello, Ms. Doyle," I said.

"Hello. I've left several messages."

"Yes, we know. We've been on the street working the case. We're both so sorry for your loss."

"Thank you. Have you arrested anyone?"

"Not yet, but we are working on several leads. Would you mind if we asked you a few questions about your brother?"

"No."

"Thank you. When was the last time you talked to him?"

"We talk about once a week, usually on the weekend, so the Sunday before last. I tried to call him last Sunday evening, but he never answered. I figured he was out."

That Saturday or Sunday would be around the time of the homicide. I wrote that down in my notebook.

"Did he ever return your call?"

"No, but I didn't think much of it until about two days later because he was always good about calling me back. I tried to call him again, but he didn't answer so I left another message. I called the police the following day. I mean, we talked every Sunday, sometimes on Saturday for almost two years, after our mother passed away. We got closer because of that."

"When you did last talk to him, did he mention anything unusual?"

"I don't believe so, but I don't quite understand what you mean."

"Like was anything bothering him or anyone he might be having a problem with?"

"No, not at all."

"Do you have any names of his friends or people he was known to hang out with?"

"Just an old college friend we both knew, but he lives in Philadelphia now."

"Do you have a name and phone number for him."

"I think I still do. Hold on."

We heard the phone being set down.

A couple of minutes later she picked it up and said, "John Reese," and provided a number.

"Thank you. Was Chris in a relationship?"

"No. I know that because we both talked about wanting to be in relationships."

"He ever talk about who he was dating?"

"Sometimes. Yes. He did meet a lot of girls."

"He ever give you any of their names?"

"I know he was interested in this one girl, but for the life of me I can't remember. She was light-skinned. That was a couple of months ago. Why are you asking about the women he was dating?"

"We need to get a better understanding of his life. You never know what might be helpful. For instance, we could not find anything about him regarding what he did for a living."

"He's been out of work for three months and living off his savings. He's..." She paused for a moment and then continued. "He was a financial advisor for a group in DC. They let a lot of people go. He was one of them."

"What was the name of the firm?"

"Bendon Financial. I don't know where they're located, but it's in Washington."

"Did he ever mention any of his associates there?"

"No. He didn't really talk about work. I know he was unhappy there, though, and after he was let go he just wanted to take some time to himself before he started looking for another job."

Kelly looked at me with an upward nod, which I understood as her asking if there was something I would like to ask. I shook my head.

"Well, thank you, Ms. Doyle, and again, we're so sorry for your loss. Could we call you again if we think of anything else you might be able to help us with?"

"Of course. Please find who did this. Chris was a decent, loving man." She cried softly after.

"We're doing everything possible, and thank you for your time."

"Okay, please keep me informed."

"We will. Take care, Ms. Doyle."

I was happy Kelly did those interviews. I had to sometimes, but wasn't as good at it as her. I didn't come across as someone caring like her. Kelly could sound so loving sometimes, and then turn the other direction and crawl down your throat. She had a way about her, but I trusted her with my life.

"We need to fucking find Arthur," she said like a demand.

"I know. Listen, something important came up with my mom last night. I hate to ask this of you, especially now, but I need you to cover for me again. I have to go to Richmond."

"Your mom okay?"

"Getting a little worse. There's just some damn paperwork I have to go over and sign in person and before a notary. It can't wait. Won't be more than half the day. We can go to Bendon Financial and interview Wakeling's girl when I get back."

"Take the day. We'll get all this shit done tomorrow. I have some things I can take care of here in the meantime."

"Appreciate it, Kelly."

"Do what you have to do. We're there for each other, remember. You do it for me. If the sarge asks, I'll tell him you're following up on some leads for Arthur."

Damn, all that made me feel even more guilty.

14

It would take a little more than an hour and a half to get there. Traffic always backs up on 95 just outside Richmond. Sometimes bumper to bumper. I'd still have plenty of time to set up in the parking lot and wait. It could end up being a total waste of my time, but a son's gotta do what a son's gotta do to protect his mother who no longer has enough sense to protect herself.

Over two hours. Exhausted from lack of sleep and thinking too much about Arthur and Celeste. I couldn't shut it out of my head. Lord knows I tried. He kept popping into my head. I knew it was the right thing to do, just like I knew what I was doing here was the right thing to do. I gotta let that part go or it'll eat me up.

I backed into a spot in the parking lot that faced the front entrance. It's a nice facility. Couple hundred rooms. Well-kept garden area in back. The neighborhood is safe so I don't have to worry about that. I've got about forty-five minutes before he's supposed to show. I got a good parking spot and the only way in for nonresidents was that front door. I roll down the window, let some of that cool breeze in, and light a cigarette.

A couple of cars pulled in and out. No one that entered met his description, though it wasn't quite time yet. Still about ten minutes until he was supposed to pick her up for lunch, if he even was going to. For all I knew, Richard was a figment of my mom's imagination, maybe a past lover remembered. A part of her life that her brain recovered for comfort.

Three cigarettes later, I noticed a black newer model sedan pull into the lot. A male driver. He parked in a space ahead of where I was parked. Spent a couple of minutes in the car before he decided to exit. He looked to be in his early to mid-forties, fairly attractive, with wavy light brown hair cut over his ears. He wore navy blue pressed slacks and a white button-down shirt with an out-of-date plaid sport coat that had a light blue handkerchief poking out of the breast pocket. He straightened his jacket, brushed off the front of his pants, and walked toward the front.

About ten minutes later I saw him exit with my mom. Her arm was wrapped under his right arm as he escorted her to his car and opened the door for her, then he helped her in and closed the door. I fucking felt sick inside. Something inside hit me like a rush of warm blood to my brain and all I wanted to do was beat the fuck outta him. Don't know where that came from. Maybe how he smiled at my mom, or just the way he looked and what in my mind I perceived were his intentions.

I grabbed my notebook and a pen and quickly noted the make, model, and tag number of his car.

He backed out. I waited for him to get to the exit before I pulled out of my space. He made a right. I allowed a car to pass and got behind it and followed.

What the fuck am I doing?

A few blocks later they pulled into the parking lot of an older corner diner. I pulled in shortly after and backed into a space a few spots from them, where I can see the front entrance. I put the car in park just as they were walking toward the front door. Again, her arm comfortably wrapped under his. Made me feel ill. He opened the door for her. *That damn smile of his.* I wanted to wipe it off his face.

They were in there for over an hour. My mom exited with him with a wide smile on her face. She looked so happy, but what's a son to do. I followed them back to the retirement home, backed into the same space. Turned the car off. A few minutes later he came out. I stepped out of my car and got to him just as he opened the driver's-side door. He turned to me. I blocked him in front of his open car door. He could only go into his car or try to go through me.

"Can I help you?" he asked.

I wouldn't have looked like a threat to him because of my suit. I moved in closer to him. The proximity changed the expression on his face.

"Yeah, I think you can."

He smiled uncomfortably that time.

I pulled my jacket back with my right hand to show him my holstered gun.

"What's this about?" he asked nervously.

I snatched the cars keys out of his hand.

"Just take the car. I don't have any money."

"Do I look like a fucking carjacker to you? We're just going to talk, but you try to get out or do anything stupid, it'll become more than a conversation. You get me?"

"Yes, just tell me what you want."

"That was my mother you were with. What are your intentions?"

His face went blank, almost pale.

"I won't ask again."

"I have no intentions. I sell medical supplies to this facility and sometimes take the elderly folks out for lunch because I want to help. It makes them feel good."

"Really?"

Again with that look, but then he said, "Yes. Maybe I should call the police, because I feel like I'm being threatened."

"Please, call them. I'm not going anywhere."

I could tell he didn't know what to make of that.

"Call them. I'll have no problem explaining to the police what it is you're up to with my mother."

"I don't know what you're talking about, sir."

I gut-punched him. Hard. He bent over, groaning, and fell back, but his butt was caught by the edge of the seat. Out of nowhere he vomited, nearly hitting my shoes. I backed away a step. His whole lunch left his body through his mouth. Fucking disgusting, but I've seen worse. I looked around me to make sure it was clear. A couple more heaves and he tried to straighten up but couldn't look at me directly.

"You good now?" I asked.

He didn't answer.

"Stand up."

He had a hard time catching his breath.

"Please," he whimpered.

"Stand up on your own or I'll help you the hard way."

He struggled to stand, still slightly curled over and holding his stomach. I took him by the shoulder and turned him so his back was toward me.

"Please. What are you going to do?"

I patted his back pocket, felt his wallet, and pulled it out.

"Turn around."

He obeyed.

I searched his wallet and took out his license.

"Richard Loughman."

I tossed his wallet on the ground near where his vomit was. I kept the license, set it on the roof of the car, and pulled out my notebook and my pen. I noted his name, date of birth, license number, and address, then dropped the license to the ground. This time in the vomit.

"Very simple, Richard. You ever get with my mom again, I'll come for you. I won't go easy on you next time. Anything ever happens to my mother, even if it appears to be an accident, I'll come for you. I'll also find out everything about you. What company you work for, whether or not this is a current address—everything. I highly suggest you get with your company and have someone else assigned to this facility. Actually, not a suggestion. You understand me?"

"Yes, but—"

"You understand what the fuck I'm saying, Richard?"

"Yes, I understand."

"You stay away from here, because I will find out. Pick your shit up and go."

He was slow to move, but picked his wallet up first, and then carefully picked up his license like he was afraid of touching his own vomit.

"Get in your car and drive."

He sat on the driver's seat, placed the wallet and the license on the passenger seat.

"Have a nice day," I said, and slammed the door shut.

I felt queasy myself after he left. Everything was getting to be a bit much.

I drove out and made my way back to DC.

I got back to the office in time to get with Kelly and check off.

"Everything work out?" she asked.

"I believe it did. Thanks for covering for me."

"We always got each other's backs, right?"

"Always."

15

The following day was hard on my body and mind. So much going down. Started to question who the fuck I was.

Unfortunately, Arthur was the only decent lead we had, but what could I do. Celeste was the most important thing. I had no choice but to play it out. There were other things we had to cross off our list, though, like visiting Maria and Bendon Financial. Maybe he made some enemies there. Even a friend or two could lead to something helpful. John Reese was quickly ruled out. They hadn't talked in over a year. He was hit hard to hear about his friend's death. So Bendon was our first stop. The offices were on the tenth floor of a building downtown on K Street NW.

The receptionist was a young twentysomething girl, with eyeglasses that seemed too big for her face. We showed her our identification.

"We're investigating a homicide," I began, "and the victim used to work here. We'd like to talk to the office manager or someone in HR."

"Is this the murder that's been on the news?"

"There've been a couple of murders on the news, but probably," Kelly told her. "Can you see who is available to talk to us, please."

"Of course."

She picked up the phone and tapped in a couple of numbers.

"There are some detectives here who would like to talk to someone about a murder." After a few seconds she said, "Yes, a murder. I don't know why, but they said they need to. Okay." She hung up. "Have a seat and he'll be right out to see you."

We sat on the sofa under a large black-and-white photo of downtown DC. Financial magazines were on the coffee table and folded over one another like playing cards. About five minutes later an overweight man in a suit walked in from a hallway behind the receptionist's counter.

"Bill Myers," he greeted us.

We all shook hands.

"Detective Blum," I introduced myself. "And this is my partner, Detective Ryan. Is there someplace more private where we can talk?"

"Of course. I'm assuming this is about Chris Doyle. It's been on the news, but I don't know how I can help you."

"Just a few questions. We have to follow up on everything," Kelly said.

"We can go to the conference room. Please, this way."

A large wooden table with ten chairs was centered in the middle of the room. Myers sat on a chair on the other side, near the head of the table. We sat across from him.

"We won't take up much of your time, Mr. Myers. Just a couple of questions."

"That's fine."

"Did you personally know Chris Doyle?"

"Yes, I did, but we were not friends. I was the one who had to fire him."

"Fire him?" Kelly asked.

"Yes. I had to have him fired."

"Why and how long ago?" I asked.

"About four months ago. Something was going on with him. Maybe he was an alcoholic or maybe drugs. I don't know, but he became very difficult over a short period of time—missing work, calling in sick all the time, every day it was something new. He appeared to be unraveling."

"When did you first notice this behavior?"

"A couple of months before he was fired. Honestly, I had no choice. We gave him every opportunity, but when he started to neglect our clients—his clients—and the complaints started rolling in from them and his co-workers, I had no choice but to take it up the ladder. The decision was to let him go, so that's what I did."

"Is there anyone he worked with that you might consider a friend of his?"

"We have over fifty employees. I don't keep track of things like that. I can say that a lot of his co-workers complained about him, especially his appearance. Some even advised me that he smelled, like he wasn't showering."

"He ever get in an argument with anyone here?" I asked.

"No, not that I know of. I really didn't see much of him, even before all that behavior started. He always kept to himself. His cubicle. He was a good worker for a while."

"How long did he work here?"

"About two years."

"We'd like to talk to his co-workers if you don't mind."

"There were only three who worked directly with him, and I'm the last person who would want to hinder a murder investigation."

We both thanked him and interviewed the three co-workers. Total waste of time, but we had to do it. Forty or so minutes later we were in the car and off to see Maria. She lived in an apartment building just north of Columbia Road, on 16th.

Both of our pagers went off simultaneously about three minutes before we hit 16th. We both checked, fearing the inevitable.

"It's the LT," I said.

"Yeah, me too. Fuck."

I took my cell out and tapped in his number.

"What's up, Lu?"

"Alexandria detectives want you two to respond to a small park along the Potomac River, a couple of miles before the Mount Vernon estate on the parkway."

"What on earth for?" I asked like I didn't know.

"They're hoping you can identify a body. Possibly related to your case."

"What body could be related to our case?"

"Just get over there. Can't miss it. It's where all the units are along the parkway."

"Just drive along the parkway toward Mount Vernon? No physical address?"

"Again, I think it'll be hard to miss."

I felt my heart sink, like it was all happening too soon.

"Copy that. On our way."

"Keep me posted."

I flipped it closed but held on to the cell.

"What?" Kelly asked with reluctance.

"I don't know, but I don't think it'll be good."

Several marked Alexandria PD vehicles and two Park Police vehicles along with an ambulance were on the Potomac River side in a parking area for a small park and a trail that followed the river from Mount Vernon to Old Town. A uniformed officer lifted the crime scene tape that allowed us to drive in. Traffic was backed a bit in both lanes because of the looky-loos. A couple of local news vans were parked off the road on the other side. Cameramen and their accompanying reporters were kept by two officers from coming to the other side.

A couple of Park Police officers were standing on the grass area above an incline that led to the river.

We parked alongside one of the Park Police cruisers, walked toward the Park Police officers, made sure they saw our badges hanging from our necks.

"Detectives Blum and Ryan, with MPDC," I said. "We were told to come here."

"Right down there," one of them told us, pointing down the incline.

We both scooted down toward them. One of the detectives was Frank Marr, a hardworking DC detective I knew from Narcotics. I wondered why he was way out here.

He turned from the two Alexandria uniformed officers he was standing with and said, "Blum. Been a while."

"Yeah, it has. You still at the branch?"

"Always."

"This is my partner, Kelly Ryan."

"Frank Marr," he said, and extended his hand to shake hers.

"What the hell you doing here?" I asked.

"Let's step down to the river's edge and you'll see."

When we got there, a detective in a suit was crouched down looking over the body that was front-side up, clothes drenched, obviously pulled out of the water. Probably got himself tangled in the large driftwood poking out of the water like a sculpture.

I looked down to the body. It was Arthur, of course.

16

T hat's Arthur," I told Kelly.

"Fuck me," she said.

She bit her lower lip and shook her head.

The detective leaning over the body stood and faced us.

"Detective John Thomas," he said, extending his hand to Kelly first, then me.

"Alexander Blum," I introduced myself.

"Kelly Ryan."

"I know Frank here," Thomas began. "He helped out on a case of mine a few months ago that led to DC, and we worked using his CI here. Obviously, I called Frank and asked him to be here because it's his CI."

"Yeah," Frank began, "but because you guys put the BOLO out, they obviously need you here too."

"Arthur was your CI?"

"About a year after you left, Arthur was released. He tried to contact you at the branch 'cause he liked the money you paid. I picked it up and signed him back on. Couldn't let someone like that go, right? He's been working with me ever since. I got the BOLO. Was gonna call you because I hadn't heard from him for a few days. I knew something was wrong."

"I tried to get in touch with you there, hoping you might have some information on him, but you weren't available, and your cell number belongs to some detective at Intel now."

"Yeah, they gave all of us detectives those Nextels so I got a new number. Sorry I didn't have a chance to get with you, but our supervisor's got us jumping through hoops and it's been a bit crazy."

"We're going to need to sit down and talk, Frank."

"Yeah, definitely. I got a feeling this is some bad shit."

"At least we know the approximate time of death," Kelly advised.

"How would you know that?" Thomas asked.

"Because we have an approximate time when he made a call to his girlfriend a couple of days ago."

Thomas knelt back down, careful not to soil his suit pants, and turned the head sideways a bit to reveal what appeared to be three small entries to the back of the head. The river took care of cleaning the blood away.

"Wounds almost look like they were cleaned," Thomas said, like he read my mind. "But probably from the water washing over his head."

"No exit wounds," I said.

"Yeah, small caliber. Execution-style, you know."

"How was he found?" Kelly asked.

"By the couple up there with the dog."

We looked up. Another detective was interviewing them by an unmarked cruiser.

"He was facedown in the creek, caught up by the driftwood over there so he wasn't taken farther by the current. Damn, just a few more feet back and this would have been on Maryland."

"Sorry it landed on you all," I said.

"So this might not be the crime scene?" Kelly asked.

"Right. Crime Scene Search is canvassing up the river for any sign."

"It goes without saying that based on the relationship we know he had with our other decedent, our cases are probably connected," I said.

"That's fine with me," Thomas said. "My partner, Malcolm, and I could use all the help we can get."

"We'll let our LT know," I told him.

I kneeled, looked at his face. Eyes were open. Uninhabited. What was once there expelled. That expression frozen on his face almost looked like he'd waited for the end to come. Seemed horrified. I felt sickened.

"Find anything in his pockets?" Kelly asked.

Thomas straightened up and turned to her, said, "Just car keys and a key that probably goes to his house. I'm assuming you have an address on him?"

"Yeah," I said. "No car though, huh?"

"Not in the parking lot here. Unless he was driven by someone. I have a couple of officers with the keys canvassing the area, though. Marr here said it's an early-model black Toyota Camry."

"Anything else? Cell phone? Wallet?" Kelly asked.

"Nothing other than what I said."

"I'm going to catch up with Crime Scene, see what they have," Kelly advised me.

"Okay."

She walked upstream, looking down toward the ground as she moved carefully.

"I need a smoke," Marr told me. "You wanna join? We can talk."

"Yeah, I could use one too. Talk to you in a bit, Thomas."

He nodded. "I'm not going anywhere soon."

"Appreciate it."

I followed Marr up the incline and to his black Ford Explorer.

We passed a couple of Alexandria PD supervisors, but they didn't pay much attention to us. Couple of news reporters with their cameramen were now closer to the yellow tape. Cars still slowing to look over.

I stepped into the passenger side of Marr's SUV, closed the door. He started the engine, rolled his window down halfway. I did the same. He grabbed a pack of cigs, tapped one out and offered it to me. I took it. He grabbed one for himself, found his lighter in his front pants pocket, lit mine and then his. I took a nice long drag. The waft of smoke I exhaled was quickly pulled out the window.

"I'll need you to share what you were working on with Arthur."

"Won't be a problem. Can't believe anything I had him working on would be related to this. They got us doing mostly quick hits now. It's all about stats. Not working anything long-term. Just getting Arthur into places he knew or heard about, making a couple of buys, and then rammin' in the doors a couple days later."

"The name Chris Doyle ever come up?"

"Nope. Your other body, right?"

"Yeah. Looks like he was dealing heroin. Surprised Arthur never brought him up."

"You know better, Blum. They always keep a couple to themselves. How else he gonna get his personal shit?"

"You're right. It's been a while. So, he didn't have to piss anymore?"

"No. Did his bit and that was that."

"What about a Raymond Wakeling?"

"Don't know him either. Was he an associate of Doyle?"

"No. Arthur. They used together and both bought from Doyle. He's in jail now, being held on an FTA and PWID."

"Sounds like someone I might want to have a chat with. That good with you?"

"No problem but it'll have to wait, 'cause we can't rule him out in connection with Arthur until we get an approximate time of death from the coroner."

"Goes without saying."

"You ever meet his girl, Celeste?"

"Oh," he huffs. "She's a piece of work. Former stripper. That's how Arthur met her. Next thing you know, she's living with him. He thought the world of her, but I don't think she thought much of him, just a place to bed down and not have to pay for. Wasn't she with Arthur when you worked with him?"

"Yeah. I just wanted to check if you knew her. Is she still an addict?"

"I'm sure she uses. Never really got to know her, though. Only met her a couple of times. Tried to stay away from his home. Damn, he was good, though, but you already know that."

"One of the best. Don't know what this is, though, but he got himself into something."

"That he did, my brother," Marr said back. "That he did."

17

K elly showed up at the window on my side. I rolled it down all the way.

"Crime Scene found a possible location where it looked like the body could've been dragged into the creek. Nothing confirmed, but it looked good to them. They found a small canvas zip bag containing works, a used syringe, cigarette butts, and condoms. They bagged them. Couple of footprints too they'll have to pull up. Couple of the prints were scratched away with wood or something, though, so probably won't be useful."

"You wanna hop in the back and join the party?" Marr asked.

"Why not. Need to sneak a smoke before our damn whiteshirts decide to grill us."

She stepped into the back seat, shut the door. I turned to her as she lit a cigarette, blew the smoke in my face, but not on purpose.

"Sorry," she said. "So you got anything, Frankie?"

"'Fraid not, but like I told your partner here, I'll share everything I worked on with Arthur. I'll also look into Chris Doyle if you want me to."

"Appreciate that."

One of the supervisors I passed approached on Marr's side, bent down to speak. Marr opened the window all the way.

"See the media there? Cameras are probably catching you all smoking it up nice and cozy in the car while a body is still on the scene. This might be something regular in DC, but not here. Copy?"

"Copy that, sir," I said, and we extinguished our cigs.

"Damn smoke streaming out your windows looks like you're smoking a blunt. I also expect you all to fill in my detectives with everything you know."

"We'll be sure to do that," I advised.

He walked away.

"Piece of shit," Marr said.

"Well, I guess I'll be filling him in, then."

Kelly snorted out a chuckle. I turned back to her.

"You owe me."

"You fucking owe me too much already," she told me.

"Such love between you two." Marr smiled.

"I'll leave the both of you to catch up," I said, and opened the door and stepped out.

I walked back toward the crime scene, but another supervisor, a captain this time, stopped me and said, "So, what can you tell me?"

"Just that it's the guy from the BOLO we put out. I'll make sure my supervisor fills you in if we learn anything more."

"Our chief expects me to talk to the media and that's all you have?"

"'Fraid so, Captain. Anything else, sir?"

He turned away from me without saying a word. I made my way down the incline. A uniformed officer was standing near the body.

"They're all up the creek a bit, where the crime scene might be."

Up the creek. I had a good comeback for that but didn't say it.

Thomas and Malcolm were a few feet away from where the crime scene techs were working the scene. One of them was taking photos while the other, kneeling down, was pouring the substance into a footprint to lift it.

"Alexander Blum," I introduced myself to Malcolm.

"Walter Malcolm," he returned, and we shook hands.

"Does look like something was dragged. Footprints I can see don't look that large," I mentioned.

"More than one, but hard to determine the others." Thomas was pointing here and there along the river as he said this. "It's something, though. Dog prints too, so the footprints might belong to one of the folks who discovered the body. We'll rule them out. They did recover a bit of blood from the grassy area over there."

"We'll see then, I guess. Fucking only lead we had: dead."

"Tough break. For both you and the decedent," said Malcolm.

After the body was removed by the ME and we cleared the scene, we met Marr at Buffalo Billiards at Dupont Circle to have lunch. It was going to be another long one for me and Kelly. We both needed something to sustain us, and I loved their turkey burgers. After lunch Marr returned to the branch to do his write-up and Kelly and I made our way to Arthur's home to notify Celeste. It had to be done in a timely manner just in case it hit the news. Never was a good thing when people were informed about the death of a loved one over the news. *Loved one. God.* The difficulty was not in having to inform her about it but having to act normal.

She answered the door wearing the same outfit as the last time I saw her, except with different socks. She seemed surprised to see us.

"Can we talk inside, Celeste?" I asked before she could say anything.

"Something's wrong," she said intuitively.

"Let's talk inside."

She allowed us in, shut the door behind me.

"Is this a sit-down conversation?" she asked with an odd half-smile.

"We can sit," Kelly said.

A full smile this time and we followed her to the living room. She sat on the purple armchair. Kelly and I sat on the sofa, with me closer to Celeste.

No sense in beating around the bush, so I got right to it and said, "We found Arthur. I'm sorry to say that he wasn't alive."

Her head dropped into her cupped hands.

"No."

She looked up, eyes red, but no tears.

"What happened? Did he call you like he said he would?"

"No, he never called, and I also tried to call him several times. Did he call you back, or did you try to call him?"

"No. I was tired and fell asleep."

"He never called you back?" I asked again. "Said he was going to meet someone or anything."

"I said no."

I believed her.

"You didn't tell me what happened."

"We won't know for sure what the cause of death was until there's an autopsy."

"Autopsy?" she asked.

"Yes, that's the only way we can determine how he died."

"Was he murdered?"

"We don't know that."

"Like Detective Blum said, we'll have more information after the autopsy."

"Where was he found?"

"In Alexandria, off the parkway at the river," I said.

"Why would he be all the way there?" she asked.

"I don't know," I began. "We were hoping you could tell us."

"I've never known him to go to Alexandria. Was he alive when he was found?"

"No. Celeste, I know that Arthur's mother passed a few years ago, but don't know of any other living relatives who should be notified. Can you help us?"

"Arthur said he was an only child. I don't know about his dad or any other relatives. I'm sorry. What's going to happen to me? Am I going to have to leave? I have nowhere to go."

"I'm sorry, but we don't have an answer for that," Kelly answered flatly. "There are some other questions we have if you don't mind."

"Okay."

I sensed something different about her. Didn't look like grief. Scared, maybe. Afraid she was going to have to leave the house. Or was it relief? She was finally free.

"You have no idea why he'd be in that area?" Kelly asked.

"I said no. That's why I'm surprised to hear it."

"What about any friends you know that might hang out in that area? Anyone else we can talk to?" Kelly asked.

"I don't know of any. What's going to happen to his body?"

"We'll make every effort to locate a living relative to claim the body."

"We're sorry for your loss," Kelly said.

"I don't know what I'm going to do now."

Since his murder was now linked to the murder of Chris Doyle, we needed more than Celeste's consent to search the house. She slept in the same bed with him and had an expectation of privacy. There was a big chance we'd find some drugs in the house too. Aside from seeking information that might lead to a relative, we stayed clear of all that. There would have to be a search warrant.

She walked us back to the front door, and like she did before I left the last time, she turned to face me and hugged me hard. I patted her gently on the back with my right hand, noticed Kelly watching like *What the hell...*

I made eye contact with Kelly and shot her a look with raised brows. Uncomfortable.

"We'll be in touch," I said.

I gently broke free and we were out of there. Kelly said nothing as we walked to the car. Maria was our next stop before heading back to the office.

18

We had a lot to write up, so we figured we should include Maria too.

"You mind driving? I'm getting worn down."

"I don't mind."

I climbed in the passenger side of the cruiser.

"What's with that hug she gave you?" Kelly asked after starting the ignition.

"I don't know. Grief. Needed some comfort. No big deal."

"Yeah. Okay."

"What the hell you suggesting?"

"I don't know, partner. Looked a little more than needing a little comfort to me."

I knew she was trying to push my buttons, so I just said, "Fuck you."

She huffed out a chuckle and pulled away from the curb. I lit a cigarette, rolled down the window enough so I could flick the ashes out.

Lot of traffic when we hit U Street and continued west toward

16th. Everything was changing in the area. New restaurants, clubs, and businesses popping up. Other spots closing down. Velvet Lounge and Polly's and a few other places held tight, though. I was thankful for that. Despite the changes, the drug boys were still obvious, bound to their corners on 9th and 10th, a block or so north and south of U Street. Some of them strolling along, passing shops, smoking blunts and peering through shop windows like they were regular folks. Some things would never change no matter how much effort was put into it. I knew that for a fact. This was my home, but I could care less about those boys on the corner, as long as they didn't affect me. I wasn't always like that. I lightened up when I got into Homicide. Change of focus or some shit like that.

Maria lived on the fourth floor of the apartment building on the east side of 16th. It was an old building, not well maintained. Kelly was shouldering her black leather satchel. We took the stairs. They were littered with empty dime-bag zips, pint-sized liquor bottles, and a few used condoms. That was just a bit of what we saw, but something we were more than used to seeing. Felt more comfortable here than in the house on the block where Chris Doyle was murdered.

A couple of the doors along the hallway toward her apartment looked like a battering ram had been used on them at one time. We glanced at each other and smiled knowingly as we walked by.

Kelly knocked on the door of Maria's apartment. Shortly after, I could hear light footsteps approaching and stopping. I was sure whoever was on the other side was peering through the peephole.

"Can I help you?" a muted female voice with a slight accent asked.

"I'm Detective Ryan with the DC police. I spoke to you over the phone the other day about Raymond Wakeling."

Kelly lifted her badge hanging around her neck and directed it to the peephole.

"Just a couple more questions that can hopefully help Raymond out and we'll be on our way."

The door opened, but only a bit. I could see the silver chain securing it.

"We won't be long," Kelly said with a comforting smile.

"Let me see identification from both of you, please."

We both removed our police ID from our wallets. Kelly showed hers first and then me.

We heard her unlatch the door and then she opened it.

She was short and small-framed. Attractive, with full lips and large brown eyes.

"This is my partner, Detective Alexander Blum."

"What else can I help you with? I already told you I was with him."

"I think it's best we don't talk about it in your hallway. Can we step inside? You can leave the door open if you want."

She was hesitant, but then stepped aside to let us in.

"I have to be at work soon."

"We won't be long," Kelly assured her.

She allowed us in. We stepped into the small foyer. The living room a few steps away. All I could make out was an older light blue sofa and a scuffed-up wooden coffee table. It looked clean inside, though. I removed my notepad from my rear pocket and my pen from my shirt pocket to take notes.

"Just a couple more questions and some photos we'd like you to look at and we'll be on our way."

She didn't respond.

"I want you to know that we don't care about your drug use, but this does involve a homicide that might be drug related, so we do very much care about where Raymond got his heroin from."

"I don't know anything about that. I swear."

"I want to show you some photos. Tell me if you recognize any of these people. Okay?"

"Okay. I have to go to work soon, though. Can we make this fast?"

"Of course."

Kelly flipped her satchel open while it was still on her shoulder. She showed her the image of Arthur with Doyle first.

"Do they look familiar?"

After a brief glance, she touched the image of Arthur and said, "Just him. That's Artie, a friend of Raymond's."

"Raymond Wakeling?" I asked.

"Yes."

"When was the last time you saw Artie?"

"I don't even know. More than a week ago. I can't tell you what day."

"Where did you see him?"

"At Raymond's house."

Kelly took the photo back and put it in the case jacket, removed the photos of the women, still with the sticky notes on them. She handed them all over to Maria.

"Please don't remove the sticky notes. I'm sure you can tell the women in these photos are naked."

She shook her head as if that troubled her, looked at a couple of the photos, and stopped at the third one.

"I know her. Ivy. That's just her stage name, though. I don't know her real name."

"Stage name?" Kelly inquired.

"She's a stripper?" I asked.

Kelly looked at me. I shrugged.

"Yes."

"How do you know her?" Kelly asked.

"She's come over to Raymond's a couple of times with Artie."

"How many times have you seen her with Artie?"

"Three, four times."

"What club does she work at?"

"I don't know the name of it. It's downtown on K Street, though."

"Do you know any of the other women?"

She looked through the remaining photos and said "No."

Kelly retrieved them and placed them in the case jacket.

"I really have to get ready for work."

"Are you a dancer too?" I asked.

"No," she replied as if offended. "I work at a restaurant on 14th Street."

"Okay," I returned.

"If we have any more questions, can we contact you?"

"I guess, but please call first."

"Thank you," Kelly said nicely.

She nodded and we stepped out. She closed the door. I heard her locking it. We headed back to the stairs.

"I guess we'll be going to a strip joint later."

"Guess we will. Don't sound pleased."

"I could care less. You know I'm not into that."

"Every man's into that."

"I'm not fucking every man." I smiled like I was pleased with myself.

19

At the office I drafted the affidavit in support of a search warrant for Arthur's home. I was going to take it to AUSA Theresa Hargraves at the Triple Nickel the next day to have her sign off on it, and then to the judge at superior court.

It was past our shift. Kelly notified the LT that we had to work overtime so we could go to the strip club and interview a person of interest that came up during the course of the investigation.

We didn't know if Ivy would even be there, but the end of the workday on a weekday was usually peak time for most strip clubs. Lot of men hitting them before heading to their cozy suburban homes. We'd give it a shot. At the least find out when she would be working.

Took us longer than expected to get there. Traffic was a beast. No rush-hour parking near the club, but we stuck the bubble on the dash and parked anyway. Kelly tucked her badge, secured to the chain, under her blouse. Mine was hooked on a leather holder and affixed to my belt. Wouldn't be seen unless I lifted the bottom of my suit coat to reveal it. Didn't matter. It's not like we were trying to go undercover, and we'd certainly badge our way in if there was a cover charge.

The doorman, a large bald man who spoke with something like a Russian accent, gave us each the once-over and then opened the door for us to enter.

The dance music filtered in from the main room but was still loud and sudden. Before entering the main room we had to make our presence known to an attractive blonde wearing a revealing schoolgirl-type two-piece with a very short black-and-white plaid skirt, and black boots to her knees.

"Identification, please."

We showed her our police identification so she couldn't see our personal information. She seemed hesitant. I revealed my badge and a bit of my holstered gun.

"Unfortunately, it's business, not pleasure." I smiled. "We need to talk to one of your girls who goes by the name Ivy. She's not in trouble. Is she working?"

"I should get the manager," she told me.

"Whatever it takes," Kelly said.

She pulled out a small walkie-talkie from a shelf under the counter, pressed down on the side button with her thumb.

"Shelby, can you come up front please. The police are here."

"Police? Be right there," a filtered female voice replied.

Two loud talking men in expensive suits entered the front door and stood behind us. The man with a serious bald spot looked Kelly over. When she turned toward him and caught him, he smiled like he thought it could go somewhere. She turned away. He lost his smile.

"If you don't mind, could you wait over there," the schoolgirl said, directing us to the other side of the small room near a wall.

"No problem," I said.

The two men had their IDs ready. The schoolgirl shot them her best sexy smile.

"You know the way, gentlemen."

The bald spot man handed her a folded bill. She rubbed her fingers across the palm of his hand as she accepted and then slipped the folded bill under her bra strap, where several other bills were held. I noticed Kelly as she rolled her eyes.

"C'mon, Ryan. I know about some of the places you frequent."

"Oh, you do, do ya."

"Yeah, I do."

She rolled her eyes again. One of those places of hers was a hidden S&M spot on U Street, right across from the Third District and on the second floor of another club. She had her action spot and I had mine. She didn't know about mine, though. At least I didn't think she did. I didn't take the conversation any further for fear of finding out.

The manager stepped in. She dressed professionally, wore a black skirt that fell a bit below her knees, and a black button-down silk shirt. She had long dark hair kept in a ponytail. She smiled at the two men like she knew them as they made their way into the main room.

She looked at the girl behind the counter, who motioned with her head toward us.

She approached and said, "Can I help you with something?"

"I'm Detective Blum with the DC Police, and this is my partner, Detective Ryan. We're investigating a homicide and need to talk to one of your girls."

"A homicide?"

"Yes, but the girl we want to talk to is not in trouble. Her name came up during the investigation and she may have known the victim. It's important we talk to her. Her stage name is Ivy. Is she working?"

"Yes, she's one of our busy girls, but I certainly don't want to interfere with a murder investigation. She's onstage, though."

"We don't want to interfere with her money, so is there some-place more private where we can talk to her when she's done?"

"Of course. You can use the office in back. Would you mind waiting outside the office, though, until she's done and makes her rounds? This is a busy time."

Another man entered. It was obvious the manager didn't want us standing around making our presence known.

"I can take you back there."

"No problem," Kelly said.

"Appreciate it," I responded.

We stood in the narrow, dimly lit hallway, careful not to lean against the wall for fear of what might cling to our clothing.

The music soon changed to another equally loud and annoying song. Hopefully that meant the end of her set. I knew after Ivy stepped off the stage she would visit all the customers at the tables and say something like "Thanks for watching me," even if they weren't. Most of them would tuck a couple of dollar bills under her thigh strap.

After a few minutes, Ivy stepped in. She was wearing three-inch platform heels that made her about my height. She was very thin, but with large round breasts poking up and almost through her black lace bra. She looked young, maybe nineteen years old. She had a long see-through black shawl draped over her shoulders and covering most of her body and thong. A small glittery purple purse hung from her left shoulder by a chain and hugged her hip.

She walked toward us like a model on a runway and stopped inches from me, made eye contact, then without moving her body peered toward Kelly.

"You're here about a murder?"

Her breath smelled of mint.

"Yes," I told her.

"I wouldn't know anything about something like that."

"Let's step inside the office," Kelly said. "I like to see who I'm talking to."

She opened the door and walked in first.

The fluorescent light was on. It was a small office with a cheap wooden desk and a chair on rollers. Years of framed black-and-white and color photographs of strippers hung on every wall. There was a black leather sofa that seemed older than the desk at the other end against a wall, with a glass coffee table in front. There was a large glass ashtray at the center of the coffee table with ash and cigarette butts in it. No other chairs in the office except for the one on the other side of the desk. Kelly and I looked at each other knowingly. I couldn't make out any stains on the sofa cushions, but that didn't matter. We both knew what happened there regularly.

"Have a seat," I told Ivy.

She sat at the far end of the sofa on the left. Kelly shot me one of her upward nods and so I looked down at the cushion first and then sat in the middle near Ivy. Kelly stood by the wall at the front right side of the sofa.

"Like I said, I don't know anything about a murder, so I'd appreciate it if we could get right to it. I'm losing a lot of money."

I reached for my wallet, pulled out several twenties so she could see, and slid one to her.

"I can appreciate that," I said, and smiled after.

She accepted the twenty without hesitation, opened her small purse and wedged it in front of what looked like a couple hundred dollars in ones. I noticed a cell phone in her purse too.

"We already know you knew the victim, so let's not beat around the bush," I advised.

20

C hris is dead?"
  "Yes," I said.
   She handed the Polaroids of her image, the other women, and
the one with Doyle and Arthur back to me, and I handed them
off to Kelly.
   "And you're sure you don't know the other women?"
   "I'm positive. Why was he killed?"
   "That's what we're trying to find out. You met Chris here
I assume."
   "Yes. He was a big spender. Always took me to the back room.
Got a bottle of Dom. He was very nice. Not grabby or demanding
like the other man in the photo."
   "What was the other man's name?"
   "I don't remember. I didn't like him."
   "Why?"
   "Because he was rude and grabby and talked bad."
   "Do you know a girl who goes by the name Celeste?" Kelly asked.
   "No. Why?"

"Just another name that came up during our investigation."

"Tell us about you and Chris?"

"He wasn't like a friend or anything. You saw the picture. I did special parties for him on occasion and posed for him. Am I in trouble?"

"We don't care about what you did for him. How you make your extra money. That's the least of our concerns. But we do need you to tell the truth, because we may already know the truth. And that could get you into trouble. Lying, I mean. Did he pay you in drugs or cash?"

She made direct eye contact with me again. Her eyes were big. Seemed too big for her thin face, but God made her look good despite that and the overly large fake breasts.

"The drugs were just party favors. I don't shoot up. I like to smoke heroin. Track marks aren't good for business."

"Just heroin or did he deal cocaine, too?"

"He didn't deal cocaine, but he had it around."

"So you know he dealt heroin?"

"I guess, but I had nothing to do with that."

"We don't care if you did." Before she could say anything to that I continued with "How long have you known him?"

"At least a year."

"What about the other man in the photo with him?"

"I met him a few times, but only here. What I did with Chris was only for him."

"And you haven't seen Chris for over two weeks?"

"Something like that."

I handed her another twenty. She put that in her purse beside the other one.

She smiled and said, "Thank you."

"Was he involved with any other girls here at the club?"

"Not that I know of."

"Did you ever see him dealing drugs?"

She looked at me like she was surprised by the question. Looked down after. After a second, she looked up again. I knew then she knew more than she was letting on.

"I said I don't have anything to do with that."

"But you said that you knew what he did?"

"Yes, but I wasn't a part of it."

"Ivy, we only care about who murdered him. We need answers to certain questions. You need to be honest with us. We haven't even asked you for your real name or any personal information. We can keep it that way."

"But I wasn't involved with all that."

"Okay. You weren't."

"I forgot my cigarettes."

Kelly moved toward us, pulled a pack out of her satchel. Offered her one. Kelly lit it for her and we watched Ivy take a long, deliberate drag, blow the smoke out away from my face. She didn't make eye contact after.

"But you do know who his supplier was, don't you?" I asked because I had a feeling. "And your name will never come up."

She looked at me hard and said, "Yeah, like I can trust you two."

"You can trust us, Ivy."

"I don't know anything about that kind of stuff. How many times do I have to tell you?"

"Listen," Kelly began. "We can continue this conversation here and you can get back to work, or we'll take you to our office, where you will definitely lose money tonight. Your choice."

"You can't make me go anywhere."

"We most certainly can," Kelly told her.

"You're the bad cop."

"I'm whatever I have to be."

"Just give us his contact."

"You're going to get me killed."

"You'll never come up again," I advised her.

"He'll find out. He's dangerous, and he's not afraid of the police."

"You know him well, then."

"Well enough to know not to fuck with him."

"He one of your clients here?"

"Yes. He's a real big spender. More than Chris."

"He ever take you to his home?"

She hesitated again, took another drag from the cigarette and tapped off the ash into the ashtray.

"Hotels only."

"When was the last time you were with him?"

"Last week. Thursday."

"Did he ever hang here with Chris or the other man in the photo?"

"Yes. They sat with him sometimes. I didn't mean to lie. I'm just scared."

"We understand. He call you on your cell when he wanted to get with you?"

"Yeah, or just here."

"Did Chris introduce him to you or did you introduce him to Chris?"

"I met him through Chris."

"Give us his name and number."

"Don't make me do that."

"Ivy, he's a possible suspect in a murder investigation. Like Kelly said, we'll take you to the office if we have to and go through the court to get the information we need from you. Let's just do this the easy way and we'll be out of your hair."

She snuffed out her smoke in the ashtray. Looked like she was thinking hard.

"You promise to keep me out of this, and I won't have to go to court."

"You don't exist," I said.

She looked at me again like she wanted to trust me or like she knew she never did exist. She opened her purse and retrieved her cell, flipped it open and scrolled through her contacts. Kelly had her pen and notebook ready.

"His name is Trevor. I don't know his last name, but I remember Chris calling him Miles once."

She gave us his phone number and after I asked, she provided his description, too.

"You ever seen him with a gun?" Kelly asked.

"Yes. Several times. He liked showing it off. You have to believe me. He's very dangerous."

"We believe you," I said. "What nights does he usually come in?"

"He's a regular. Usually Tuesdays or Wednesdays."

"Around what time?"

"Late. Maybe midnight. He likes to stay till closing."

"Okay. Give us your cell phone number so we can call occasionally to check in on you."

"Remember, you promised."

"I did."

We left the club and walked to the car. There was a ticket on the windshield. Kelly huffed and pulled the ticket out from under the wiper. It wasn't MPDC. They'd never do that to one of their own.

"Damn DPW," Kelly said.

She crumpled it up, and I thought she would toss it, but she stuffed it in her satchel.

"LT will write that off."

"Yeah, I know, but it's just more paperwork we have to do."

"I'll give Marr a call on the way home, see if he knows anything about this Trevor dude."

"Good idea."

21

Marr knew Trevor Miles. Said they could never get to him. Not that he was all that smart, but "just lucky," according to Frank. He hadn't been arrested in the last two years. Maybe he'd been in jail. He did have an extensive record back then, though—PWID cocaine, PWID heroin, carrying a pistol without a license, several possession charges, and an assault on a police officer. He didn't do much time, if any. His record spanned a few years, but then nothing after 1997. Maybe he cooperated or spent a bit of time in jail. But now here he was. Frank wanted him bad. Offered resources. Couldn't turn that down. We didn't have much in the way of resources here, or manpower. Always nice to find help where you could get it.

When I got home, I listened to the messages from my mother. She was worried about her *friend* Richard, because according to my mom, he was supposed to come visit and never showed up. I'd give her a call tomorrow. She went to bed early.

I poured myself a scotch on the rocks. Didn't feel like TV or music, so I just sat on the sofa, finished my drink and poured another.

After I finished, I placed all my shit on the dresser and undressed. I hung up my suit and dropped the shirt in the dry-cleaning bag and went to the bathroom to take a long, hot shower and then off to bed.

I woke up early.

I had the affidavit in support of a search warrant with me. I called Kelly and advised her that I was going to 555 4th Street NW and then court to get it signed.

"I'll let the sergeant know," she said.

I found a parking spot about two blocks from the Triple Nickel. My mom called while I was walking. I stopped to answer.

"Hi, Mom."

"Alexander, I'm so worried."

"What's wrong?" I asked like I didn't already know.

"My good friend Richard is missing. He was supposed to take me to breakfast, but never showed. I'm so worried, Alexander."

"I'm sure he's okay, Mom."

"Can you use your contacts as a detective and see if he's okay?"

That's not how it worked, but I didn't tell her that. I only told her what she wanted to hear.

"I'll make a couple of calls. What's his full name?"

"Richard Towns."

Piece of shit. Didn't even give her his real name.

"I'll take care of it. Don't worry."

"Thank you, son. I love you."

"I love you, Mom. I'll call you later."

I wasn't that worried. I hoped that her brain would get jumbled up and forget about him soon. I would just have to throw some comfort her way in the meantime.

It took a couple of hours, mostly waiting for the judge in chambers to read it and sign off on it. I returned to the office, warrant in hand. Kelly and I could handle it ourselves. Didn't need manpower for this one. If we found anything major that could be used as evidence, we'd radio for Crime Scene to show up. I had a feeling that wouldn't be necessary, though.

We still had Arthur's cell phone, and Kelly found a contact on it for Miles. Now to figure out what to do with it. First thing was to get this search warrant out of the way, so I grabbed the backpack that had everything we might need in it, and by eleven a.m. we had made our way to Arthur's home. It took a few knocks before Celeste finally opened the door. She seemed surprised to see us, and even more surprised when Kelly advised her why we were there.

Before we entered, she said, "I don't know what he has hidden in here so I have nothing to do with what you might find."

That statement was a good indication that we might find something illegal, but I knew before Kelly answered that we wouldn't arrest her for anything bad we might find.

"You'll be okay," Kelly assured her. "But if you know about anything like drugs or weapons in here, now is the time to tell us."

"I've never seen any kind of gun or other weapon in here and he never shared any secret places where he might hide anything either."

"Okay then."

We entered. I went straight to the armchair and sofa, unshouldered the backpack, and set it on the floor, lifted the cushion to the purple armchair and then the sofa and the other armchair. I looked under and around them but found nothing to be concerned about.

"Why don't you have a seat here," I told her, directing her to the purple armchair.

She obeyed. I could tell she was nervous.

"This is part of the job," I said. "Just sit tight and we'll be out of here in no time. By the way, do you know anyone who goes by the name Trevor or Miles?"

She shook her head and said, "No. Why?"

"Just another name that came up. You're sure Arthur has never mentioned the names before?"

"I'm positive."

Couldn't tell if she was being truthful. I gave her a slight but hopefully reassuring smile, turned to Kelly.

"I'll start in the living room," I told her.

"I'll hit the kitchen and the second bedroom."

I picked up the backpack, walked into the dining room and set it on the dining table, then returned to the living room to begin my search.

"Am I going to have to leave this house?"

"I can't answer that. I don't know."

"I have no income and nowhere to go."

"I'm sure you'll be okay" was all I could think to say, and realized quickly that was not so comforting.

Why the fuck should I care anyway? Oddly enough, I sort of did. Well, a little more than sort of. It was an odd attraction I had, but then I always fell for the dangerous ones. The ones who could never fully be had.

There wasn't much to search in the living room. Celeste stayed quiet after what I last said. I'm sure she was genuinely worried about her future. I wanted to reach out, but I kept my mouth shut. It'd only get me in trouble. I still couldn't help but be drawn to her. I finished up in there.

"You sit tight, okay?"

"I won't budge."

I went to the dining room and opened a couple of cabinets but found nothing. Kelly walked in when I was almost finished, stood close to me so Celeste couldn't hear.

"Found a lot of syringes and other paraphernalia. Looks like personal use. Nothing I want to waste our time with recovering and putting on the book."

116

"I agree. No drugs, though, right?"

"Not even residue."

We took our time in the master bedroom, sorting through papers, bills that looked like they were paid off, and photos. The photos were mostly old family photos, and a couple of Celeste that looked like they were taken in Georgetown. I recognized one of the shops. I did find a ten-pack of what appeared to be heroin in small clear zips. It was secreted in his top dresser drawer under his underwear. I left it there. I don't know why. I convinced myself it wasn't worth the paperwork and was nothing more than personal use. If Celeste knew it was there that was also okay. Let her have that escape. I closed the dresser drawer.

"This area's clear," I said.

"This place is clean," Kelly said, sounding a bit disappointed.

22

The search of Arthur's home was a bust, except for some paper-work verifying that it was his house, and of course what I left behind. Arthur never was a real player. He just knew the big boys and had access to them. He learned a lot from working with guys like me and probably Marr too, and that was to keep your house clean. Never bring anything related to whatever illegal activity you're involved in to the place where you bed down. Good rule to follow.

I called Frank from the car. We decided to meet at the branch to figure out how to work Trevor Miles.

The older officer at the front counter recognized Kelly and me and asked us to wait. He made a call on the phone to advise Marr that we were there, and a couple of minutes later he entered from an open door to a hallway that led to several offices and the main rooms where the detectives and officers had their cubicles. He was carrying a thin manila folder.

"Hey," he said when he saw us. "C'mon back."

We followed him a short distance to a small conference room

with a table and several chairs that took up most of the room. A large, clean ashtray was in the middle.

"Sit anywhere."

Kelly and I sat at the side of the table where we could see the door. Frank sat across from us. The hallway was busy, someone looking in every few seconds. A thin, attractive young woman who looked more like a teenager, wearing an unbuttoned faded red flannel shirt over a navy blue T-shirt and equally faded blue jeans, entered. She smiled at us.

"This is Erin Molek. She's a UC here and hopefully'll be working with us for a bit."

"Hello," she said.

"Hey," I returned.

Kelly nodded an acknowledgment her way.

She sat down across from us and near Frank.

"Fresh out of the academy?" I asked her.

"Sort of," she advised with the same kind of smile.

He handed each of us a live scan printout of Trevor's photo.

"Photo's a couple of years old. I'm sure you already have one, but printed these out anyway."

We had it. I look it over, though. Looked like he'd been around the block. Smirking for the photo like it meant nothing.

"Well, needless to say," Frank started, "I got a lot on this boy Trevor Miles. He used to be nothing but a corner slinger from the fourteen hundred block of Fairmont, but after a brief stint at Lorton, he got out. Must have made some good contacts there and got a good education 'cause he quickly graduated to weight when he got out. Mostly heroin and crack but has a good hand in cocaine too. So you know I'd like to get him."

"We don't mind you having him, but we want to get him in the box with us first."

"Goes without saying."

"And we'd like to figure out a way to get him there so he doesn't figure out the charge right away. By the way, we just got back from searching Arthur's. It was clean. Do you know of any other place that he might bed down at?"

"No, just the house, and I'm surprised you didn't find anything. I know he was using."

"Nothing," I lied.

"Must've been trying to score then," Frank said. "Got anything on his death yet?"

"No, but we hope to sometime today."

Frank pulled out a pack of smokes from the pocket of his untucked long-sleeved shirt, offered one to Kell first. She took one. Offered me one. I did too.

He lit our cigarettes with a Bic lighter, then lit his, took a long drag.

"Back to Mr. Miles," Kelly began. "We know that he's a regular at the strip club on K. Goes there most Tuesdays and Wednesdays. Our source said they've seen him with a gun a few times."

Erin had a notebook out and was writing in it. I could tell she was a rookie, probably not even close to being vested. They made the best UCs, though, because they were fresh, not having spent enough time on the street to harden and get that certain look that came with it. A look that can usually be made by smart players. Maybe Trevor being one of them. She was quite attractive, too. I was sure she could win our boy over with those looks and that smile. She looked up after taking notes. Caught me staring at her. I smiled that time, turned back down to the photo of Trevor after.

"That might be tough, introducing Erin into a strip club," I said.

"Naw," she began. "Girls go to strip clubs all the time."

I shot her a look like how the hell would she know.

"Yes, they do," Frank agreed. "But there are still ways to strengthen the ruse."

"Maybe going there to find Arthur because I can't get in touch with him, and he gets me my shit."

"That's good, Erin," Frank told her.

"And if Trevor is there, I can make my way to him, work that into the conversation."

"He's a suspect, though. Have to be careful working in someone he may have murdered," Kelly advised.

"Nothing more has to be said other than she's trying to find him. In her head, he's just missing."

"Yeah, and unlike Chris Doyle, Arthur's name hasn't hit the news," I mentioned.

"Only thing is, most of the dancers get a bit pissy with outside women hitting on their clients," I said, and again got that look from Kelly. "Prostitutes go there sometimes, and the dancers don't like to see their money go anywhere else other than them."

"You know a fucking lot about this sorta shit," Kelly said.

"Yeah, well, we all got our thing, right? I used to hang out."

She snorted out a little chuckle.

"Nothing wrong with killing a bit of off-time at a strip joint," Frank added. "Nice atmosphere in most of them." He smiled. "And come on, Ryan, I know you gotta know."

She took a drag from the smoke. Didn't have to say anything.

"Why you all making such a big deal outta all this shit like a bunch of old farts," Erin said.

"Old?" Kelly busted out. "Early thirties ain't old."

"For her it is," Frank said.

"Back to it," Kelly said.

Ventilation in this little room was piss-poor. Smoke started hanging. Made my eyes sting and water.

"Not a guarantee the target will show. Might take more than one night. Your sups good with you guys working midnights until we get what we need?"

"They're good with whatever I need to do as long as I produce. And I got a good feeling about this one."

"How many people we going to have with us?" I asked.

"We have to have at least six. Eyes on her till she gets in and when she gets out and back to the meeting spot. Button camera that'll record and we'll have ears on her from our car. You two can get in with me and hear."

"So next Tuesday then?" I asked.

"That's more than enough time to make it work."

Frank snuffed out his cig, followed by Kelly. I smoked mine to the filter then followed.

"Good fishing, then," Frank said.

"Yeah, looks like we have good bait." I smiled at Erin.

She rolled her eyes.

23

It was hard to find solace at home, just the echoes of my mother's voice bouncing off the walls and then into my head. At least we'd had a regular shift today, but who knew what next week would bring. I got Friday/Saturday for my weekend so I'd catch up on my sleep tomorrow.

I gave myself a nice pour of scotch, with a couple of rocks this time, and turned the CD changer on but moved it to the third disc. Nick Drake. Nothing like a little melancholy for the melancholy. Somehow one had a way of short-circuiting the other.

My cell rang.

Celeste again.

I thought about not answering, but that side of my brain wasn't functional, so I paused the music and answered.

"Hello."

"This is Celeste. Is this a bad time?"

"No. Not at all. Everything okay?"

"I guess. I hate to keep bothering you. I don't know what you must think."

"You're not a bother. What can I do for you?"

She didn't respond, but I could hear her slight breathing.

"Celeste?"

"I don't know. I don't know why I called you. I'm sorry."

"Talk to me. What's going on?"

"I'm sorry. I gotta go." And she disconnected.

I didn't understand. I finished my drink but couldn't stop think-ing, so I called her back. It went to voice mail. I tried again, but no answer.

"What the fuck?"

I poured myself another drink. A double.

I downed it quickly, got up and decided to drive over to her house. Wasn't thinking straight. Of that I'm quite sure.

I drove past the house. I could see the dim yellowish glow of light seeping out through the closed blinds. The patio light was also on. I parked. I was still fairly buzzed after downing that double. Before I could think too much about it and change my mind, I locked the car and headed to the house.

I had to knock several times but eventually heard her stepping toward the door.

She opened it and didn't seem surprised to see me. She smiled and allowed me in without a word. Closed the door behind and locked it. We stood there, just looking at each other. I already knew what was going to happen and so I leaned in and kissed her. She wrapped her arms around me, and I wrapped mine around her, slid my right hand down to her lower back and pulled her into me tight. We fit well. It seemed natural. Expected. To say we kissed would be an understatement, though. It was the kind of kiss that I felt could never be duplicated with anyone else. Something I had not experienced. I was taken in. Done.

Sex with her was the same way. *Sex* is too dirty a word for it though. It felt to be much more than that. I had to admit, but only to myself, that I had wanted it since the first time I saw her again.

After, we spent an unclear amount of time naked, side by side on top of the covers and simply stared at one another, taking in each other's breath. We got lost in each other's eyes.

"I love your blue eyes."

"I love your green eyes."

She smiled.

Felt corny after I said it. I never talked that way. Didn't care, though. Her smile told me everything I needed to know. No one could fake a smile like that. At least I hoped not.

She stroked my hair with her fingers, stopped at the back of my head and pulled slightly. Never took her eyes off me. We were so close I lost focus, but that didn't matter. Those fucking eyes were something else.

I wanted to tell her that I'd never had it as good as I'd had with her, but that would make me too vulnerable, so I kept it to myself. I didn't feel guilty anymore. About anything. I felt good with the way it all turned out. I knew then that I cared for her deeply and all that happened didn't matter anymore. All that mattered was she was safe, and with me. And I wanted to take care of her.

24

I couldn't get Celeste out of my head. I couldn't wait to see her again. I gave her a bit of money to get her through the week, buy groceries, pay bills. She was thankful and said she would start looking for a job. I told her I would take care of her like that until she did. She was like a fucking drug and only after a couple of hits I was addicted. There was no turning back. I agreed to see her again. Told her I wouldn't be available until Friday because I was consumed at work with the two cases. She didn't want to wait that long. That actually felt good—that she wanted to see me so bad. Equally addicted? I caved and said maybe sooner, but that would depend on the next couple of days. I didn't mention what was going on, of course. I hadn't totally lost my mind. I did know that Tuesday and Wednesday might be crazy with what we had planned with Frank and his UC and the hours we'd be working beginning tomorrow.

"Maybe Thursday," I told her on the phone on Monday.

"Okay. That would be nice."

"I'll let you know."

"I can't wait."

Kelly walked back in carrying two cans of soda. I flipped the cell closed as she handed me one of them.

"Who was that?"

"Nursing home," I lied.

She sat down, cracked her soda open. I did the same. Took a swig.

"How's your mom?"

"Up and down. Only a matter of time before she loses it completely."

"I'm sorry."

"Yeah. Thanks."

I picked up the ME report again. It was still on my mind. We'd got it in earlier that day. Arthur's death was officially ruled a homicide, and the manner was gunshot wounds to the head. Two .22 caliber rounds were recovered from his head. In addition, opiates in his blood.

I was tired when I got home, but it was too early to sleep. Drinking didn't help. Only made me more tired. I had to try to stay up as late as possible and sleep late too. We shifted our tour to evenings, with the likelihood of going into the midnight shift. I knew all too well how these types of ops worked out. Usually never how you wanted them to. Frank Marr had a good rep. I knew he'd work it through. He spoke highly of Erin, so I hoped she could work her way to Miles. He had to show up, though. That would be the hardest part—waiting for that to happen.

I woke up on the sofa. Early-morning light was barely making its way through my closed blinds. I poured myself what remained in the bottle. Finished it off quickly and went to the bed in a desperate attempt to find more sleep.

25

I dressed in tan khakis and a forest-green hooded pullover. I brought a jacket in case the temperature dropped during the night. I drove to the branch, noticed Kelly's take-home parked in the lot with her still in it and the window rolled down as she smoked.

"You got here early," I said as I opened the passenger door and sat inside.

"So did you."

"Can I get a smoke?"

She shot me a look and said, "Why don't you ever buy your own?"

"Because then I'd smoke too much."

"Shit."

She reached for the pack inside the pocket of her black puffy jacket. I took it and tapped one out, handed it back to her. I used the vehicle's cigarette lighter, rolled the window down a bit and took a nice drag.

"Haven't done an op like this in a while," I said.

"Yeah. Let's hope it works out."

"Such a pessimist."

"A realist."

She seemed distracted.

"Things going okay with your daughter?"

"Always something."

"It'll get better."

"Oh, it will?"

"Yeah, I've heard it does."

"Are you dating a single mother I don't know about? Someone who has a teenage daughter?"

"Yeah, right."

She looked at me with a crooked smile. "Long as I've known you you've been single. You even dating at all?"

I avoided the question, took another drag. Smiled.

"The master of avoidance."

"You need more sleep."

"Fuck you," she said without anger.

"Fuck you too, partner."

She took a last drag and flicked her smoke out the window and almost hit the car parked beside her.

"Well, you ready to get this started?" she asked.

"May as well."

"And yes, I do need to get more sleep," she said as she stepped out of the car.

Everyone was in the conference room. They were all dressed down. Most of them didn't look like cops. None of them familiar to me and I'm assuming Kelly either because she didn't acknowledge anyone. They must have shaken things up at the branch. That often happens with new leadership. Two officers with scruffy beards were leaning against the wall. Four other officers were sitting together on the other side of the table. One of them was a heavyset female. Marr and Erin were not there.

"This is where we're meeting Frank, right?" I asked.

One of the officers leaning against the wall said, "Yes. He'll be here in a couple."

"I'm Alexander Blum and this is my partner, Kelly Ryan. Appreciate the help."

They looked serious and were uncomfortably quiet, like they didn't want to be there. A couple of the guys sitting at the table waved, though.

There were four chairs available. We sat beside each other, set our packs and vests on the floor next to us.

Frank walked in with a mug of coffee in one hand and a manila folder in the other, and said with a smile, "Happy you all could make it."

"Just another fun evening with you, Marr," one of the officers leaning against the wall said.

"Ain't nothin' but a thing," an officer sitting next to the heavyset woman said.

"Never could figure out what the fuck that means," Frank told him.

The officer shrugged like he didn't give a shit. Tough crowd, but I suppose they have to be.

He sat next to me, set the mug on the table and opened the folder. I could see that it contained several live scan photos of Trevor Miles and some other papers. He handed the photos to me.

"Take one and pass it around," he told me.

I took one and passed the stack over to Kelly. Everyone got a copy.

"Trevor Miles, a possible suspect in two homicides, one of them a CI of mine and a former CI of Blum's. Blum and Ryan are handling the homicides. He's also a known heroin dealer. That's why we're involved. See if we can get him on some good charges. Give these two some leverage when they question him. We're sending in Erin with the hope that if he's there, she'll make a connection."

Marr pulled out some printed maps of the area on which the strip club was highlighted. He passed them around.

"Ragland and Cortez, you'll be parked across the street with eyes on the entrance."

"What if we don't find parking?" Ragland asked.

Ragland was sitting at the table beside another officer who I assumed was Cortez.

"Then fucking park illegally or at the bus stop. Just make sure you have eyes on the front and can see the UC walk in and out."

"Copy."

"Tyler, Danny, you two park in the alley rear of the location. There's a rear exit and stairs leading up to another door on the second floor. The girls step out for smoke breaks and weed. Lights out, okay?"

The hefty female said, "Got it."

"You two mutts," Marr said to the two leaning against the wall. "You go inside."

"Sweet," the one who spoke before said.

"Nothing sweet about it. You find a cozy spot where you have eyes on Erin. No fucking around with the girls."

"What if they want to fuck around with us?"

Marr pulled out a thick stack of dollar bills from his coat pocket. The bills were held tight with a rubber band. He tossed it to him. He caught it with one hand. Smiled after.

"Give me half of those," his partner said.

"Tip money. All you got is a hundred so don't go crazy. And don't draw too much attention to yourselves. Use your pagers if you have to message me. Keep them on vibrate in case I need to get with you. Just fucking pay attention please."

"What about drink money?"

"No money for that from me, but what I can't see I don't know. Nothin' hard, though, if you know what I mean."

"It's Miller time, boys," the big girl said.

That got a couple of chuckles.

"Ryan and Blum are with me. We'll get with the UC at our spot and advise when she's out. Questions?"

No one responded.

"Let's roll then."

26

E rin was dressed to kill. Damn, I'd offer her the world if I ever saw her at a bar. We met her at a spot Marr had picked out and was about a fifteen-minute walk to the club. She'd walk there and back after leaving the club. We'd have eyes and ears on her at all times. I sure as hell hoped she knew what she was doing and was schooled well. Erin sat in the rear seat on the driver's side. The rear windows had a heavy tint. I stepped out of the back to let Marr in so he could wire her up. I took the driver's side, watched them through the rearview. Erin took her coat off and pulled up her black lace V-neck top. She was wearing a black lace bra under it. Marr taped the wire so that it was secured up her torso and between her cleavage under the bra strap. She pulled her top back down and Marr inspected her to make sure the wire was not showing.

"How does it feel?" he asked.

"Good."

"Be careful if you take your jacket off. Don't want to shift anything around."

"I will."

"Okay, step out of the car and let's check audio."

She got out of the car, walked a short distance across the vacant lot. Marr turned the recorder on.

She came over the little monitor clearly with "Hello, hello. This is a voice check. Hello. Helloo."

She walked back to the car, opened the door.

"Was that good?"

"Yeah. Get in and let's go over this one more time."

She sat beside him and shut the door. He handed her the live scan photo. She looked at it.

"This was a couple of years ago, but not so long ago that he woulda changed that much. He's pretty distinctive. Hair might be different."

"I'll recognize him."

"You've done this before, but never in a spot like this. You know what to do, though. Girls that work there might be on you, so be prepared."

"I can handle them."

"Respectfully, right?"

"I got ya, Frankie."

"I mean, they might think you're working or something, and if you move in on Miles, there might be some interaction because he's a client and a big spender."

"You worry too much. I got it."

He handed her some twenties and a thick stack of ones with a rubber band securing them. She folded up the twenties and wedged everything in her tiny purple sparkly purse and snapped it closed.

"Okay. Remember, under no circumstances are you to go any-where private with him or leave with him. If he follows you out—"

"I'll take care of it," she interrupted. "And I know—never get in a car."

"Don't be a smart-ass."

"Copy that, Frankie."

Their interaction made me smile a bit, but I was still nervous. I felt she was too young for something this big. I trusted Frank so tried to push it out of my head. Kelly was quiet. That made me think she felt the same way.

Frank's pager buzzed.

"Boys inside said it's a slow night and they haven't spotted the target."

"It's still early," I said.

It was a Tuesday evening so not much going on downtown. Rush hour was pretty much over and those who were out looked normal enough. We weren't in a part of DC where you'd have to worry about corner thugs, just a few homeless people. Tall, well-lit buildings, one against the other, lined the blocks. Once we got closer to the club, the atmosphere changed. Even more panhandlers and a few prostitutes. Frank went over the surveillance channel to let the others know where Erin was. When she got to the block he notified everyone again. The two officers on the block acknowledged when they saw her. We drove past her just as she walked up to the doorman.

Frank kept the handheld radio at his lap and keyed it in and said, "You guys got eyes on her?"

"Yeah," said someone I didn't recognize.

"Lost sight of her," Frank said. "Finding a parking spot."

"I'm supposed to meet someone here," we heard Erin say over the monitor.

It was a bit crackly, but we could hear well enough.

"See some ID," the doorman demanded.

"No prob."

Shortly after, we heard her walk a few steps and what sounded like a door opening. Loud music in the background.

"She just entered the building," the officer responded over the radio. "Didn't look like she had trouble at all."

"Copy that," Frank acknowledged.

Frank spotted a parking place along the curb near a crosswalk on the other side of the street. He waited for a couple of cars to pass and made a quick U-turn. Pulled to the curb and quickly turned the lights off.

"Identification," said a female voice that sounded like the same girl we met at the front counter.

It was a bit hard to hear, but we could make it out. It was recording to a small device taped near her crotch, so the quality could probably be better.

"I just showed my ID to the doorman, but here."

"You been here before, sweetie?"

"No. I'm meeting a friend who comes here all the time, though."

"Oh, who? I might know him."

"Artie."

"Oh, Artie. He hasn't come in yet."

"I'll wait for him. He told me he'd be here."

"So, you like girls, sweetie?"

"I'm just here to meet Artie."

"You dance?"

"No."

"Let me know if you ever want to. I'll set you up with the manager. You'd do well here."

"I will."

"Straight through the door there, sweetie."

"Thanks."

Music got much louder. A couple of seconds after, Frank's pager buzzed.

"They got eyes on her inside."

We could hear clothing rub against the mic as she walked. A

little more scuffling and then it stopped. Maybe found a place to sit. Movement every so often though.

Frank lit a cigarette. Kelly followed suit.

A homeless man pushing a grocery cart passed us.

"We come here every so often for the prostitutes so no big deal," Frank advised.

The homeless man disappeared around the corner.

"Sometimes the pimps use them as lookouts. But no worries. It's all good if that's what they think we're here for."

"So much for an undercover car," Kelly said.

"Oh, it ain't the car. It's the occupants inside it and just hanging out. Not that hard to put two and two together."

"Got that right," I said.

"Hi, honey. What can I get ya," said a distorted female voice.

"Vodka soda."

"You wanna start a tab?"

"Not right now. Just cash. I'm waiting for somebody."

"No worries, honey. We get girls in here all the time. As long as you're not hustling, all right?"

Erin chuckled softly and said, "Naw, that ain't me."

"Be right up, then," the muted waitress said.

A taxi pulled up to the front of the club. A couple of men wearing suits stepped out and walked to the doorman. They shook hands and the doorman let them in right away.

"Whore just came up and read us a menu for services," Tyler, who was parked in the alley rear of the location said over the radio.

"No chatter, unless it has something to do with our UC, copy?" Marr said gruffly.

"Copy that, Frankie. Just sayin'."

"Fucking idiot," Marr said.

"Gotta wonder what's on the menu tonight, though," I said.

Frank and Kelly chuckled.

"Here you go," the waitress said.

"Thank you, doll."

Frank's pager sounded again.

"They said the two suits walked in and sat at the table near the UC."

Frank typed a response on the keypad of the pager then set it back down. Just as he did, it sounded again.

"Shit," Frank said, and picked it up. "One of them scooted toward the UC."

"You working, sweetheart?" a faint male voice asked.

"I'm here waiting for my boyfriend and he wouldn't appreciate you asking that," Erin responded.

"I'm just asking, beautiful, and wondering why a girl like you is sitting here all alone."

"Well, now you know. Bye-bye."

Pager went off. Frank read it.

"Dope moved back to his table," Frank advised.

"You like my dance?" a female voice was heard asking over the monitor.

"You're wonderful," Erin said.

More shuffling heard.

"Thank you, darling," the female voice said.

"She better go easy on those tips. Make them last," Frank said, and flicked his cigarette that was smoked close to the filter out the window.

"You're not like most girls we get in here," she said. "Hope you're not scamming."

"No. No, I'm just waiting for someone. You know Artie?"

"Fuck yeah. Everyone here does. He your man?"

"Well, yes and no."

"I see. I gotta make my rounds, but I'll sit with you for a bit if you want."

"Yeah, I'd like that. Sort of uncomfortable here alone."

"I got ya, baby. Be back soon."

"All right."

"Good girl," Frank said to himself.

Two prostitutes walked by, dressed in skirts up to their crotches, bras, and platform shoes. One of them stopped, peered at Kelly through the passenger-side window like she was considering it, then moved on like she knew better. They both looked at each other and giggled, then crossed the street to the other side and continued down the block, not toward the club.

"You'd have to be outta your mind to go with something like that," Kelly said.

"Yeah, most men are," Frank said.

27

The stripper from earlier sat with Erin. Erin engaged her like a
pro. Got her to share her life story. The one-year-old with an
unsupportive father that she had to take care of, who was at home
in Southeast with Grandma. The crack habit she also had to take
care of, and occasionally heroin.

"That's why I'm here and tryin' to get with Artie," Erin told her.

"You mean crack? Artie ain't into crack. And he ain't no
dealer either."

"Heron," she advised, using the slang. "And I know he ain't a dealer,
but he takes care of me with what he gets from someone else."

"Oh. Well, I hope he shows for ya. He comes around most of the
time but hasn't been here for a while."

"He said he'd come by tonight. I don't know what I'll do if
he doesn't."

"Well, we'll just have to see then."

"What do you mean?"

"Don't push it, Erin," Frank said to himself.

"That we'll just have to wait and see is all. I'm up next. I'll get
back with you. Hope you like my dance."

"Wait. Here—for you."

Shuffling, and then the stripper said, "Thanks, baby. Every bit helps."

"Come back and sit with me. I'll take care of ya. I don't like sittin' here alone."

"Well hell, these other men here sure as hell ain't gonna take care of me. I'll be back, sweetheart."

"See ya soon, doll."

"My stage name's Sparkle."

"See you soon, Sparkle. My name's Jennifer."

"Fucking Sparkle?" Kelly snickered.

"Don't give the hardworking girl a hard time," Frank said.

Kelly lit another cigarette instead of responding.

"They do work hard," I added. "Seriously."

"I'm beginning to wonder about you, partner," Kelly told me.

"Hand me a smoke" was all I said.

She grinned at me but gave me one along with her lighter.

"Thanks, sweetie."

"Fuck you again," she said.

"You two are something else."

"Love him like the brother I never wanted," Kelly said back.

Frank smiled.

A tall man dressed in red pants and a long fur coat walked by smoking what looked like a Swisher Sweet. He was accompanied by a much shorter, stout man dressed in dark clothing. They both looked hard at us. Thought I was back in the seventies for a minute. The short, stout man spit on the ground near the front end of the car.

"Fucking knuckleheads," Frank said.

I finished my smoke and flicked it out the window. It hit the sidewalk and embers lifted a couple inches. The stout man turned after it hit. They turned the corner and were out of sight.

"You want another?" the waitress asked.

"Thanks, but I'm still nursing this one. Maybe in a bit."

"Can't take up the seat and not drink, baby, so not long. Okay?"

"Okay."

A group of four young men were walking up the block toward the club.

"Four dudes coming your way. None of them meets the description," the unknown officer from the car down the block advised.

They walked to the doorman.

"We got 'em in sight," said Frank. "None of them match the description."

Doorman didn't ask for ID. They walked right in.

A few minutes later we could hear them yapping over the loud music. Sounded like they already had a few.

Frank's pager buzzed.

"Negative on the four that entered," Frank read to us from the pager.

The four men were loud in the background, like they were sitting close to Erin. We could make out the waitress asking what they'd like and two other female voices calling them all "baby" and "lover" and asking if they'd buy them a drink. It sounded like one of them agreed and that the two girls joined them.

A couple of minutes later we heard:

"What are you doing here all by your lonesome, beautiful?"

"Waiting for my boyfriend," Erin told them.

Shuffling and then—"I can keep you company until then. Someone like you shouldn't be kept waiting."

"I'm fine, but he won't be if he catches you sitting next to me, so bye."

"Aww, c'mon now, baby. How much would it cost me to take you to a nice hotel tonight? I guarantee you won't be disappointed."

"I ain't no prostitute and my boyfriend'll be pretty damn upset with you suggesting that."

"You think I should be scared?"

"I think you should."

"Well, I'm the police and I don't scare that easily."

"Fuck me," Frank said.

"This doesn't sound good."

"If any of them knew her we'd know by now," Frank said.

"Hopefully," Kelly added.

"You got nothin' to say to that?" he asked.

"You think I should be intimidated or somethin'?"

"No, baby, just that I can take care of you. Maybe better than your boyfriend."

"I don't need that kinda taking care of."

"Hey, doll," we heard Sparkle say. "Let me squeeze in here next to this lover."

"You're lovely," he told her. "Yeah, come on in and join the party."

"You aren't Artie," Sparkle said.

"No, I'm Bobby. Who the hell is Artie? This beautiful girl's boyfriend?"

"Yes, that's my man," Erin told him.

"So what do they call you, darling?"

"I'm Sparkle. How about buying me a drink?"

"Oh, that feels good," he said. "Reach your hand up a bit higher. Yeah, like that. You can have as many drinks as you want."

"I see you in here a lot," Sparkle said. "But you're always surrounded by the other girls."

"Happy you're here now, Sparkle."

"I need to get with the mutts," Frank said, and grabbed his pager and started typing.

"What do you think they can do?" Kelly asked.

"Maybe get closer to the other three and pick up on their conversation. You know us cops always talk shit about work. We need to know who they are."

"Just because they're in a strip club doesn't mean they're dirty," I said.

"No, but it puts Erin in danger of possibly getting herself burned."

Based on what we were hearing over the monitor, it sounded like Sparkle had his attention. The waitress was also heard asking what Sparkle would like to drink.

Frank's pager buzzed again.

"They'll work it somehow," Frank said after reading the response from the two inside.

"Tequila shots all around," Sparkle said.

"Erin's going to get herself real drunk," Kelly said.

"Trust me, she can handle it."

"Sounds good to me. Make it Cuervo. The good stuff," Bobby ordered.

"You got it, sweetheart," the waitress said.

Frank grabbed the handheld and said, "Cortez, when those four boys exit the front, I want photos, all right?"

"Copy, Frankie."

"Even if Erin leaves and all of us follow her back, you two stick around until they get out and follow them to their vehicle to get a tag, all right?"

"Got it."

Yeah, this was going to be a long fucking night.

28

The cop who went by Bobby was busy with Sparkle. According to the mutts, the other boys who were with them had three girls at their table. They couldn't make out where the boys worked or if it was even with DC police, but they sounded like "a bunch of rookie SLAPs" one of the mutts messaged. And, aside from Bobby, none of them paid much attention to Erin. The message advised that she was sitting beside Sparkle, who seemed to be keeping the other cop away from her. Erin appeared to be okay.

About two hours in, a shiny black Camry with heavy tint pulled to the front of the club. Frank had his small binos out and called out the temporary DC tag. Kelly wrote it down in her notebook. If they were thugs, then the temporary tags were probably bought off the street for a buck fifty and would be impossible to identify.

Two men exited the rear of the vehicle.

Cortez came over the radio almost immediately after with "Looks like our target. Three-quarter black leather coat, blue jeans…"

"Got him," Frank advised.

I peered out the rear window with my binos.

"Sure does."

Frank got on his pager and messaged the mutts.

The Camry drove off and the two men knocked knuckles with the doorman like they were pals. Looked like the one who might be Trevor slipped him a bill. The doorman opened the door for them.

They entered.

Seconds later the pager shook. Frank read it.

"Appears to be our guy. Walked in like he owns the place. The two men passed the so-called cops and greeted them, then went to sit at a corner table to the left of Erin."

Pager sounded again.

Frank read, "Four girls went to their table right away along with the waitress."

"I gotta go say hi before I go dance, sweetie," Sparkle said.

"I understand, babe," Bobby said. "You come back, though."

"I will, doll."

"Looks like it's just you and me again, little girl."

No response from Erin.

"Also looks like you have interest in the man over there."

"What makes you think that?"

"You keep lookin' his way, and I'm guessing that you're here for something more than to meet your boyfriend, if that's even real."

"Oh, it's real and he's always late. And what else do you think I might be here for?"

"I'm a cop, girl. I know a user when I see one."

"User?"

"Drugs, baby."

"If that's what you think I am, then why would you be interested. I mean, being a cop and all."

"'Cause I like beautiful girls and I couldn't give a shit if you use drugs."

"Well, no offense, but I don't trust cops. I definitely don't trust you."

"No offense taken, and I can understand that. Let me at least try here. You wanna meet the man over there? I can make that happen."

"Fuck me," Frank said.

"I don't know about this," Kelly said.

"Let it roll," Frank added.

"I mean, I really don't think your boyfriend's gonna show. You been sitting here for a bit."

"Who is that man over there and why would you know him?"

"He's the guy who can get you whatever the hell you need, and I'm not your average cop."

"I think this is a setup."

"What're you into? Blow? Crack? No, I think you like heron."

She didn't answer. Probably still running scenarios through her head.

"This guy worries me," I said.

"If he is a cop and works vice on the district level, he wouldn't be setting her up like that—through a known dealer. In his head she's just a user, and certainly not a big player. He's bad news, but I trust our girl in there. Pretty sure all he wants to do to her is fuck her," Frank said.

"It's always all about sex," Kelly said.

"I don't do crack" is all she said.

"C'mon. Meet Trevor. You can wait for your boyfriend at that table as easy as this one."

The sound of movement, but not her.

"C'mon, sweetie. You're safe with me."

It sounded like she was moving.

"Okay. I'll play," Erin said.

Frank's pager went off again.

"She's walking over to the target's table," he told us.

29

W hat's up, Miles?" Bobby said.
"My boy, Officer Bobby. I seen you sittin' there. Who's
this you got with you?"

"I'm Jennifer."

"Bobby have to arrest you to get you here with him?" he joked.

Bobby was heard laughing.

"Naw, I'm here of my own accord."

"Come and sit. Have some Champagne. You too, Officer
Friendly."

"Don't mind if I do," Bobby said.

"Ooh, Dom," Erin said.

"Always the best here. Scoot over, girls. Let 'em sit."

"Squeezing closer to me is all right," said an unknown man.

"I got an extra glass here, Jennifer," Trevor told her.

"Thank you."

"Hi, girls," Bobby said.

Couple of hellos from unknown girls.

"Where'd you and Bobby meet?"

"Just met here," she said.

"And what brings you here? Girls do come here, but usually not all by their lonesome."

"I was supposed to meet up with a friend, but I think he got caught up with something or someone else."

"He's a no-show, sweetheart," Bobby told her.

"And why you meetin' up with this friend here?" Trevor asked.

"'Cause he said he wanted to meet me here. That he usually comes here on Tuesday."

"Who is this friend? Maybe I know him."

"I gotta go dance, lover," one of the girls said.

"All right, baby. Here ya go."

"Thank you, love."

"His name is Artie."

"Shit. Artie. I know him. Haven't seen him in a bit, though."

"Must be some kinda stupid to stand you up, girl," the unknown man said.

"Got that right," Bobby added.

"This looks like the table to be at," Sparkle said. "Did you enjoy my dance, Trevor?"

"Always, girl."

"Can I join?"

"You know my table's always open."

"Thanks."

"Squeeze in next to me," Bobby told her. "Continue where you left off. And here's a little somethin' for you."

"Thank you, dear."

"You look like you like to party, Jennifer," Trevor said.

"I've been known to."

"I got a nice room at the hotel down the street for a little afterparty."

"That sounds nice, but I got a kid with my mom that I have to

149

pick up so I can't stay late. I was just here to meet up with Artie and get a little something to hold me over."

"Get a little somethin'? From Artie? What little somethin' you get from him?"

"You can tell him," Bobby advised. "He's good people."

"But you're a cop."

"Sheeeit," Trevor said. "Only thing Bobby here cares about is pussy and makin' money and he don't like dirty pussy but doesn't care if the money is. Ain't that right, Bobby?"

"You got that right," he chuckled.

"Fucking dirty cops. Shit," I said.

"Don't worry, we'll take care of that part. You got the homicides to deal with. We'll work these guys and let IA know about it. It'll be a pleasure."

"But still, how do I know you don't work for the police?"

Trevor busted out with a deep laugh and said, "Baby, it's the other way around."

"And if it were like you said," Bobby began, "it sure as hell wouldn't be for some user and simple possession charge shit."

"I like heron. I just need to get a couple of dime bags to get me through until I get paid tomorrow."

"Dime bags. Shit, that ain't nothin' for me."

"That's all I can afford until I get paid tomorrow."

"What you do for work?"

"I work for a rich family. Walk their dogs. Take care of their house. Whatever they need. They pay me every Wednesday under the table."

"Sounds like you're a hardworking girl," Trevor said.

"I do work hard. Take care of my baby boy and other things."

"Bull, hand me a couple of them greens, will you," Trevor said.

"Sure thing, boss."

A moment later Trevor said, "Here ya go, baby."

"I can't afford two. I can tomorrow, though."

"Other ten's on the house, baby."

"Oh my. Thank you, sweetie."

"We can go in back," Sparkle suggested.

"I can't go get my baby boy high. My mom would know. She's a nurse. Have to get my mom outta the apartment and make sure he stays asleep." A couple of seconds later she said, "Here, Trevor, and thank you."

"Good girl," Frank said.

"I'm here for ya, doll."

"Can I get in touch with you somehow?" Erin asked.

"I'm here Tuesday and Wednesday. This place here is somethin' like my part-time office."

"And we're all very happy about that," an unknown girl said.

"Why don't you call your mom, say you got caught up with something, and come to the hotel?" Bobby asked.

"I wish I could now, Bobby. Maybe some other time, after I get paid and can afford a babysitter."

"I'll take care of that babysitter for you tomorrow. You don't have to worry about that. Come by tomorrow."

"We'll see."

"Another bottle, Trevor?" the waitress asked.

"Yeah, another bottle for the table," he replied.

30

C ouple more hours passed. Bobby was heard trying to get Erin into a private room with Sparkle several times, but she managed herself out of that well. Certainly had a knack for this kind of work. I could see why Frank took to her. She was a natural and someone to hold on to. She worked her way up to having to leave because her mom had an early shift the next day.

"Can we exchange numbers, Jennifer?" Bobby asked.

"This boy just don't give up," Trevor said, followed by chuckles around the table.

"Yeah, we can," Erin said.

"Oh, you go, boy," Bull said.

"Hold on, I got a pen here. Hand me that napkin, sweetie."

"Here ya go," Sparkle said. "I think I should be jealous, though."

"Naw, I'm always yours, girl."

After a few more minutes of conversation, she said her goodbyes. Frank's pager went off.

"On her way out," Frank advised us.

Shortly after, she was seen exiting the front door. Cortez came over the radio with "UC's out."

"Got her," Frank said. "She knows to walk a couple blocks so we can see her from here. Make sure she's not followed, then I'll take the lead, then you guys in the rear. Cortez, you two watch the front to make sure that dope Bobby or someone else doesn't come out to try and find her."

"Copy."

"Think it's too late for that," I said, and right after, Cortez came back over the radio.

"One of those possible cops just walked out."

"Shit," Frank said. "Get pictures."

"Copy that."

"Let me walk you to your car," Bobby said.

"I don't have a car. I walk home. It's only about ten blocks."

"Ten blocks? Shit, it ain't safe this time of night. I'll drive you."

"I need to know you better, Bobby. I can take care of myself so I'm just gonna walk."

"You gotta give me somethin' here, girl. I just hooked you up."

"You got my number. I'm worth waiting for, okay?"

"I ain't the patient type."

"I gotta go. I'm gonna try to come back tomorrow."

"All right then, but you call me when you get home okay?"

"How sweet of him," Kelly said sarcastically.

"I will, baby."

She walked away. He watched her for a bit and then entered the club.

"Damn," Frank said. "Okay, keep eyes on her and then I'll make my way around."

"I got her," I said.

After she walked a couple of blocks Frank went back over the radio and advised, "I'm turning the block. Watch her until I get around and back into view."

"Got her," Cortez said.

"And Cortez, you guys wait for Trevor to leave and tail him to try and get an address on him."

"Got it."

Frank pulled over to the curb when he got too close, stayed at least a block behind. She followed the route back to the pickup spot. At the curb, we made sure none of the cars stopped for her. She walked strong, kept walking, like she belonged to the city. Good. Thugs had a way of picking up on those who looked like they didn't belong. Not many of them were out, though, on a boring Tuesday night in downtown.

31

After we picked Erin up we headed back to the branch to meet everyone in the conference room for a debriefing. Frank put the clear narcotics evidence bag that contained the two small green zips that Erin purchased from Trevor on the conference room table. He tested the powder beforehand, and it was positive for opiates. Ragland and Cortez were the last to arrive.

Cortez closed the door behind him.

"Great job, everyone, especially you, Erin," Frank said.

Erin smiled.

"Got a little sketchy there for a bit," Frank added.

"Yeah, and should I call that Bobby guy to let him know I got home?"

"Yeah, let's do that now. Quiet on the set," Frank joked. "And radios, cells, and pagers off."

Frank retrieved a recording device from his coat pocket. It had a thin cord with a small mic that could be held near the cell's mouth-piece, but before he allowed the call, he pushed the record button on the device and gave his name and the date and time, and advised what the call was for and who it was being made to.

He paused the recorder then and said, "Don't push for his full name or agree to meet anywhere other than the club. You don't want to spook him. This is about Trevor. We're gonna let IA take care of Bobby. Tell him to help you with Trevor because you want to buy a bit more next time so you can make some money on the side. Let him carry the conversation. Again, don't push anything."

"Okay. I got it."

"We have enough now on Trevor already," Kelly began. "All we need is an arrest, search warrant, and to get him in the box."

"I have to justify our time, too, and try to get enough to get him held. I know I said we're doing a lot of simple buy/busts, but this one's different. Trevor is a major player."

"Let them roll with it, Kell," I said.

Kelly could be hardheaded, but this time she let it go.

Frank handed Erin the mic and she pressed it against the mouthpiece and tapped in the number.

Bobby answered on the second ring with "Hey there, babe."

Loud music in the background filtered through the earpiece.

"I told you I'd call."

"I appreciate that. It took you a while. What's up with that?"

"I had to wait for my mom to leave."

"I wanna see you again. A drink somewhere other than here, though."

"We'll see, babe. I really need to know you better, but maybe I'll see you tomorrow at the club again."

"Get a babysitter this time. Hang out with me after."

"My mom already said she was going to take care of my kid. I told her I have to work late. She likes to be with him. I couldn't say no."

"Why you being so difficult?"

"I'm not being difficult, Bobby. I appreciate what you did for me, but I have to trust you more. We just met, and I can't get the fact that you're a cop outta my head."

"I don't know what else I can do to make you trust me."

"I'm getting paid tomorrow. Hook me up with Trevor again so I can get some more. Maybe enough for me to make some money on the side. I really need some money now. I know Artie would help, but he doesn't get back with me."

"Sounds like he's not much of a boyfriend."

"He's just not dependable is all, but I know he'd help me out if I could just get in touch with him."

"So can I. Help you out, I mean. How much you looking to get?"

"I don't know. I've never done this before, but I know people who would buy from me."

"That's a dangerous business, Jennifer. I don't know if you're cut out for it, and I wouldn't want you to get yourself hurt or arrested."

"I'm not stupid. And what, you sayin' you're going to arrest me?"

"Ha! Definitely not, babe. And I ain't sayin' you're stupid. Just let me take care of you. That's all."

"What do you mean, take care of me?"

"Help you out and make sure you do it the right way so you don't get yourself in trouble."

"Why do you want to do all this for me?"

"I think you know why, baby."

"I want to trust you."

"I told you, I'm not your typical cop. You can trust me. Come by tomorrow."

She paused for effect and then said, "Okay."

"I work midnights, so I'll be here early. About six. Can you do that?"

"Yes. Will Trevor be there?"

"He usually is."

"Okay then. I'll see you tomorrow."

"Bye, sweetie."

"Bye, Bobby."

She disconnected, folded the cell closed. Frank took the mic back and called out the end time, pushed the stop button on the recording device.

"Nice," Frank said. "Very nice. It looks like we're going to play again tomorrow."

"Whoop-de-doo," Ragland said, twirling his index finger in the air. "Let me and Cortez go in this time so we can have fun."

"Negative. We're keeping it like it is."

"Fuck, Marr."

"Yeah, fuck, fuck, fuck," Frank snickered.

"Man, that boy is into you, girl," Kelly told Erin.

"I told you she's good," Frank said.

"Maybe you should take a bow, Erin." Cortez smiled.

"Go on, now," Erin said like she was embarrassed.

All I could think was just another night I wouldn't be getting with Celeste. Wanted to put this to bed, but her even more.

The debriefing lasted about forty-five minutes. Kelly and I still had a couple of hours in the shift to get through, so we made our way back to the office to write our end up. I went home after and gave myself a good pour of scotch and plopped my tired ass down on the sofa. Of course, all I could think about was Celeste.

32

Celeste called in the early afternoon before I had to go to work. "Can I see you tonight?" she asked.

"As much as I want to, I can't tonight. I'm working a late shift. What about Friday night? I'll take you to dinner."

"Seems so long to wait."

"Only a couple of days. Just a couple of days. I'm off Friday so we can have all night and through the next if you want."

"I do want. That'll make it worth the wait."

"Yes, it will. Can't wait to see you."

"Me too."

Made me feel good that she called. I had something to look forward to.

We set everything up for the club op at the same time as before.

"I have a feeling Bobby's gonna push me to be with him," Erin told Frank.

"He will, and you know never to get in a car, right?"

"Hundred times over, Frankie. Yes."

"Okay," he said, and then to Ragland and Cortez, "you guys switch up to uniform and take a marked cruiser just in case it goes sideways. And if it does, you guys act like you're working prostitution. Just like you've done before."

"Copy that," Ragland said.

"Park it outta sight from the club. No one's gonna think twice."

"Got it."

They got up and left the room.

"We'll cover the front," Frank advised.

We set up. Even found the same illegal parking spot with a good view of the front. Erin was inside and met with Bobby. He was there alone this time. No buddies. Sparkle was at the table with them. Bobby pressed for a private room for the three of them. Sparkle was all in, but Erin said it wasn't her thing. Bobby eventually backed down. Sparkle went to the stage to do her thing at the pole.

"She's got nice tits and ass, but not as nice as yours," Bobby told Erin. "You'd do well here, probably better than any of the girls."

"I do okay with the job I have. Even better after you hook me up with Trevor again."

"Like I told you, that's a dangerous business."

"Not if I have you by my side."

"Now we're getting somewhere."

"Don't touch me like that," Erin told him. "I'm not like one of your girls here."

"Never thought you were."

"Then give me some respect."

"You got all my respect, babe."

"Where are your other friends, anyway?"

"They got families. Not like me. I'm all by my lonesome."

"They work with you?"

"Yeah, we all came on the department together. Why you so interested?"

"Just curious is all."

"Well, we always got each other's backs and now I have yours and hopefully more."

"You take care of me, Bobby, and I'll more than take care of you, but like I told you, it's all about time and gaining trust. If you want me, you hafta be patient. Okay?"

"I'll try, babe."

After about an hour of that shit, Trevor and Bull showed up. And after another hour or so of more bullshitting, the deal was made through Bobby for a ten-pack of heroin and an eight-ball of coke. Marr was more than pleased.

"This is all good, right? 'Cause it's a lot of money for me and I gotta turn it around fast."

"It's all good shit. Better than you're gonna get anywhere. You can cut 'em up and more than double your money," Trevor told Erin.

"You can trust him, Jennifer," Bobby added.

"More business you do means the more business I get," Trevor said.

"I need money for my baby boy is all, so I wanna make it good."

"You know how to cut it, right?" Trevor asked.

"I have a friend that does."

"Oh, you have a friend, huh?" Bobby questioned. "Is it that Artie dude that never showed up?"

"No, I never heard from him. It's a girlfriend. Someone I trust."

"That's all good, then."

"You two need to fuck already," Trevor said with a laugh.

"What makes you think we aren't?"

"Ha! I know better, Bobby-boy."

Another couple of hours and Erin advised them she had to go get her kid from her mom.

"I'm gonna walk you out," Bobby said.

"Fuck," I said to myself.

"She knows what she's doing," Frank said.

"I can manage, Bobby."

"Yeah, I got the feeling she can handle herself, Bobby-boy."

"I'm walkin' you out."

"Whatever makes you feel good then."

Couple of minutes later they were both out the front door. They walked past the doorman toward the middle of the sidewalk. We had eyes on her. Bobby tried to hug her and kiss her on the lips.

"I don't know you like that yet, Bobby," she said as she pulled away from him.

"After all I done for you, not even a kiss?"

She leaned in and kissed him on the cheek. He tried to hold her again, but she pulled away.

"Patience. I'm worth the wait."

"Well, I'm giving you a ride home."

"No, I'm gonna walk. You go back inside and have fun. I'll call you when I get home."

"I'm not takin' no for an answer. You come to my car with me. I'm just up the street."

He took her by the arm.

"No, Bobby. I'll be all right."

"Cortez, Ragland, might need you to roll up to the front and do your thing. Stand by," Frank said.

"Copy."

"You can't go walkin' around carrying like that. It ain't safe."

"I told you, I can take care of myself."

"Let's go, baby," he said, grabbing her arm and trying to lead her.

"Stop. I don't like you holding me like that."

"I done a lot for you. All I'm askin' in return is to take you home. Now c'mon."

"Roll by, boys," Frank ordered. "Make it look good."

"Copy, Frankie."

Erin kept insisting, but he was pulling at her arm. Didn't look like she could break away, but also didn't look out of control. The doorman was right there but didn't do shit.

"That hurts, Bobby. Let go."

"I'm taking you home, Jennifer. Said I ain't taking no for an answer."

"Okay, just let go of my arm then."

Cortez rolled ahead of us and made the left toward the front of the club.

"A police car is there," Erin said.

"You'll be all right. I might know them and we're just hanging out. They're just working their beat."

"I can't get arrested," Erin said.

"Don't worry yourself. They gonna roll by."

They pull the cruiser up to the front and stop in the middle of the road. I saw Cortez poke his head out of the passenger-side window.

"Hey there, Jenny," Cortez said. "Found yourself a new spot, huh?"

"I'm not working, Officer. I'm just here with my friend."

"Working?" Bobby questioned.

"Give us a break, sir. We know better."

"I don't know what you're talking about?" Bobby said like he was genuinely confused.

"We're with the prostitution unit, so why don't you roll on back inside, sir, before we arrest both of you for solicitation."

"You're a fucking prostitute?" Bobby blurted.

"Not anymore. I don't do that anymore."

"Get the fuck outta my sight," Bobby said.

"Good advice, sir. You move on up the road, girl, and if we catch you anywhere around here we're gonna lock you up again. Got it?"

"You won't see me," she said, and started walking the same direction as before. She didn't look back.

"Fuck you," Bobby called out to her, and quickly turned to walk back inside.

"Have a nice day, sir," Cortez said.

They both stayed there as Erin continued walking.

"Stay there until we're out of sight," Frank said over the radio.

"Just like the old days, Frankie," Cortez chuckled.

We took the right to quickly make our way around the block and get behind Erin. Saw that same pimp and his boy walking in the opposite direction sharing a blunt. Both wearing the same clothes as the night before. What a life they lived.

33

W e picked Erin up at the spot. She hopped in the back with Frank. She seemed relieved. I was at the driver's side, peering through the rearview mirror. Frank took the wire off her and placed it back in the box it came in.

"He's blowin' up my cell," she said.

"Yes, we heard it over the monitor, ringing off the hook. Glad you didn't answer. Let me get the phone tap."

"Of course I wouldn't answer."

He got the wire out and gave her the tiny mic to place on the mouthpiece of her cell phone.

"What should I say?"

"Just let him do the talking. Fuck himself up. Take it from there. I don't want to waste more time on this dope. IA will take care of him."

Frank cued the radio and went over the surveillance channel with "Making a UC call so we'll be off the air."

Everyone copied that. We all made sure our radios, cells, and pagers were off. Marr hit the record button, provided his name, date, the time, and who the call was being made to. Handed the mic to Erin and she made the call. She kept the cell away from her ear so that we could hear most of what he said, if he even answered.

He did.

"So what the fuck?" Bobby said loudly. Music was not heard in the background.

"I was telling the truth when I said I don't work anymore."

"You're a fucking whore! You played me, bitch."

Hard to hear, so Kelly and I leaned over the front seats and closer to Erin.

"You there?" he asked.

"Yes."

"Man, I'm glad we didn't fuck. You'dve given me clap or something worse."

"No, I wouldn't have. I'm clean. And I do appreciate you hooking me up with Trevor for the drugs."

"Fuck that! You owe me, bitch. You coulda got me locked up. Somethin' like that would get me fired. Solicitation. Shit."

"I said I'm sorry. Doesn't sound like you're at the club. Where are you?"

"I'm heading into work early now 'cause I'm so pissed. See if I can get some overtime or something. I mean it, you owe me."

"I'll take care of you, baby."

"Damn right you will."

"Where do you work? Maybe you can come over when my kid is sleeping."

"My beat is Georgetown. Where do you live?"

"I'm in Northeast off Florida Avenue."

"I don't know if I can get that far out. Depends on how the night goes. I'm almost at work. Don't do too much of that heron, 'cause I might just call you later. Hear me?"

"Okay, Bobby. I hope you do, and I'm sorry for what happened."

"Yeah, yeah. Maybe I'll forgive you after you suck my cock."

"You keep me hooked up with Trevor and I'll do more than that, baby."

"Yes, you will. Gotta go now."

"Bye, Bobby."

He disconnected without saying anything. Frank took the mic, gave the end time, and then stopped the recording.

"Fucking idiot," Frank said.

"Works the Second District," I advised.

"Yep. Sounds like it," Frank said. "He ain't our problem anymore. Like I said, I'm passing all this shit off to IA. You did good, Erin. You mind driving back, Blum?"

"Not at all."

"We're good to go with Trevor then, right?" Kelly asked.

"More than enough to get him in the box with you two, and with his backup time, I'd say we got enough to get him held. You guys want to draft the affidavit for the arrest, and I'll do the search warrant?"

"I'm good with that."

"Yeah, me too," Kelly added.

"I'll confirm the address that Ragland and Cortez got on Trevor, then. We should give it a couple of days before we hit, though, try to keep him from thinking the arrest had to do with Erin, and give you guys more to work with."

"Sounds good," Kelly said.

"And who knows what the search warrant might yield," Frank said. "Might feel like Christmas."

I loved the thought of that.

34

C eleste was heavy on my mind and I would see her soon because it was Friday. But we'd go to my apartment after dinner, not Arthur's home. That just didn't feel right. Not that I felt bad after the first night with her at his house, just that I've had time to think about everything and didn't want to be somewhere with her where I might feel his presence, or for that matter, she might feel his presence.

It was early evening and chilly when I left to pick her up. Preferred this time of year over any other season, especially the summer and that wall of humidity that DC was so well known for.

Celeste looked nice. She wore a waist-length teal jacket, dark, thin-cut blue jeans, and black leather heels. She hugged me and kissed me lightly on the corner of my lips. She didn't seem high, but I could honestly say that I wouldn't care if she was. I believed her when she said she only smoked heroin on occasion. I didn't notice tracks on her body when she'd lain naked beside me before, unless she stuck the needle between her toes, which I somehow doubted. I didn't know why the thought of smoking it seemed a lesser offense than shooting it, though. And Officer Bobby kept popping in my head after I thought about it. I tried to convince myself that I was nothing like him, but then I realized that I wasn't because maybe I was worse. I let the thought go. Kicked it right outta my fucking head.

I didn't want to take Celeste someplace where there might be the chance of running into someone I knew. She was still a bit like forbidden fruit, and I had to keep whatever kind of relationship we had to myself, at least until the investigation concluded.

I wanted to impress her, so I made a reservation at Restaurant Nora, on Florida Avenue, in Northwest. I had been there before on a date and loved it. Traffic was always rough on a Friday evening, and parking even worse. I gave myself enough time for both, so the drive there wasn't made stressful for me. Nora was a couple of blocks from my apartment, so I decided to drive to my private parking spot at the building.

We walked to the restaurant.

"I missed you," she said after lighting her cigarette.

"I missed you too."

She handed me the cigarette like she knew I wanted a drag. I accepted, handed it back after.

"Where are you taking me?"

"Everywhere." I smiled.

The front door to Nora opened to the tiny bar, which had one of the best selections of single malts in the DC area.

"Fancy," she said as the hostess walked us to our table.

"Not so fancy. Just incredible food that I wanted you to experience."

She turned to me and showed me that wonderful smile and said, "The quilts are beautiful."

It was busy. We sat and when the waiter showed up to advise us what the specials were and take our drink orders, I talked her out of a vodka soda and into a vodka martini. She agreed.

"One for me too," I told the waiter. "Make them Grey Goose, please."

"Of course."

He turned and walked away.

Celeste looked at her menu.

"Be adventurous," I told her.

I felt her foot rub gently up my calf. Made me smile.

"It's been a long time since I've had salmon," she said.

"Everything here is good."

"I can't wait."

I couldn't take my eyes off her. She knew it, too. She'd occasionally take her eyes off the menu and look up at me without tilting her head, but only for a second, then back down to the menu. Before she could take me away too far, I glanced at my menu.

"Do you want an appetizer?"

"You choose," she said.

The waiter returned with our drinks. I ordered the appetizer and advised him we needed more time to decide on the entrée.

"Of course."

I lifted my martini toward Celeste. She lifted hers.

"Cheers."

"To a beautiful night," she said.

We clinked our glasses.

"Do you like doing what you do now at work more than what you did before?"

I don't know why she asked that. An attempt at table conversation?

"I do. This is where I've always wanted to be."

"Isn't it depressing? All those dead people?"

"If you think about it too much, yes."

"So you numb yourself?"

"No, you just realize it's a job. Something that has to be done. You have to care, though."

"You're an empath."

I just smiled because I couldn't tell her I was far from an empath.

"You know, I've never really questioned how you got to be here, where you're originally from," I said, as delicately as I could.

"I'm originally from Bethesda."

"The nice part of Maryland."

"You're not a Maryland fan. I get it. Most people from DC aren't."

"No, just PG County. So that's where your family is?"

"That's where my family still is. Yes."

"Do you talk to them?"

"No."

She looked down, then picked up her drink and sipped.

"Sorry if it's a sensitive subject. I just want to know more about you."

"Well, here goes, I guess." She smiled. "I was raised in the house my parents still live in. I have one brother. Last I heard he was in Fairfax working in construction. I left after I graduated from high school. Tried to never look back."

"Why? You weren't abused, were you?"

"Not physically. You know, I was a state champion in junior tennis." She said it like she wanted to change the subject.

"No kidding?" I suddenly remembered the trophies. "So those trophies in the dining room are yours?"

"Yes. I even had a scholarship to almost any university I wanted to go to in this area."

"What happened?"

"I got a calf muscle tear and had to have surgery."

"And you couldn't play anymore?"

"It was a long recovery, but that wasn't the real problem. I sort of got myself addicted to pain meds."

"Shit. How old were you?"

"Fifteen. No, I'd just turned sixteen. That's what I never

171

recovered from, really. My dad disowned me because of it. And that I wouldn't go back to playing."

"I'm sorry, Celeste."

"It is what it is." She smiled but couldn't hide the sadness behind it.

I didn't push the conversation after that. I knew how painful it was for her and that the addiction was more than likely the reason she got into all this other shit. I felt even closer to her, though, and looked at her with a genuine smile.

She rubbed my calf with her foot and that alone was good conversation. I felt compelled to tell her how sorry I was when Arthur was my CI and I wanted to explain why I never stepped in when I learned of the abuse she was suffering. I couldn't go there, though, because that'd bring Arthur back, and he was gone now. Far from both of us. And it felt damn good. If I were an empath, I would have done something about it.

"I've never seen a dead body."

"That's a good thing. The first body always stays with you."

"See, you are an empath."

"Stop with that."

"No, I won't stop with how good I believe you are."

Guilt began to set in. Made me feel uncomfortable.

"I'm glad I know you, Celeste."

"I'm glad I know you, Detective Blum."

After dinner we walked back to my building.

I enjoyed thinking through the plans I had for her while I opened the door to my apartment. It barely registered when she walked past me and into the small foyer. Her purse thumping to the ground caught my attention. She walked into the living room as if she had done it several times before. I closed and locked the door and walked toward her. For some reason when I faced her, I froze, completely and utterly, and all the plans I had made in my head vanished. Some aspect of my subconscious recognized the hunter had just become the hunted. She didn't speak or move. She didn't have to. She was in complete control, and I knew it. I allowed it.

Finally, she moved closer to me, trailed her hand across my chest, down my left arm to my hand. She captured my hand and drew me into the bedroom. *Does she always walk like that?*

Slowly, while never breaking eye contact, she stripped me of my clothes. When I moved to help, she stilled me with a look. Words were not necessary, and I knew better than to try that again. She slid out of her clothes after. I remained perfectly still, knowing it was what I needed to do. Knowing it was what she was demanding. With a hand on my bare chest, she pushed me back to the bed. My legs caught on the side of the bed, and I started to fall. I never stopped.

35

We spent most of the Saturday morning naked in bed, drinking screwdrivers and doing other things that I'll keep with me for some time. We had to force ourselves to eat. I scrambled some eggs and burnt some toast. We ate on the sofa in nothing but our underwear.

I made her another drink after. She looked different when I handed it to her. Pensive. It was sudden.

"What's wrong?"

"Nothing's wrong." She tried to smile.

"I'm a detective. I can read people well."

"You want to interrogate me, Detective?"

"I want to know you better. You can talk to me."

She set the glass on the end table after taking a couple of sips.

"I like you," she said.

"You keep sayin' that."

"Because I want to make sure you know."

"Well, I like you too. But I sense something's wrong."

"Empath."

"Stop."

"Okay then. I'm worried about what'll come of me. Arthur's house. The bills. He took care of everything."

I scooted closer to her, set my drink on the coffee table, kissed her lightly on the forehead.

"I'm gonna take care of you."

She looked at me directly.

"You don't even know me."

"Yes, I do. I want to know you better, though. I don't want you to worry about anything."

"I want to trust you."

I faced her toward me. We kissed.

"You can. You have nothing to worry about."

She hugged me. I hugged her back and we held each other.

"I have certain other needs too," she told me.

I understood what she meant, and I didn't care. I mean, I cared that she had a drug problem and would've liked to see her beat it, but it wasn't something that would keep me from being with her.

"I know. We'll figure it out."

I dropped her back at the house the next day while on my way to work. I walked her to the door, and we hugged, but she wouldn't let go. I held her head back and kissed her.

"I have to go," I said.

She released herself from me.

"I left something for you. In Arthur's top dresser drawer tucked under his underwear."

She looked at me confused for a second, but then smiled wide like it suddenly came to her. She kissed me hard, but with passion. I could tell she didn't know the heroin was there.

"You'll find what you need. It's more than enough to get you by. I left it there when my partner and I searched the house. I don't know why. Well, I guess I do. It's for you."

175

"You are such a sweetheart. I know I can trust you now."

"I really have to go."

"When can I see you?" she asked.

"Couple of days, but I'll call you when I get off work. Okay?"

"Yes. Please."

I smiled and walked down the stairs toward the car. I looked back toward her when I was on the sidewalk.

"Thank you, love," she said.

I realized then how much I had really fallen. I didn't much care, though. I had already been consumed.

It was getting colder. Would probably keep most people tucked inside. Hopefully bad things wouldn't happen. Sundays were generally peaceful. I stopped thinking about it for fear I would jinx it and the tour would take a turn.

Kelly was at her cubicle when I got in. Few other detectives too, almost a full house.

"What's up?" I asked.

I hung my coat on the coatrack.

"Just reading through Marr's write-up again. Got an email from him today too. You should have one in your box. He confirmed the address for Trevor."

"That's good news. We'll hit it soon, then."

"Probably Tuesday early morn."

I placed my suit jacket over the back of my chair and sat down.

"He did good for us," I said.

"Yep. Your weekend good?"

"Excellent. Could not have been better. Yours?"

"Good."

"You?"

"Same ol' shit."

"Too much to drink then?"

"Something like that."

I wanted to share how I was feeling—the budding new relationship and all that shit. Ill advised, though. Illicit love, but I've said something like that before.

As far as Kelly and our supervisors were concerned, Trevor was a solid lead. Doyle purchased the dope he sold from him. Arthur purchased the dope he used from Doyle and knew Trevor. Good connections all around. Lot of possibilities that would lead to murder. Money is the biggest. Always a good motive. Maybe Doyle didn't pay up. Maybe he stole from him. Arthur could have known. It made our day easier. All good, especially when I had in my possession the one nail for the coffin that would seal the deal, and hopefully keep it airtight.

First thing I did when I got home was pour myself a drink, dress down to my boxers and a T-shirt, and call Celeste. It was past eleven so not that late. I had a feeling she'd want me to come over, but I was still uncomfortable sleeping where Arthur bedded down, and she sounded like she was high. As much as I wanted her, I didn't want it like that.

"I'm all alone in bed," she said.

"I'm sitting on the couch and wishing I was there."

"Then come over."

"I really want to. You sound like you might be a little out of it right now, though."

"I feel wonderful."

"I'm sure you do, and I want nothing more than to see you, but you wore me out the last couple of nights so I'm gonna hit the sack here in a bit."

"You're sounding like an old man."

"Ha! Older than you, but still not so old."

"I want you."

"I want you too, sweet thing. In a couple of days. I need to get through some shit at work. I'll feel better about everything after."

"Feel better about what?"

"About us. About finishing things up."

"So you know who murdered Arthur?"

"We have a suspect."

"Who?"

"I can't say right now. You know that."

"You don't trust me?"

"Not saying that. I'll tell you soon enough."

"Okay, lover. I understand. I miss you."

"Miss you too."

She was mine now and she was free and needed me. I was worried she was going to blow through that stash too fast, though. I didn't know what I'd do if that happened. How far would I be willing to go for her? I'd gone too far already. What I had done has made it even more dangerous for me. I would have to live with that, but I believed I could.

36

An ice storm broke out on the evening before the search warrant was to occur. I heard it breaking like glass on the ledge outside my window. It stormed through most of the night. Kept me up. I had to get up at four in the morning so I could get to Narcotics at 0500 and in time for the briefing. We'd be ramming in Trevor's door by 0630 hours. I hoped we would not lose power. Would make the search difficult.

Most of the main roads were treated prior to the storm, but not so much on the side streets. Slippery as hell and made for a slow going. They treated the parking area at Narcotics. Made it up the ramp and found parking easy enough. I had my shoulder pack with me that contained what I would need for the search warrant, and more.

Four new officers and Officer Roman, a CSS tech I knew well, were in the conference room along with the same crew as before, minus the UC, of course. Kelly was there, drinking coffee and smoking a cigarette. Marr had not shown up yet. I stepped in.

"Morning," I said.

"What's up, Blum," Roman said, a little too cheerfully for this early in the morning.

A few more *good mornings* from other folks, including a tired-looking Kelly. I sat in a chair beside her, set my pack on the floor and my 7-Eleven coffee container on the table.

Marr was fashionably late again. Stepped in the room with a smile.

"Happy to see you all made it despite the road conditions," he said.

"You're the only one I know who'd have a search warrant on a day like this," Cortez grunted.

"Just for you, my brother."

He set his pack down, leaned against the wall near the door, and said, "What you say we get started." He lit a smoke.

A few officers took their notebooks out. Marr passed out two flyers. One was a photocopy of a picture of Trevor's home and the other was of him.

"Don't know if his associate Bull stays with him, but the mutts know what he looks like . . . Kelly and Blum will be with me. We'll also be the only search team. We don't wanna tear this place up. Gonna be methodical here."

"What the fuck?" an officer I didn't know asked jokingly.

"Means you fucking won't be searching," Marr replied. A few chuckles and he continued, "Cortez, you'll be on ram. I got a no-knock warrant so we're going straight in. The target has been arrested for gun charges in the past so be on the alert. I staked it out overnight. He does get in-and-out traffic, mostly girls, but I did see his boy Bull enter in the early evening and stay overnight. Don't know if he has any dogs. The scope of the search warrant is good because it involves not only narcotics and weapons but also possible evidence related to homicides."

Marr gave out the rest of the assignments including entry team, front and rear cover.

"Questions?"

"Yeah, the two homicide detectives springing for lunch after?" Ragland asked.

"Only if you like pizza," I said.

He shot me a thumbs-up.

"Everyone get ready. We'll line up out front," Marr said.

On the way to the car, Kelly turned to me and said quietly, "You got my back, right?"

I looked at her hard.

"What the hell you asking something like that for? Of course I have your back."

She stared evenly at me. "Good."

That's when I knew she was worried about my involvement and suspected more. I tried to maintain my composure.

The ice hung heavy on the trees lining the short block off Benning Road NE, where Trevor lived. We stopped a few houses down from his and double-parked, blocking in several vehicles but allowing enough room for other cars to pass. We exited and silently closed our doors. Cortez and Ragland ran toward us and behind Marr, who would lead the way. Our guns were out and in a tucked position. Rear team made their way behind the house, jumping a short chain-link fence to get there. Front team stopped at the yard and scanned the windows.

His home was an old two-story town house with a neglected small front yard. Five steps led to an old wooden patio and the front door. The patio would be slick from frost. There was a cast-iron security gate. Ragland had the pry bar. Marr gave the signal and Ragland tried the handle to see if the gate was open before prying it. It was locked. He secured the pry bar between the top bolt and the main lock, forced it open with one pull, bending the bolt and latches out. Ragland quickly moved aside, holding the security gate open, and Cortez busted the door in on the second hit. He dropped the ram on the patio to the left and stepped aside to allow Marr in first.

"Police! Police!" Marr called out several times as we all ran in.

Closet doors were opened and cleared. I made my way upstairs with Marr and Kelly. Everyone else stayed downstairs to clear the rooms. Three naked women were running out of two different rooms on the second floor, screaming. Kelly stopped all three and put them against a wall between the two bedrooms.

"Shut the fuck up," she commanded.

A tall man in nothing but his underwear burst out of the room to the right of what might be the master bedroom. He had a sawed-off shotgun. I was a bit to the left and headed to the other bedroom. Without hesitation, I swung around as Marr fired several rounds, hitting him in the chest. He still tried to lift the shotgun. I fired two rounds, striking him in the chest. The shotgun fired a burst into the floor just ahead of the tall man's feet, blasting into the wood. He was thrown back and collapsed back inside the room.

Without thought, and acting purely on adrenaline, I continued forward and kicked in the partly open door to the possible master bedroom. There was Trevor in the bed, under the covers like nothing was going on. I wondered what the fuck he was thinking. He didn't even try to get out the bedroom window. It wouldn't have been that long of a drop, but the boys covering the rear would have nabbed him. I had my weapon pointed at him. His hands were under the covers. I scanned right and left with my eyes and immediately back to him.

"Let me see your hands! Let me see your hands!" I ordered.

"What the fuck" is all I heard him say.

I felt a hand on my back left shoulder and Kelly said, "Kelly."

She moved to my left side, gun also on him.

"Get your fucking hands out, now," I commanded again.

"All right, all right. Don't fucking shoot me."

He slowly removed his hands out from under the covers.

"Reach for the ceiling. All the way up."

He obeyed. I moved to the right, with my gun still aimed at him. Kelly cautiously stepped toward him.

"Don't fucking move," she ordered.

"I ain't fucking doin' nothin'. Just don't shoot me."

Kelly grabbed his left hand, squeezing his fingers tight.

"Aww, fuck. You're breaking my fingers."

She turned him toward her, and he fell out of the bed halfway, head and shoulders on the ground. I stepped over to him, put my gun to the back of his head.

"Don't fucking move."

Kelly holstered her weapon and grabbed the cuffs secured in her pants at the small of her back. She cuffed him.

"Fuck, that's tight! Take it fucking easy."

Kelly grabbed under his right arm and with my gun still in my right hand I grabbed him under his left arm with my free hand. We dragged him out of the bed.

A .38 revolver fell out of the bed with him, landed on the wooden floor with a thud.

"Shit" was all he said.

37

After the area was cleared and before it got chaotic outside, I went with Kelly to Marr's car to get our packs. EMT and an ambulance were called to the scene. Internal Affairs was also on the way to investigate the shooting. The suspect Marr and I shot somehow survived and was transported to DC General. Detective Caine and his partner, Jac, were called in by our LT to assist and go to the hospital with the suspect. The three girls were all allowed to get dressed and were seated on a sofa in the living room after it was searched and cleared. A bald old man in pajamas and a bathrobe was sitting on an armchair. He was found in a small bedroom on the first floor. Trevor's grandfather, and the owner of the house Trevor took over from him. Trevor was in the living room too and sat on a chair brought in from the kitchen. He was still in his underwear with no shirt and complaining about why he couldn't get dressed and why we had to "murder" his cousin. Everyone's hands were cuffed behind their backs.

The rear cover team was brought in to stay with the suspects in the living room while I coordinated the search with Kelly. Marr was busy with two officials concerning the shooting. It was a good shooting. There'd be no question. Cortez and Ragland were with the other officers out front, containing the area. Lot of people from the neighborhood approached the house. Two marked cruisers were holding them back.

Roman had his work cut out for him, especially since a shooting was involved. Two other CSS techs were called in to assist, freeing Roman to seize the weapons and whatever other evidence we might find. Roman was meticulous, infamous for page after page of numbered handwritten notes. Happy he was here. Made our jobs easier.

Marr joined us before we got started.

"They're going to need to talk to us again when we're done here," Marr advised.

"Of course."

"You two good?" Kelly asked.

"I'm good. I have no problem with what I had to do."

"Me too."

"Yes. You two are still here," Kelly said. "I'm going to take the old man into his bedroom and interview him, see what he has to say about his grandson. I'll search it first, though."

"He's probably clueless," Marr said. "My experience they usually are and only care that the bills are paid. But then, you never know."

"Okay. I'll take Trevor's room," I said.

"I'll take the other one. CSS already took the photos they need. Just need to watch where I step."

Trevor's room reeked of sex, cigarettes, and skunk weed. At least I hoped it was all that and not a ripened body under the bed. He kept his dirty laundry in large black garbage bags. There were three of them at the end of his bed. I set my pack down on what looked to be a clean area of the floor. I already had latex gloves on.

I tossed the sheets, looked under the pillows, and then lifted the mattress, but didn't find anything. I looked under the bed. More clothing, but underneath some jeans was a shotgun. Nothing else I could find under there. I would call Roman up for photos and to take it once I finished the rest of the room and after I did what I had made my mind up I would have to do. Didn't want to do that too quickly, though.

I had already cleared the bathroom and the closet after we detained Trevor, but they still needed to be searched. I started with the bathroom. That man did not believe in cleanliness. I wouldn't be caught dead in that tub. Fucking toilet looked like it had black mold inside the bowl on the porcelain. I lifted the tank cover but didn't find anything. I searched the cabinet and still nothing. I went back to the bedroom, cleared an area on the floor away from my pack and tossed the clothing out of the dresser onto the floor. Found another handgun in the third drawer. A 9mm Sig Sauer with duct tape wrapped around the grip. Left the closet for last. Bunch of shoes piled on one another on the floor. Funky, colorful shirts and Redskins jerseys on hangers. Top shelf was cluttered with odds and ends and a couple of shoeboxes. I took them down, set them on the bed and opened the first one. Bunch of court papers and mail matter with his name on them and the address we were at. That was good. Meant he lived here even though the house was in his grandfather's name. I'd be taking that shoebox. I set it near my pack and returned to go through the second one. Photos. Of course, mostly naked women and pictures with him and boys from his crew. That'd go with me too. I placed it on top of the other shoebox and returned to the closet.

Marr entered and said, "Found the mother lode."

"Yeah. What?"

"Kept the stash in his cousin's room. Probably half a kilo of powder cocaine, an ounce of crack, at least a pound of weed all compressed, and then a few ounces of heroin. Looked to be uncut. Haven't tested everything yet, though. Ton of green zips of all sizes too, couple of scales and a lot of syringes. Fucking pharmacy."

"Sweet. Made your day, huh?"

"Got that right."

"So far I got a shotgun under the bed, another nine from the dresser, and the one he dropped out of his bed. Lot of mail matter with his name and address on it."

"But nothing linking him to either of the murders."

"Not yet, but I got hope. Gonna get back to the closet."

"I'm going to check in on Kelly and the old man. It was a good hit, brother."

"Yeah, so far. Let's hope for something Kelly and I can use."

"Worst case is you got him to take back with you."

"Yeah."

"I'll be downstairs."

"Talk in a bit."

He left. I returned to the closet and searched the rest of the shelf, checked the walls for secret panels, and then went through all the pockets of his clothing. This was the perfect time. I went to my backpack, made sure no one was around. I unzipped a side pocket and removed the .22 I shot Arthur with and Celeste allegedly shot Chris Doyle with. I quickly returned to the closet and placed it in the side pocket of a puffy black winter coat. I took the coat off the hanger and put it on the floor in the cleared area.

I went to where Kelly was.

"I found a twenty-two caliber pistol," I told her quietly.

"Fuck yes."

38

Trevor's cousin, Terrence Holden, never made it alive to the hospital. He was pronounced in the ambulance. He had seventeen years of backup time for interstate trafficking of narcotics, numerous gun violations. Sure he thought he had no choice but to try to shoot his way out.

IA confiscated my weapon and all my magazines, as well as Marr's, because of the shooting. They interviewed us but told us we'd be interviewed more thoroughly once we finished up at the house. We both knew the time was going to come soon when we'd get put on administrative leave and no contact but hopefully be allowed to continue our work in our own offices. It was a good shooting. Nothing I could think of that would make IA stretch out the investigation. I already felt naked without my gun. Marr had been through it once before when he was in uniform, so he knew the process.

"Nothing to worry about," he told me.

"I know."

We spent most of the day at the house. The grandfather had

nothing to offer, and his living space and the common area were clean. Both Trevor and his cousin had to have a lot of confidence to keep that kind of shit in their rooms. After we took statements from Grandpa and the three girls, confirmed their identities, we released them from the scene. I stood with Trevor in his room while he got himself dressed. He remained silent but didn't lawyer up. He didn't know yet how very bad it was going to get for him.

After transporting him, we left Trevor in the interview room to stew on his own for a bit. Kelly and I decided that I should go in alone with him first, and she would watch on a monitor from the recording room. Some defendants are best to go at one-on-one. Felt like he was one of them.

I picked up the thick case jacket that I didn't have to make any thicker to look good and stepped into the room. He was uncuffed and cradling his head in his folded arms on the table. Can't count how many times I've seen that from a guilty man.

"I'm Detective Blum, Trevor," I advised him.

He looked up but didn't say anything. Rubbed the sleep out of his eyes. I sat in the chair across from him, set the case jacket on the table. I chose not to use my notebook. I use it primarily with victims and witnesses, not defendants. They can get uncomfortable with what they say being written down.

"Hope you got a little rest while I was getting everything together here."

Before he could respond with probably something stupid, I asked, "Do you know why you're here?"

He snickered and shook his head, like he had been through this several times.

I had a feeling and got right to his rights. I pulled out the waiver card.

"You are under arrest. Before we ask you any questions, you must understand what your rights are. You have the right to remain silent. You are not required to say anything to us at any time or to answer any questions. Anything you say can be used against you in court. You have the right to talk to a lawyer for advice before we question you and have him with you during questioning. If you cannot afford a lawyer, a lawyer will be provided for you. Now, this is important, so listen up. If you want to answer questions now, without a lawyer present, you will still have the right to stop answering at any time. You understand what that means, right?"

"Yeah, I know my fucking rights," he said.

"It means even if you sign this waiver and agree to talk, you can stop talking or refuse to answer. Just because you sign this waiver doesn't mean you have to talk."

"I know my fucking rights, I said."

I set the card before him along with a pen. He stared at it but didn't pick the pen up.

"You want to know everything about why you're here, and like I said, I want to hear your side too."

"I don't even know where here is."

"Do you need me to explain your rights again?"

"How many times I gotta tell you I know them? And I know I don't have to talk to you if I don't want to. This card here means shit."

He picked up the pen and defiantly signed the waiver. I picked both the pen and the card up and put them in the case jacket.

"So do you know why you're here?"

"I said I don't know where the fuck here is. It ain't no district station that I know of."

"No, it's not a district station. Can you answer the question?"

"What question?"

"What you think got you here?"

"What the fuck. I suppose 'cause you somehow got a bogus warrant to search my grandpop's house and you got me on unregistered gun charges. Ain't no denying that part."

"Little more involved than that."

"I ain't got nothin' to do with what my cousin was doing, and why you had to kill him?"

"You seem like you're familiar with the system, so you know we'll find out if one of those guns was used in a shooting, maybe come back to a body. That shit'll fall on you and you'll catch the charges."

"I ain't worried about that happening."

"I like your confidence."

"Yeah, well I ain't stupid."

"Never suggested you were, but then maybe we're a little smarter and that's why you're here."

He blew out a huff like a laugh.

"One of the guns we got out of your bedroom closet was a twenty-two pistol."

He gave me a sideways kinda look, like he was confused.

"What?"

"Yeah. What. Two of the murder victims we're investigating that happen to be associated with you were both shot with a twenty-two."

"I don't know what the fuck you're talking about. I don't own no twenty-two. That shit ain't right."

I felt that if I pressured him he might decide to lawyer up. I took a different path.

"How long you been living with your grandpop?"

"Tell me why you had to kill my cousin, and for that matter about some twenty-two you said you got outta my closet?"

"We didn't try to kill him. He gave us no choice but to defend ourselves."

"Yeah, right. Who shot him? You?"

"Trevor, I'm sorry for your loss, but you have to worry about yourself right now. You're in some serious trouble and you have backup time."

"How long you lived at the house with your grandpop?"

"I been there most of my life."

"He raised you?"

"Yeah, pretty much."

"Since how old?"

"Maybe five, somethin' like that."

"Where are your parents?"

"What the fuck all this gotta do with why I'm here?"

"Just some background on you is all."

"Well, what happened to my parents got nothing to do with anything I can think of, so why don't we just move on."

"You got a job?"

"I'm currently unemployed."

"How do you afford such a nice car? Shit, I could never afford an Escalade."

"That's my cousin's car. Registration's in his name."

"I'm gonna be honest with you, Trevor. The charges against you are a lot more serious than unregistered firearms."

"Oh yeah, so what do you think you got me on?"

"We got into your house with a search warrant and an arrest warrant for you, not your cousin. Detective Marr also got a warrant for Bull."

"Bull? How do you know him and what's he got to do with all this shit?"

"We know a lot of things."

"You don't even know his name. How you get a warrant on him?"

"Don't need his name."

"What the fuck you gonna arrest him for?"

"All you need to know right now is he's going to be arrested soon and we'll be talking to him too."

"This some bullshit here. I don't know what you're talking about. For what?"

"We'll get to that. I need to ask you a few more questions, though. You want a soda or something? Maybe a Snickers bar?"

"Yeah. You got orange soda?"

"I believe we do. Snickers bar too?"

"Yeah, that's good."

I picked up everything from the table and walked out of the room, locked the door behind me. I stopped in the monitor room before heading to the soda and snack machines. Kelly was sitting at the counter where there were several monitors. Caine and Jac were in there too. Marr was putting the narcotics on the book with a couple of the officers from his office. I noticed through the monitor in the room where Trevor was that he was cradling his head again.

"He's going to be tough," I said.

"At least he didn't lawyer up."

"That's why I backed off about the twenty-two, but I'm afraid he will once I start getting into the homicides again."

"Work the connections between all of them first. Get that established. Maybe we'll get lucky and one of those guns will come back to the decedents."

"Maybe, and at least we'll get him back again, but he'll be with his defense attorney next time."

"That twenty-two comes back to one of our decedents or both, then he's good to go. I could care less if he brings a whole legal team with him."

"Let me get back to it."

"Have fun." She smiled. "Work the connections."

I returned to the room with a Crush and a Snickers bar. He lifted his head. I set them on the table in front of him. He took the soda and popped it open, took a swig and said "Ahh" after.

"Refreshing, huh?"

He nodded. I let him enjoy another sip.

"Tell me about how you met Artie?"

He hesitated briefly, giving himself the time he needed to figure out how to respond. Then he looked at me like he didn't know who I was talking about.

"I don't know any Artie."

"You see that camera up in the corner there?"

He looked at the camera to the right of the door. The red light at the bottom is on.

"It's recording everything said in here and it's going to go to the prosecutor and the judge. Last thing you want it to catch is your lies. We have a lot of information and evidence, so it's important you tell the truth, because what we have will show you're lying. That's the last thing you want. It won't look good for you, Trevor. In fact, it'll really hurt you—getting caught in all those lies."

He was thinking hard.

"Remember, I might already know the answer to the questions I'm gonna ask you, so be careful. How do you know Artie?"

"Shit. I don't even know what you think that loser has to do with me. He a fucking snitch?"

"You knew him then."

He looked confused, probably my use of the word "knew." Maybe he wasn't that stupid.

"Yeah, I know him, but don't know what that has to do with why I'm here."

"You just asked if he was a snitch. Why would you ask that?"

He sipped his soda, shook his head after, like it didn't matter. I had a feeling he wasn't about to admit to anything yet—dealing drugs.

"How do you know him?"

"Ain't like we're friends. He hangs out sometimes at this club I go to."

I grabbed the BOLO out of my case jacket and slid it over to him. He picked it up.

"Yeah, that's Artie. What he get himself into, and again, what you think he has to do with me? He's a fucking addict is all I know."

"What club you talking about where you both went?"

"Strip joint on K Street, downtown. Name escapes me."

He knew the name, just downplaying it.

"When was the last time you saw him?"

"Fuck, I don't know. Had to be at least a couple of weeks."

"Who did he go in there with?"

"Fuck if I know."

"Camera, Trevor. Camera," I reminded him.

He looked up at it like it was something ominous. Gonna snatch his ass up.

I took the BOLO, placed it back in the case jacket, and removed the photo with Arthur and Chris Doyle. I slapped it down on the table in front of him.

"This guy?"

He went silent for a moment, and I thought I was about to lose him. He didn't pick up the photo that time but looked at me direct.

"Yeah, I seen him in there with that guy," he advised, and took another sip of soda. Seemed nervous, like he knew he was dead. "His name was Chris or something."

"Was?"

"I seen the fucking news."

39

I want you to know that I don't work narcotics. I'm a homicide detective."

"Homicide detective? What the fuck you think I have to do with anything like that? You think just 'cause I seen a guy on occasion at a club I frequent I got something to do with his killing?"

"Two people."

"Huh?"

"Artie's murder didn't hit the news, but he's been murdered too."

"Yeah. Okay, but still…"

"Why would a murder victim you say you've seen on occasion at a club you frequent have your cell number and call you so much? I mean a lot of times."

He doesn't answer.

"Maybe you need to eat that Snickers bar, get your brain to working a bit. Sugar might help."

He looked at the Snickers but didn't pick it up.

"We already went through your cell and know how many times you've talked to Doyle. Artie not as much."

"So I see 'em at the club. We talked sometimes. Exchanged numbers. Doesn't mean I killed them."

"We know you were Chris's supplier for heroin, Trevor. Did he owe you money?"

"Fuck that. I don't deal drugs."

"Or did Bull have something to do with it?"

"Bull ain't do nothin'."

"Well, your defense attorney is gonna get strong evidence that says otherwise. I mean, about both you and Bull. In fact, the warrant you've been arrested on is for distribution of heroin. Several counts. Conspiracy too."

"Conspiracy? You kiddin' me. You don't got no evidence. You trying to trap me in some shit. All that you got was in my cousin's room, not mine."

"Doesn't matter what room it was in. We got such good evidence on you that I don't need your confession on dealing drugs. It works better for us here to catch you lying. Make you look bad. That what you want? Again, how do you think we know about your boy Bull?"

"This some bullshit."

"I like the word choice."

"Huh?"

"When was the last time you saw Chris?"

"I didn't have nothin' to do with him being killed."

"Then you shouldn't worry about telling me when it was that you last saw him."

"I don't remember the last time I saw him."

"That's convenient."

I take out the Polaroids of the naked women, this time without the sticky notes on them. I set them one by one on the table in front of him. He looked very interested. Seemed to like what he saw.

"Let's change it up a bit. You know any of these women?"

"What, they dead too?"

"Not that I know of. You know them? Chris Doyle certainly did."

I let him look them over a bit longer.

"Doyle met them through you, didn't he?"

"I ain't no pimp."

"I don't think you are, but I do believe he met most of these women through you. Isn't that right?"

"Couple of these women here work at the strip club. He probably met them there, got something goin' on the side with them."

"Which girls work at the strip club?"

"These ones here," he said, pointing to three of them.

"What are their names?"

"I only know what names they go by there is all. This one here is Angela, this one Trish, and this one here is Alisha. And you can find them there and ask them directly if I had anything to do with introducing them to that Chris dude."

"I will, thank you. I appreciate you being honest."

"Yeah, okay."

"You know any of the other ones?"

"No."

I picked up the photos and returned them to the case jacket. He seemed disappointed.

"Those three girls you pointed out, do they use drugs?"

"Fuck, all those girls do."

"We will talk to them. Tell them you've been arrested for distribution and other charges. You know how they like to talk when they get nervous."

"Sheeeit."

"Don't really need anything from them, but it can't hurt, especially when it comes to learning more about your connection with Chris Doyle."

"Go on now. Keep fishin'."

"Damn, you really don't have a clue, do ya? We have recordings, Trevor. Got you dealing direct from the club."

He was thinking hard, like maybe Chris was the one wired, or even Artie. Hell, maybe he was even starting to realize it was our UC.

"I ain't saying shit no more. This is like entrapment and where I stop and say I want my lawyer. So go on, fuck yourself."

"Magic words."

"'Fuck yourself'?"

"No. 'Lawyer.'"

"Yeah, and I got a damn good one."

"Good luck with that. We're done. Enjoy the rest of your soda and the Snickers bar. You won't be seeing any of those for a long while."

I started to gather all my stuff from the table.

"So you ain't gonna tell me about all this evidence you say you got on me, especially about some twenty-two I don't own?"

"We can't talk anymore. You asked for a lawyer."

"This some bullshit."

"You say that a lot. You saying you want to continue talking now?"

"Naw, I'm sayin' we'll see how this plays out."

"Trust me, it won't play out well for you. When you realize that, tell your defense attorney you want to talk to us. I'm sure whoever it is will agree."

He picked up the Snickers and tore the wrapping open and took a big bite. Didn't look at me after. I knew it was over.

I walked out of the room.

We finished processing him and then had him transported to cell block. I knew how it would turn out for him, so I wasn't worried about how the interview went. He was fucked and deserved everything that was coming. I didn't feel bad about a thing.

40

M arr and I were both put on administrative leave with pay, pending the outcome of the shooting investigation. We were allowed to work at our offices because of the pending cases. Marr also said he'd take care of the prelim, which was in the morning. I was thankful, and I'm sure Kelly was too. The day was damn long, and we didn't finish up until later that night. Kelly did manage to request a rush from the firearms section, but it would still be at least a couple of days before that came back.

We all met up at Buffalo Billiards for food and drinks after we finished. My head wasn't in it, though. Celeste had taken over there. I'd called her earlier, and we made plans to get together tomorrow evening after I finished work. That made it better. I had something to look forward to.

We sat at the bar, ordered a round of whiskey shots before our burgers and fries came.

I lifted the shot glass. Kelly and Marr lifted theirs.

"Here's to life as we know it shutting down in 2000," I said.

"No. No. Fuck no. Too damn morbid," Marr said.

"Yeah," Kelly added. "Here's to the twenty-two coming back positive on our decedents so now we can bury that fuckhead."

"That's morbid too, but I agree," Marr said.

"I liked the idea of mine better," I said.

"That's because you're one dark motherfucker," Kelly said as she wiped her mouth.

"Here's to that too." Marr smiled.

We all clinked glasses and downed the shots. Knocked our knuckles on the bar top after. Marr signaled the bartender for another round of drinks.

"Wish I could've got more out of him." Don't know why I was still thinking about Miles.

"He's been through it before. He wouldn't have confessed to shit," Marr said.

"I could've done better. I think I went too hard on him too early."

"You did fine," Kelly assured me. "Don't lose sleep over this shit."

"I won't lose any sleep because I still have some hope."

I realized after, that was some shit that came out of my mouth. It was almost like I was trying to downplay what I already knew was coming.

"Gotta have hope," Marr said right when the bartender set the next round of shots on the table.

We lifted our shots and clinked our glasses again. Nice burn as it went down.

I was drunk when I got home. Ignored the blinking light on my answering machine and went straight to bed.

It was a solid sleep. Oddly, I felt refreshed when I woke up early the next morning. Been a long time since I felt like that.

The LT hit us up after roll call. Kelly and I followed him to his office. We sat in the two wooden chairs in front of his desk. He sat in his fancy ergonomic chair, propped his elbows on the desk, leaned forward and clenched his hands. I started to feel a bit like the bad guy in the box and he was out to get a confession.

"I have to brief the chief this morning. Tell me where you are."

"Getting ready to go to the Nickel to meet with the AUSA assigned to the case," Kelly began. "Plan on meeting before the preliminary hearing."

"We're sure he'll get held," I added.

"Yes, based on his record."

"Guns we recovered are also being tested. We'll check with Firearms today to see where they are."

"He's a good suspect, Lu," I said.

"Let's hope so. We need a quick closure on this."

"We're working it," Kelly answered. "But we should go, sir. Need to get with the AUSA before the prelim."

"Then go. Keep me informed."

"Got it," I told him.

We stood and walked out.

Once we were clear of his office I said, "And the pressure's on."

"I need a cigarette."

"Let's get out of here then."

Parking near the Nickel was tough. We had to park illegally near the Police Memorial across from the Building Museum. Kelly shouldered her satchel that contained the case jacket.

Theresa Graves was the assistant U.S. attorney assigned. We entered the building and made our way through security to the elevator. A few familiar faces along the way, but we managed to get to the floor Graves was on without too much conversation.

We were buzzed in another door and walked a narrow hallway lined with small offices where other AUSAs were busy working until we got to her corner office. Marr was already there, sitting on the sofa beside a small bookshelf. He was drinking a coffee from a 7-Eleven to-go mug. Graves was behind her desk, going through the paperwork needed for the prelim. She was older, with thick dark hair and a fit body. She was a runner and stayed in shape. We all knew her. I worked with her on several occasions when I was at the branch. She was good at what she did. Worked narcotics for years. Her desk was cluttered with stacks of case folders and loose papers. Framed family photographs hung on the wall to the left of her desk, along with yellow sticky notes with names and numbers.

She looked up from the paperwork to acknowledge our presence.

"Detectives," she said.

"Good to see you're on this," I said.

"Good morning," Kelly said.

"It's a strong case. Good job."

"It was all Marr," I told her.

"Aw, c'mon now." Marr smiled. "Team effort and all that shit, you know."

Graves looked at her watch and said, "We should get down there."

Our case was the third up. Trevor was escorted to the table where his defense attorney was sitting. She was a young woman who did not look like a public defender. Trevor did mention he had his own attorney. He was in an orange jumpsuit, hands cuffed in the front and secured by a chain around his waist. He nodded to his grandpa sitting on a front bench behind the defense attorney's table and a short wall. He noticed us too, sitting a couple of rows back. He shot us a nice scowl.

It didn't take long after Graves presented the case and Marr took the stand for the judge to find probable cause. Trevor was held without bond. He was not happy. Grandpa bowed his head as if in prayer. Trevor was escorted back to holding shortly after by two U.S. marshals.

Graves had another case, so she stayed behind. Marr said he was going to wait for her. Seemed like they were close. Kelly and I walked to Jack's Famous Deli on Third Street to grab an early lunch and more coffee. More familiar faces along the way. Hard to avoid when you've been on the job for a while and in court just as much along with other workers.

No ticket on the car. We decided to stay parked there, windows down to catch the cool breeze and eat our sandwiches in a spot where we'd get no interruptions.

41

G ot together with Celeste later that night. We sat at the bar of
the Velvet Lounge on U Street smoking cigarettes and drinking vodka and sodas. It was crowded, but we got ourselves a couple
of stools. Ventilation was bad. Smoke hovered over the bar, but
mostly us, like a grim ghostly fog. The slight stench of weed fanned
in from the restroom area.

I called in for the first two hours tomorrow so I could sleep in
with her. Sarge didn't give me too much of a hassle given the result
of the search warrant and getting the suspect held. That was enough
for him to justify a still open high-profile case.

"Thanks again for taking care of the electric bill," she said, and
then gave me a nice warm kiss on the corner of my mouth.

"I told you I'd take care of you."

"No one's ever said that to me. It feels good."

"I'm happy I'm the first one, then. And that it makes you
feel good."

I knew she was high, and I wanted to talk about her slowing
down because I didn't know what I could do for her after she blew

through the ten-pack. Well, there was a lot I could do, but I had to admit, I didn't feel good about having to go there. It reminded me too much of that piece of shit Officer Bobby. I didn't like the comparison. I felt sick inside having the thought of that comparison with me. Everything about him seemed vulgar. Dirty.

I couldn't help staring at her as she looked over the bar at what appeared to be nothing in particular. Seemed like she was lost in her head somewhere. She turned and noticed, smiled, and looked intently into my eyes. I could get lost in those eyes. We did get lost in each other's eyes when in bed and lying on our sides close enough that our noses touched and everything, but our eyes blurred. I looked forward to that tonight.

When she looked at me with sunken, slightly watery eyes she said, "I don't want you to get the wrong idea, but I'm glad he's gone."

"I can understand. It's okay to feel that way."

"I sometimes don't feel like it is okay, but I do feel that way."

She snuffed out her cig, immediately lit another one, looked at me again. Her face different this time. Seemed like a genuine smile.

"I like you."

"I like you too."

"So how's this gonna go? With us, I mean."

"How do you want it to go?" I asked, fearing the answer.

"I'd like to keep you around."

That made me happy.

"That's all right with me. I definitely want to keep you around."

"Good."

"Yeah, it is."

"I worry, though."

"About what?"

"About what you do for a living."

I knew what she meant. It was about her lifestyle. She was young. Didn't want to give it up. A part of me started to think I might just be a meal ticket. Someone who paid her bills, maybe provided a little more until something better came along. I shot it outta my head, though. Didn't want to believe that.

"I'll admit, I do love my work. That's not going to change."

"But I don't know if I can change right now either."

I was right about her not wanting to give it up. I still had a bit of intuition left. Maybe not enough. I was here with her, after all.

"I gotta be honest with you, it does concern me," I said.

"I would never want to get you in trouble."

"I worry for you, not me."

She leaned my way and we kissed.

She broke away and said, "Don't worry for me. I'm a strong girl now. Feeling stronger than I've ever felt before."

"That's good to hear."

I finished my drink.

"You good for another?" I asked.

She downed what remained in hers and said, "Yes. Definitely."

The tender brought us two more. I lifted my glass toward her. She lifted hers.

"Here's to feeling strong and doing what you have to do."

"Cheers to that, you sweet man."

At my apartment we had a couple more drinks and snuggled on the sofa. Her head rested on my chest. It felt wonderful. There was comfort there, but not the kind of comfort that came with contentment—it was merely satisfaction and then nothing after. I hated feeling the nothing after.

I kissed Celeste on the head, took in her scent. We finished the drinks and moved to the bedroom. I knew I'd be tired the next day, but what the hell. She was worth it. *How many times have I said that to myself?*

42

Graves notified us early the next morning before Kelly and I got to the office that the defense attorney for Trevor requested a debriefing. Trevor wanted to talk. Said he had information we would be interested in. Marshals Service would be bringing him to the B1 level of the Nickel.

I met Kelly at Graves's office. Marr was there too.

"Sorry for the late notice," Graves told us.

"No problem. This sounds good, right?" Kelly inquired.

"Depends on what he has to offer," Graves said. "And if he's willing to fully cooperate. His defense attorney is sharp."

"Yeah, the evidence is pretty damn overwhelming," I said.

"We're not narcotics detectives," Kelly said, and then turned to Marr. "No offense, Marr, but we don't have anything on him for the murders unless we get positive results back on that twenty-two pistol."

"Well, at least there's hope then," I said.

I was sure the information Trevor had for us had to do with the dirty cop but I didn't feel the need to say anything. I obviously knew firsthand that he would not be confessing to anything having to do with murder. Maybe the drug and weapons charges, though. I was sure he killed or had people killed in the past, so I had no problem with what he had coming to him. I've said that before. Probably would say it again. It made me feel better knowing what kind of man he really was. He believed he was a king in his little world, and I was happy to have a hand in overthrowing him. Knock him off that fucking throne of his.

"He'll probably give up the dirty cop," Marr said, like he'd read my mind.

"We already gave everything on him to IA, so I couldn't give a shit," Kelly replied.

"Let's see what he has to offer," Graves said.

I heard the familiar chain-hitting-chain sound as the three prisoners turned and made their way down the far end of the long narrow hallway. They were escorted by two deputy marshals. Trevor and the other two were dressed in orange jumpsuits, their movement restricted by leg cuffs and a leather waist belt that secured the hands cuffed close to their bellies. Walked like penguins being herded toward a steep cliff.

Trevor was taken first, into one of several rooms toward the end of the hallway, near where we were standing. There was another, older marshal at a desk inside a small room where there was a door that led to an even smaller debriefing room. Trevor shot us a sideways glance before he entered with an expression like he was still in control of everything. Not a worry in the world. The two marshals then escorted the other two prisoners to their rooms. After a couple of minutes, the older marshal stepped out and gave us the heads-up.

"I'll only be a minute," his defense attorney advised.

She was shouldering an overstuffed faded black leather satchel. She walked into the room where the older marshal sat. I heard the other door being unlocked and then closed.

A few minutes later she stepped out and said, "We're ready for you."

Graves followed her into the room, but before the three of us could enter we had to secure our weapons and magazines in the lockboxes in the office where the older marshal sat.

The debriefing room was tiny. Trevor was sitting on a wooden classroom-type chair in the corner, to the left of the one and only door. The door was locked from the outside. The only way out is to knock and wait for the marshal to open it. His attorney was beside him on an equally undesirable desk chair with wheels and cracked vinyl padding.

The room was pretty barren, for the only other furniture four more chairs and a large rectangular shiny faux-wood table. Graves, Kelly, and Marr were on the other side of the table facing Trevor and his attorney. His cuffed hands were resting on his lap, and he sat with legs stretched out. I was at the corner of the table at the other end. I took my notebook out of my back pocket, opened it until I got to the next blank page, and wrote the date and time on the top left-hand corner, along with everyone's name who was in the room. I underlined the date and time. For some reason I underlined the time twice. Time was heavy on my mind for some reason. It was like the job owned every second of my time and being stuck in this claustrophobic room made me realize it. Everything about this job was about time. Dispatchers verbally logged the time after every call. Evidence, statements, identifications, all information reported or notebooked was marked with the time. Prosecutors depended on precise time. Defense attorneys could tear you up on the stand if your time was off. Everything had to be done in "a timely manner." It was carved into our way of thinking. But noting the time didn't really matter much in a debriefing setting, because Graves booked a two-hour time slot, and the defense attorney was there. It was only about me and counting the hours before I could go home. I wanted all my time set for Celeste and nothing but her.

Graves plopped her large file down and pulled out the court jacket, then introduced herself to Trevor and thanked him for being there. He did not respond.

"You already know the detectives here," she said.

He nodded.

"Do we need to go over the debriefing letter again, Miss Seymour?" Graves asked.

Without looking at her client, Seymour said, "I think everything has been made clear to my client at this point."

"Do you have any questions for me, Mr. Miles?" Graves asked.

"I got good information. Will that help me with my charges?"

"I've already explained everything to your attorney and provided a letter about what we expect and how you can help yourself. Did your attorney explain everything to you?"

"She did."

He looked at his attorney, as if for approval.

"You can talk to them," she advised.

Graves looked toward us, a signal that we should take over.

"We were told you might have some information we might be interested in," I began.

"Yeah, I do."

"Okay. What might that be?"

"You already got that dirty officer Bobby on recording, but you don't know everything about him."

"What other information do you have on him?"

"Officer Bobby Hanley. He does some work for me sometimes. Gives me information, too."

"What kind of work does he do for you?"

"Protection. Information about what the police are up to, like search warrants and shit like that."

"How does he protect you?"

"I might give him information about competition. He gets it

taken care of. He will also let me know if the police are ever close to me."

"We'll need more than that. How does he get it taken care of?"

"I give him the information. He gets the work done. Search warrants. Arrests and all that shit. He'll sneak a little of what he finds on the side. Drugs, money, gun here and there. He gets the money. I get everything else."

"So you're like his special confidential informant?"

"You could say that. But he work for me. I don't work for him. What you got on recording through that undercover bitch—"

"Trevor." His attorney stopped him like a warning.

"That undercover girl with us in the club ain't shit. That just the tip of the iceberg."

"He work with any other officers?"

"Yeah, I know of one, but he mostly stay away from the club. I don't know him by name."

"You seen him before, though?"

"No. Just know about him through Bobby."

"Bobby ever do anything else for you outside of using the department? Take care of certain people in other ways?"

"You mean like what?"

"Get rid of someone for ya."

"You talking murder? Naw, I ain't down with that kinda shit."

"You used the word 'protection,'" Kelly added. "That means something a bit different than what you said he does."

"That's true," I added. "What other kind of protection does he offer you?"

He looked at his attorney again. That certain look said it all. There was more.

"You two need some privacy?" I asked.

"You want them to step out, Trevor?"

"Naw. Shi-et."

"How has Hanley protected you?"

"I said what I said. He dirty as shit. Who knows what else he gets himself into."

"Give us an example of what else he might get into."

"He don't share no details with me about what he does on his own. Just insinuates."

"Insinuates? I like that. Give us an example of what he insinuates."

He shook his head back and forth, giving himself time to think. I got the feeling he was making it up as he went. Telling us what we wanted to hear.

"I know he got a burner. Keeps it at his ankle. Called it his throwaway."

"But he still had it so he didn't use it."

That caught him off guard.

"Doesn't mean he didn't have another one before that."

"True. Anything else you know?"

"Naw. I gave you some good shit."

"Does he know Artie and Chris Doyle?"

"I seen him sitting and talking to them at the club."

"He ever with either of them at the club one-on-one?"

"Sometimes with Artie."

"And Artie knew he was a cop?"

"Hell, everyone knew he was a cop."

"When was the last time you saw him with Artie?"

"I don't recall. Couple weeks ago maybe."

"What about with Doyle?"

"Same. I don't recall dates."

"Trevor, I gotta be honest with you. Miss Graves here is already working with our Internal Affairs, and they got Hanley on conspiracy charges based on what we got with him in the club with you. We'll definitely give what you told us to Internal Affairs, though. They might even want to talk to you. You want to help yourself, we're going to need a lot more. I mean, you know why we're really here, don't you?"

He looked at his defense attorney. Seemed confused.

"This is good information, Graves," she told her.

"Yes, and it's noted."

"We need to know about Artie and Chris Doyle and your relation with them," Kelly said.

"I told you everything I know about them two."

"Mr. Miles already informed the two homicide detectives when he was arrested that he knew nothing about their deaths. You have no evidence that he was involved in any way."

"Yet," Kelly said.

"What the fuck you mean, yet?" Trevor asked.

"That's enough, Trevor," his attorney advised him.

"Well, they think they got evidence, then I want to know, because I think they're full of shit."

"I said that's enough."

"Do you need some time to talk to your attorney, Mr. Miles?" Graves asked again.

"No. You all just trying to pin some murders on me 'cause you got no one else and just 'cause I had dealings with them."

"Tell me about your dealings with them. You supplied Doyle with his heroin, right?"

"He already told you everything he knows about them. Now, we came here in good faith because Mr. Miles has reliable information about corrupt officers. This now feels like nothing more than a fishing expedition. Maybe we should talk to the FBI. You know how they like to slap their cuffs on dirty officers."

"I am handling that part of the investigation along with Internal Affairs," Graves said. "I'll relay what he provided to them and I'm sure it will be helpful."

"You mean it will help me with my charges?"

"Cooperating is always helpful" was all Graves said.

"I think maybe we're talking to the wrong people," Seymour said.

"This is not a plea negotiation, Ms. Seymour. You were made aware of that. At least it isn't yet, until your client fully cooperates with the detectives. Are you sure you don't need more time to talk to him?"

"We already know that Chris Doyle dealt heroin and that you supplied him," I said.

"His full cooperation is necessary and the truth about everyone he supplied narcotics to. It was all in the letter provided to you," Graves said.

"I had no dealings with Doyle other than seeing him on occasion at the club."

It was so obvious he wanted to remove himself from anything having to do with both victims.

"We're not going to give you another charge for dealing to him," I said. "We know you were, and if you had nothing to do with the murders, then why would you be afraid of admitting that?"

"I ain't afraid of shit. I just know how you all work and want to put one of those murders on me. I told you what I know. And you all ain't offering me anything for it."

"Let's back up," Marr began. "How about helping *me* out here. I ain't Homicide. Just Narcotics. What's Bull's real name and where is he holing up?"

"I ain't gonna give no more until I know about some plea agreement. Get my charges taken care of."

"It's only a matter of time before we pick him up. Be interesting to hear what he has to say about everything you refuse to talk about," Marr told him.

"You go give that your best shot. I came here on my own accord to give you good information about a dirty cop. One of your own, and it don't seem like you give a shit. I want to talk to the FBI.

They gonna do somethin' for me with the information you don't care about."

"The prosecutor told you she was going to give all that information to Internal Affairs. What can help you here with us is being honest about your dealings with Chris Doyle and Artie. What do you think Bull will say about that once we pick him up?"

"Like I said, give it your best shot."

"That dirty cop is going to do everything he can to save his own ass. It's gonna be all about who comes to the table first," Marr said. "Don't you get how this works?"

"I came to the table, but you don't want to listen."

"We're listening," I said. "But you're not telling us everything. What do you think Hanley will tell Internal Affairs and us about your association with Chris Doyle?"

He doesn't answer.

"I believe this conversation is over," Seymour said. "At least until you provide whatever other evidence you have that might connect my client to your two homicide victims. He's told you everything he knows."

And that was fucking that.

Strike two.

43

I had a hard time getting through the rest of the day, mostly because I knew the answers and they had started to weigh me down. Trevor, Hanley, and Bull would be nothing but a waste of time with respect to the homicide investigations, but I had to play it out, wait for the ballistic evidence to come in so we could put this to bed.

On the way home I went to my regular spot for Chinese takeout, just around the corner from my place. After I ordered and was waiting for my food I suddenly fell into an uncomfortable clouded state. I felt the ground beneath my feet spin and whatever sense of time I had was gone. There was no doubt in my mind that I was dying. That's how it felt at the time. My heart pelted the inside of my chest like it was trying to ram its way out.

Should I call 911? Try to call 911?

Oddly, I was too embarrassed to reach out for help. There were a couple of customers in there and employees behind the counter. They became nothing but a blur. Don't know if they noticed what was happening to me. I thought I was about to pass out, so I managed to get myself to one of the chairs at a table near the window. I was beginning to hyperventilate. I cupped my head in my hands on the table, and then the dread that had hit me was gone. Just like that. I found myself sitting there but didn't know for how long.

After a couple more minutes I got my food and walked home. I felt a bit better once I got there but didn't want to be alone. I was restless and wanted to call Celeste, but it was late. It was always too late. I didn't have the energy to walk to one of my haunts, and I was afraid what happened before might happen again. I knew who I was in need of and I couldn't have her right now.

Everything. It was all too much. I felt like I was going to break down, cry or some shit like that. I sat on the sofa and ate my food. That helped, but only a little.

Damn, what was going through my head? What was I trying to do?

The next day I thought about going to the doctor, but a few minutes after I got out of bed Kelly called and advised me that our captain, Byron, wanted to see us. It was my day off and I hoped to get through whatever it was I was going through and get together with Celeste later. Hopefully the meet wouldn't take too long, and I'd be able to do that.

I met Kelly at her cubicle and we walked to his office. He was reading the *Post*'s metro section, reclined in his nice chair, feet propped up and crossed over each other on his desk.

"Morning, Alexander, Kelly."

"Mornin', Cap," I said.

"Good morning," Kelly said too.

We were fortunate to have good officials at Homicide. That was something rare. Byron was a good man. Worked patrol for about twelve years, then made sergeant and after about another five years he made lieutenant. He did that for only three years, with the last eight in specialized units.

Could never figure out how old he was. He could have been

in his early forties or even his fifties. Good skin. He kept his head shaved tight. Had a glossy brown scalp like he used some sort of oil product.

He folded his paper, sat up, and set it on his tidy desk.

Everything felt odd to me, staged like I was in a TV series or a movie. I was like a character in one of a billion productions, executive-produced by God Himself, something that amused His angels and all His heavenly rulers. Don't misunderstand; I didn't think so highly of myself that I believed this life movie was any sort of hit. Far from it. It may have been masterly done because, after all, God did make it, but it was not a masterpiece and that was only because it starred a bunch of fallen humans, especially me. This movie was more like one of those quirky, off-beat films that got a very limited release. It did have its moments, though, and the best I could hope for was it'd be a sleeper and I'd make it through and allow there to be another one. I don't know where my brain was going.

"Have a seat," he said. "Thanks for being here on your days off."

I was brought back to reality. We sat in two of the three chairs in front of his desk.

"How was the debriefing with your suspect?"

I looked at Kelly and she said, "Not what we hoped for, Cap. He gave us information about the dirty cop, but nothing else."

"We believe he's holding back," I added. "He won't admit to having any connection with either of our decedents, even though the cell phone information we have suggests otherwise."

"You still think he's good for it?"

"Yes," I said immediately. Looked at Kelly again then, and she seemed surprised I jumped on it so fast.

"We are hoping for something positive with the pistol," Kelly said.

"I made a call about that," Byron said. "You should have something coming your way in a couple of days."

"Thank you, Captain," I said.

"Anything else you can fill me in on?"

"Trevor was forthcoming about a couple of the girls in the Polaroids we recovered from the decedent's home. They work at the strip club, so we'll follow up on that," Kelly said.

"And Detective Marr is working the guy we only know as Bull. He got the warrant for him."

"Why not one of you?"

"We could have but thought it would be better for a Narcotics detective to draft the affidavit. We'll be the first to get him into an interview room once he's picked up, though."

"Make sure of that."

"We will, sir," I said.

"Well, needless to say, with all that's going on in the department, and this new mayor, I want this one off my back. I need you to write something up for me today."

"We understand," Kelly advised. "No problem."

"Get me that write-up."

He picked up the newspaper and started reading it again. We stood and walked out of his office.

When we were near our cubicles, Kelly turned to me and said, "What do you mean by telling him yes? We're not even close to something as positive as that."

"I know." I felt weird again. "I guess I reacted based on a feeling. Shouldn't have said it."

"Fuck yeah. We won't look so good if it goes south."

I sat at my cubicle. Kelly hovered over me.

"Everything good with you?" she asked.

"Yes. Of course. Why would you ask that?"

"You seem off is all. You getting laid?"

"You're something else," I told her.

"Yeah, you need to get laid."

"Go on with that" was all I said.

"All righty then."

She was right, though.

My cell rang a few minutes later. It was Celeste, but I didn't answer. Had to get through this shit and out of here first.

We nearly got through doing the write-up for the captain without an incident, but then a call came in for the whole squad to respond to the scene of an unnamed off-duty officer found shot to death in his personal vehicle. Kelly and I shot each other a *fuck me* kind of glance when we heard the location. We had to go too, even though we were on a different squad.

44

Robert "Bobby" Hanley was on administrative leave without pay pending investigation, but now he was slumped over, head on his steering wheel, shot three times—twice in the back of the head and once in the chest. The car was parked on K Street, about half a block west of the strip club. It looked like an execution. Blood spatter and brain tissue like tiny pebbles caked to the windshield, dashboard, and front seats. One of the Crime Scene techs was taking pictures and the other was dusting the exterior of the vehicle for prints. News vans from almost every station were already on the scene. Crime scene tape secured the whole block, with uniformed officers at all corners. Too many fucking whiteshirts, even the deputy chief. New chief was on his way.

This was a clusterfuck.

Bodies were piling up. I had to wonder if Trevor called the shots from jail on this one, but would he give up the one ace in the hole he had that in his mind could lead to a plea negotiation? I of course knew that wouldn't happen once the ballistics came back, but Trevor certainly didn't. Maybe he got scared of what Hanley would give up to try to save his own ass. Marr did tell him it was all about who came to the table first. Typical TV phrase, but true. Trevor had a lot of garbage, and Hanley probably carried a lot of it out for him. Maybe it wasn't Trevor, though. Bull was still out. On the run. Did Hanley have something on Bull? I was sure Hanley made a lot of enemies other than Bull and Trevor. The girls who worked the club more than likely didn't care for him much either. Shooting Hanley at this location was a statement.

Caine, Jac, three other detectives, the sarge, and the LT from our squad were on the scene. I called Marr on the way, but he hadn't arrived yet. We grouped together. The sarge had Jac and Caine canvassing for possible evidence, and the other three for witnesses.

"You and Kelly come with me," he ordered calmly.

We followed him to his car, parked in the middle of the street within the perimeter of the tape. He stood at the front end.

"Internal Affairs is on the way."

"How the hell was Hanley out?" Kelly asked.

"You know how slow IA operates, and based on what I heard on the recordings he probably wouldn't have been held anyway. You should know that."

"He facilitated a drug deal with Detective Marr's UC. Marr's been working closely with IA on this," she said.

"It was not on you, but now it is. Jacoby and Caine will take the lead on this one, though. You two keep working your end but keep them informed. I'll make sure they keep you two informed. Anything on this character Bull?"

"In the wind and a possible suspect for this," I said. "Marr got BOLOs out on him in connection with his warrant. Our suspect wouldn't give up anything on his boy when we debriefed him."

"There's a reason it happened here," Kelly said. "The club doesn't open until five, so he had to be meeting someone in front."

"Or didn't even get a chance to get out of his car to go somewhere else," I added. "Maybe he was going to meet someone inside the club."

"You two go to the club, see if anyone is working. Call Frankie, too. Get his ass down here."

"Already called him. He's on the way. Also, they're a few girls who work there whose names came up during the course of the investigation. We want to talk to them if they're working this evening," I added.

"I'll have everyone who works there escorted in."

"Copy that."

We walked to the club, knocked on the steel door several times. After a couple of minutes, we knocked again but harder. A short time after, a young lady dressed in a black pantsuit answered. It was not the same woman as before. She didn't have to ask what it was about. She was older, seemed professional.

"I'm Detective Kelly and this is my partner, Detective Blum."

"Yes. Okay."

She had a slight accent. Sounded Russian.

"Can we talk inside?" Kelly asked.

"Of course," she said.

We entered and she closed and locked the door behind her.

I had my notebook and pen out.

"What's your name and your position here please," I said.

"Nadia Sokolov. I'm the head manager."

I wrote it down.

"I only heard what sounded like loud firecrackers. I didn't open the door or see anything."

"Can we talk in your office?" Kelly asked.

"I don't know how else I can help."

"It won't take long. We'll be interviewing everyone we can."

"Are you the same detectives who were here before and talked to the night manager and one of my girls?"

"Yes."

"Is this related to that?"

"We don't know yet," Kelly told her.

"My office is this way."

We followed her to her office. It was the same office we were in before.

"Do you want to sit down?"

I didn't want to sit on the sofa again. There was one other wooden chair near a desk. I offered it to Kelly.

"I'll stand," she said.

I did too.

"I never opened the door when I heard all the sirens. I figured it was more than firecrackers. I didn't know if it was safe. Was someone shot?"

"Yes," Kelly advised.

"Oh dear. There have been shootings around here before, but not on this block. Is the person okay?"

"No," I said.

"Oh my. Security and my girls are going to begin to come in. Are they in danger?"

"Everything is blocked off until we get through here. You might want to call them after we leave. We'll have them escorted in."

"This is usually a busy night. We can't afford to stay closed."

"You should be able to open once we finish here," I said.

"But you don't know how long that will be?"

"Ms. Sokolov, someone was just murdered. That's a lot more important than you opening on time, don't you think?"

"You're right. I apologize."

"No need to apologize to us," I said.

"Just remember that we're going to want to talk to a couple of the girls anyway," Kelly said.

"Yes, but why?"

"Because we have information that they might know the man who was shot. We need to follow all the leads. They're not in trouble, but they might have information that is important to us."

"What girls?"

"Sparkle, Angela, Trish, and Alisha."

"Alisha's not working tonight. Do you have to do this here?"

"We have to do this, and it would be a lot more comfortable on the girls if we talk to them here rather than taking them to our office," Kelly said. "Besides, that would take them away from working for a lot longer."

"Can you call Alisha and have her come in?" I asked.

"That's going to be up to her. She does have a child, so I can't say."

"Would appreciate if you'd try."

"I'll try," she said.

"Anyone else working right now?"

"No, I'm the only one here."

"I noticed that the two large windows in front are blacked out. So you only heard the gunshots?"

"Yes. That's what I told you."

"How many gunshots did you hear?"

"Again, I didn't know they were gunshots, but I figured they were when I heard the police outside."

"I understand. So how many did you hear?"

"I don't know—maybe three, four? It was very fast."

Kelly took her business card out of her back pants pocket.

"Here's my card. If you hear anything about what happened, you need to call."

"Of course."

"You should get on the phone and make those calls now. We'll be back when everyone arrives," Kelly said.

"I'll try to get in touch with who I can."

"Be sure to tell them it's okay to come to work and that it's safe. They'll be escorted in," I said.

"Thank you for your time," Kelly told her.

"I will show you out."

45

The cast and crew were escorted into the club. Believe it or not, it looked like they all showed up. I noticed one who had stopped before entering the club and looked at the car with the shattered driver's-side window that belonged to Hanley. She immediately cupped her face with two hands and seemed to almost fall to her knees. The officer supported her with two hands by holding her under the right elbow.

Fortunately, the body was already gone. Most of the scene was canvassed, but Jac had a sidewalk drain grate opened and was bent down looking into it with a stream light. The chief was here but staying away from the media and talking to our captain, the LT, and the deputy chief. Other whiteshirts were standing around trying to look busy.

"That's interesting," I told Kelly, and tilted my chin in the direction of the driver. "She noticed the car."

"Should talk to her first."

We waited until she entered, and then gave them a couple of minutes to settle inside. We found the sarge talking to Marr and walked over.

"Looks like they have a full house in the club," I told Sarge. "We're going back in. Marr should join us."

"Okay with me," Sarge said.

"Yeah, of course," Marr said.

I noticed a couple of news cameramen shouldering the video cameras, panning to follow us there. I tried not to be obvious when I saw them.

"Game face," I mumbled so that Kelly and Marr could hear.

"Always," Marr said.

"I fucking need a cigarette," Kelly muttered.

We knocked on the door and a stout security man in a black suit answered. We identified ourselves and he let us in without question.

"We'd like to speak with the manager, please."

"I'll get her."

He walked toward her office. A couple of minutes later they walked out together. She told something to the security guard and he disappeared into the main room.

She acknowledged us with "Yes, Detectives."

"This is Detective Frank Marr," I told her. "He's working with us."

She nodded in his direction. Frank smiled an odd, comforting smile. She maintained eye contact with him for a brief second, then looked back to the two of us. Frankie had a way about him. Never knew how.

"We'd like to talk to everybody one at a time. Can we use your office? We'll be as fast as we can so you can get back to business."

"I'm very busy with work. Would you mind using one of the back private rooms?"

"You mean where they take customers?" Kelly asked.

"That's what she means," Marr said before she could answer.

"That won't be a problem," I said. "Can we speak to you briefly in your office first?"

She seemed to hesitate like this was a bother but then said, "Yes."

We followed her there. I gazed through the slit in the curtain that led to the main room and noticed a couple of the girls standing around in their normal street clothes, including the one who broke down outside. She was on a barstool surrounded by a couple of the other girls.

When we all entered Sokolov's office, I took the liberty of closing the door behind me. She seemed to wonder about that. Not worried, just maybe because I didn't ask first.

"Thank you for making sure everyone got here," I said.

"That's my job."

"Did you know Officer Bobby Hanley?" I asked straightaway.

She seemed genuinely surprised.

"Oh my God, was he the one who was shot?"

"Yes, afraid so."

"Oh my. That is terrible. Do you know why?"

"We're looking into everything," Kelly said.

"How well did you know him?" I asked.

"Only that he's a regular here. A good paying customer."

"Did you ever meet with him, talk to him?"

"Meet with him? I would see him come in sometimes, and we would say hello. I would sometimes make sure he was escorted to his table. We considered him VIP."

"He spent that much?" Kelly asked. "Isn't that what VIP means?"

"Not necessarily. Just a good, regular customer who the girls liked. But he spent at the bar and tipped the girls. I am so sad to hear this. You aren't thinking it could have to do with anyone or anything here?"

"Like we said, we're looking into all possibilities. Nothing more."

"Do you know anything about his personal life or people here he would hang out with on a regular basis?" Kelly asked.

"I'm only here during the day. I will usually leave a couple of hours after we open, sometimes, like today, a bit later. I stay in my office. I don't hang out at night."

"Was Chris Doyle or a man they call Artie a VIP here too?"

"I don't know anyone by the name Artie. I only know the name Chris Doyle because I see his name on credit card slips."

"Do you watch the news?" Marr asked.

"Why do you ask that? No, I don't care for the news. Sometimes for the weather, though. Again, why?"

"Chris Doyle was a regular here too, and he was found murdered in his home. It's been all over the news," Kelly said. I knew now that she didn't trust the manager.

"I don't know what to say. I know nothing about that. I do my job here and I go home. I take care of the books, payroll, and staff. The night floor manager takes care of the night and hires the dancers. She might know these people. It is part of her job to take care of the VIPs and other customers, and make sure everything is running smoothly on the floor. But you've said you have spoken with her already."

"Yes," I said. "We're just following up. Can we have your number in case we have other questions?"

"Of course."

She went to her desk and picked up a card from inside a wooden bowl, handed it to me.

"Appreciate it, Ms. Sokolov," I said.

"Will that be all? I have to finish up here before I can go home."

"Yes. Thank you."

She let us out and closed the door behind us.

"She actually seemed on the up and up," Kelly said.

"You can never tell with Russian people," I said.

"That seems bigoted," Kelly said, with a sort of scorn.

"You forget I'm Russian."

"Ha!" Marr huffed out.

46

Before we went into the main room we stopped to talk about how we were going to work the interviews.

"Marr, you mind interviewing the three security guards, the bartender, and the night manager we interviewed before? We'll take the girls."

"No problem. I'll talk to them out here."

"Kelly, we should start with the girl we saw outside crying first."

"Agreed. Let's get this done," Kelly said.

We pulled the curtain aside and entered. Everyone turned to notice. I immediately recognized Ivy. She was at the bar standing beside the girl who'd been outside crying. She looked nervous when she saw us.

I introduced us to everyone and advised what was going to happen.

A girl we didn't know asked, "Why do you have to talk to us? We weren't here when it happened."

"Most of you probably already know that the person shot was a customer here. It's important we talk to everyone. It could help with the investigation."

Marr walked toward the security guards and Kelly and I to the bar where the girl was sitting. She was still teared up.

"We'd like to talk to you first," Kelly said.

She looked at Ivy, who was still standing beside her. Ivy seemed to force a smile.

"Okay," the girl said.

"The manager asked that we use one of the private rooms in back. Can you take us to one?"

She nodded.

We followed her to the back, where there were four rooms one after the other on the left side of the wide hallway. They all had black curtains.

She pulled the first curtain open with both hands and we followed her in. I was dimly lit. Not great for interviewing. I took my notebook and pen out.

"Is there any more light in here?" I asked.

She went to a wall at the other side of a purple velvet-like sofa with a large, sturdy square table in front of it. I assumed it was for the girls to dance on. She flipped a switch that allowed a little more light.

"This is as much as I can do."

"That's okay," Kelly said. "Would you like to sit down?"

She sat squarely on the edge of the table. I shot Kelly a side glance. I could tell she was thinking the same thing—that neither of us wanted to sit on the sofa. Certain small clear stains were visible, and I was sure if we moved a black light over it that it would reveal more than we wanted to know.

Kelly sat beside her on the edge of the table to the left. I chose to stand but backed up so it would not appear that I was hovering.

"What's your name?" Kelly asked.

"My stage name is Alisha," she said.

"I'll need your real name for my notes," I told her.

"Lynn Beaumont."

"Your date of birth and address?"

"Why do you need that?"

"It's just routine." Kelly smiled. "Nothing to worry about. We have to be thorough."

She provided her date of birth and address. Fucking twenty years old.

"Thanks for coming, Alisha," Kelly said. "We know it's your day off. We noticed you outside."

"I saw the news before Nadia called me, and so I was worried. When I saw the car, I knew it was Bobby."

"You were close?" I asked.

"He's the father of my son," she said, and then dropped her head down, covered her face with the palms of her hands, and began to cry again.

Kelly put her hand on her shoulder and said, "We're so sorry."

"Did he live with you?"

She looked up. Eyes puffy and tearful.

"No. He stayed on most of his days off, though. He took care of us." She sniffled. "Provided child support. We were going to get married."

She cried again.

I had to wonder if she could be that naïve. I felt sorry for her.

"Did he ever hang out with anyone else in here you know?" Kelly asked.

"You mean the girls? Yes, I knew he messed around sometimes, but he loved me. I know he did."

That answered my question. Damn.

"Aside from the girls," Kelly continued, "any other customers?"

"Clients? Even some of his other cop buddies," I added.

"Just first names. We never went out like that or anything."

"What are the names?" I asked.

"Peter, Shawn, and I think Thomas."

"Starting with Peter, can you describe them?" I asked.

She did. I wrote it down.

"Anyone else. Clients who weren't cops?" Kelly continued.

She was hesitant. I knew she knew.

When she didn't answer right away I said, "Maybe we can help refresh your memory. Trevor Miles and his boy Bull?"

She didn't want to answer.

"Alisha, we already know. I know you want to find out who did this," I began. "Did he have any trouble with Trevor or Bull?"

"He didn't get along with Bull."

"Why?" Kelly asked.

"'Cause Bull was rough on the girls sometimes."

"Do you know Bull's real name?"

"No. Nobody did."

"Did you ever hear Bull threaten him or learn that he did?"

"No. Bobby just told me to stay away from him and never to go into a private room or especially a hotel."

"Did management or security know he was rough on girls?" I asked.

"Oh, it never happened in here. Always at a hotel party."

"Were you and Bobby at any of those parties?"

"I was with Bobby once. We left early, though. Went back to my place."

"What was Bobby's relationship with Trevor?"

"They were just friends. He wasn't involved with him if that's what you mean."

"So you know what Trevor was involved in?" Kelly asked.

"Of course I did. Everyone here did. Bobby wasn't, though."

Damn, she *was* stupid, or fucking lying her ass off.

"Is there anyone you know that had it out for Bobby?"

"I don't know. Maybe Bull, but to do this? I'm sorry, I just don't know." She broke down again. "I can't believe he's gone. I don't know what I'm going to do."

"We're very sorry for your loss," I said.

"Alisha, did you know Artie?"

"Yes. All the girls knew him. Why?"

"When was the last time you saw him?"

"I couldn't even tell you. It's been a while. Why are you asking about Artie? Does he have something to do with Bobby's death?"

"No," Kelly said. "What about Artie's friend Chris Doyle?"

"I know Artie's friend Chris, but not by last name. Oh my God, he's the man who was found murdered. I saw that on the news too. What does all this have to do with Bobby?"

"We're looking into every connection, Alisha," Kelly said. "That's why it's important you tell us everything. Was Bobby friends with them?"

"Friends? No. He sat with them and had drinks sometimes. He never mentioned anything about them to me."

"Did Artie and Chris hang at a table with Trevor and Bull too?" Kelly asked.

"Yes, they did, especially Chris."

I started to feel terrible with the questions Kelly had to ask. It was starting to break me down. What was I supposed to do, though?

Nothing, and so I just tried to shut my brain down. Let it play out. It had to be played out.

47

Ivy sat on the sofa. I sat on the square table across from her, almost knee to knee. Kelly stood this time.

I looked straight at her and said, "You lied to us, Ivy."

She bowed her head.

"You knew some of those girls in the photos. Why would you hold back on us?"

She looked up, tried to make eye contact, but her eyes kept looking down.

"I was scared. I didn't want to get anyone in trouble."

"Why would you think they'd get in trouble?"

She didn't answer.

"Why, Ivy?"

She looked up at me this time and said, "Not trouble, I guess, just to protect them. Protect me."

"Protect you from what?"

"Not from danger so much because Chris was dead. Just all that happened."

"Tell us, Ivy. Why? Because of Chris?"

"Chris raped me, and Angela," she told us bluntly.

"You have to tell us everything," Kelly said. "As hard as it might be, we need all the details."

"I went over there for a private party. That's all. I only danced at private parties. Maybe a lap dance too, but never sex."

She stopped and pulled out a pack of cigarettes from her tiny purse, tapped one out. Kelly had her lighter at the ready and lit it for her.

"Thank you," she said.

"Go on," I said.

"He said he'd pay me more money for a picture with his Polaroid camera. I agreed."

"So you were there alone?"

"Yes. He was a regular for a long time and we did several private rooms together, sometimes with Sparkle, too. I trusted him."

She dropped her head like she was suddenly embarrassed to admit that.

"How did it happen?" Kelly asked.

"He brought me to his bedroom. I reminded him again that there'd be no sex. He said not to worry. He had me pose a certain way and then took a picture. Next thing I know he's on top of me. I was pretty high. He was strong and holding me by the wrists over my head with one hand, while he took his pants off. I told him to stop, that he was scaring me."

She took a long drag from her cigarette. Was obviously having a hard time.

"He didn't stop. He turned me over and raped me from behind. I started to cry. He was violent. When it was done, he tossed a bunch of money over my body and told me to get dressed and go. I told him I was going to call the police. He just laughed. It was awful, his laugh. He said something like, 'Yeah, you go do that. See what they say. You're nothing but a whore who I paid.' I told him I wasn't a prostitute and he said they'd never believe me."

"I didn't know what to say. I got dressed as quickly as I could and ran out."

"I'm so sorry, Ivy," Kelly said.

She finished her cigarette and snuffed it out in the ashtray at the corner of the table.

"That's okay. It's over and done with."

"How did you learn that Angela was also raped?" I asked.

"Not until I went back to work a couple of days later. I warned all the other girls about him. That's when Angela told me it happened to her too. I got mad at her because she never said anything. Never warned me. All she did was apologize, even though she knew I was going over there. Angela never liked me anyway. She's older and been here forever."

"What about Alisha or Sparkle?"

"He'd never touch Alisha. He was afraid of Bobby."

"You never talked to Bobby about it?" I asked.

"No, just the other girls to warn them."

"And Sparkle?" Kelly asked.

"She never said anything, but she always considered him her client when he showed up. Sat with him all the time."

"Did you tell anyone else that Chris raped you?" Kelly asked.

"I told his friend Artie."

"What did Artie say?"

"He just said I should never have gone to party with him, like he didn't care. Like it was no big deal. He also said that I should just shut up about it because it would cause me too much trouble."

"Did he say what kind of trouble?" Kelly inquired.

"I didn't ask."

I had this weird feeling. "Why would you tell Artie, knowing that they were good friends?" I asked.

"I was at a table with him, and he was buying me drinks. I guess I was just drunk and wanted him to know. I don't really know why."

"Were you and Artie close?" Kelly asked.

"No, not really. He was just a paying client. Bought me a lot of drinks."

"Do you know someone by the name of Celeste?" Kelly asked.

"No. Who is she?"

"No one of importance," I told her, and noticed Kelly look at me after.

"Did you ever tell Trevor?"

"No. Of course not."

"Why?"

"He wouldn't give a fuck. Why would he?"

"Do you know if Officer Bobby ever went to Chris's house, or hung out with him in places other than here?" I asked.

"I don't know anything about that. I'm sorry. Bobby was a good guy. Liked to party a lot, but always tipped us good."

"What about his relationship with Trevor?" Kelly asked.

"They seemed to be friends."

"Did you ever see him leave with Trevor?"

"I'm sorry, but it can get pretty busy in here and I don't pay attention to that. I do my thing onstage and try to entertain the clients."

"What about Bull?" I asked. "You know anything about him?"

"Just that he's Trevor's boy."

"Do you know his name?"

"Listen, I never give my real name to nobody that comes in here, so I don't ask for someone like Bull's real name. I know better."

"Do you know anybody that would want to hurt Bobby, someone he may have had bad words with here?"

"No, of course not."

"We appreciate your honesty," I said.

She just nodded.

"Can I go get ready for work?"

"Yes," Kelly said. "Thank you."

She got up and walked out.

"Would you ask Angela to come in here," Kelly said.

"Sure."

She stood up and pulled the curtains back and walked out.

"Damn," I said as if to myself.

"Damn yeah," Kelly said, and lit her own cigarette.

The interview was about the same with Angela. It took a little bit longer to get it out of her, but she finally admitted that Chris raped her too. There was nothing else she could offer, or the other girls we talked to, so that was that. One thing most of them had in common was wanting to stay away from Bull.

We got with Marr in the main room and went outside. Bobby's car was being towed to the lot by our department. Crime scene tape was still up and there was a big uniform presence. Media, along with civilian onlookers, was beyond the tape. The chief and his deputy appeared to be gone and so was our captain. We did notice the LT and Sarge standing by the LT's cruiser talking to Jac and Caine.

"Got good news about Bull," Marr told us while walking. "One of the security guards knew him and gave up his name."

"That's excellent news," I said.

"Damien Leonard."

"Hopefully he'll be in the system," Kelly said.

Marr chuckled and replied with "If he's not in the system I'm gonna change my line of work."

"Well, let's hope he is then," Kelly responded.

When we got to the cruiser, Caine immediately advised us that he found two witnesses at two different businesses near where the shooting occurred. He gave us the description of the suspect.

"That sounds like it could be Bull," Marr said.

"Damn right," I said.

Caine leaned against the hood of the car and said, "Both witnesses stated that the suspect walked slowly on the sidewalk from behind the vehicle. Seemed calm, and when he got to the driver's-side window he shot twice, then took a couple of steps, turned like he was facing the decedent, and shot one more time."

"Did they say they could identify the suspect?" Marr asked.

"They did," Jac responded.

"Damn good, 'cause I got a name for Bull."

Caine took his notebook out and then his pen from his shirt pocket. "Fuck yeah. Give it to me."

"Damien Leonard. According to the security guy I interviewed, he's in his early thirties."

"We're outta here, LT," Caine said.

"Go. If he's in the system, get that photo array and get back here ASAP."

"Copy that," Caine said with a nod of his head.

"I'll go and make sure the witnesses don't leave," Jac advised.

"What do you need us to do?" Kelly asked.

"Give me a brief synopsis of the interviews and then stand by until Caine gets back."

"Got it," I said.

"And by the way," LT began, "IA was here briefly. For once they actually moved quicky. You and Marr are cleared. You can pick up your service weapons."

"Won't feel so damn naked now," Marr said.

"Ha."

"Yeah, that's good news," I said. "Won't need Kelly's protection anymore."

"You'll always need me."

I knew that was true.

48

We gave the sarge and LT everything we got out of interviewing the girls. The LT seemed surprised that Chris Doyle raped two of them.

"You need to look at them and anyone they're affiliated with for a possible suspect in the murders. And how is this other guy involved, the one found in Alexandria?"

"We're on all that," I told him. "We do believe there's a definite connection between the two."

"I'm heading back to the branch. See if I can get an address on Bull."

"Appreciate the help, Frankie," LT said.

Kelly and I sat in our cruiser after our short meet, to smoke cigarettes and wait for Caine and Jac to return. I don't usually smoke. I'm a social smoker, and this cig feels damn good right now. Almost comforting. Have to be careful or I'll get myself addicted like Kelly and Celeste.

"Still can't wrap my head around why your boy Arthur was murdered."

"He never was *my boy*," I told her. "And I don't believe Doyle's murder had anything to do with the rapes. Doesn't appear that Arthur was involved with any of that, and their murders are too similar. We're looking at one suspect for both, and my opinion is it's all about drugs and money. Chasing those girls and their connections is gonna be a waste of our time."

"That's why you like Trevor for them?"

"Yeah, I think he and maybe Bull are good for both."

Damn, I was getting too good at this shit.

"LT's right, though. Have to follow through with every lead. And them being raped by Doyle is a lead."

"I suppose you're right."

"'Suppose'? Of course I'm right."

The crime scene was eventually cleared, and traffic allowed through as well as pedestrians. The media had already left. The sarge stopped by to visit and share a smoke.

"Caine is on his way. Good thing, 'cause the witnesses are getting antsy and want to go home."

"Let's hope for an easy closure," I said.

"We always hope for an easy closure," Sarge came back.

A few minutes passed and I noticed Caine pull around the corner in his cruiser. He found a spot a few cars up from us and parked. Stepped out of the car and walked up to us. He was carrying a manila folder.

"LT gone?"

"Had to get with the chief at headquarters," Sarge said.

Caine opened the manila folder and handed the array with nine photos on the page to the sarge. He glanced at it and passed it over to me. I held it so Kelly could see too. Sure enough, there was Bull in the number three spot.

"That's our guy," I said.

"Fucking hell of a record too," Caine said. "CPWL, assaults,

PWID. I could go on. Don't know how the hell he's walking around."

"Because it's DC," Kelly said. "They all eventually walk. That revolving door here never stops moving."

"I found an address too, but need to confirm if it's a good one."

"Get with Marr on that. He's also trying to confirm an address," Sarge advised.

Caine nodded and then asked, "Where's Jac?"

"He's at the building where you found your second witness. They allowed them to use a couple of their offices."

"On my way."

"I want good news when you return," Sarge said.

Caine looked back at him while walking and sneered.

"I'll keep my finger on his photo when I hand it to the witnesses," he joked.

"I didn't hear that," Sarge said.

Less than an hour and we saw Caine and Jacoby walk out of the building across the street and head our way. Sarge immediately stepped out of his vehicle to meet them. We noticed him smile. Had to be good. We stepped out of our car and met them on the sidewalk.

"Judging by the looks on your faces, it went well," I said.

"Damn right," Jac said. "Couldn't get more positive hits."

"Yep," Caine added. "Pointed him out without question. He's good to go."

"Get back to the office and draft the affidavits. Also, get with Marr and see if he got an address for the search warrant."

"Judge in chambers is gonna be gone, so will the AUSA," Caine said. "I'll call the AUSA over the phone, we'll have to go to the on-call judge, probably at their home, to get it signed. It'll be an early a.m. hit if we confirm an address."

"I know the procedure. Do what you gotta do."

"Will let you know when we're done," Jac advised.

"Copy that, gentlemen. Get outta here."

And then they were gone.

"We'll head to the office too, see if we can help," Kelly said without consulting me first.

Another fucking late night, and Celeste was hard on my mind. This was gonna be rough.

49

Since it was after hours the warrants got signed by the AUSA on call and then the on-call judge at his house. Kelly and I went with Marr and managed to confirm the address. He lived on the second floor of a small multistory apartment complex on the 1300 block of Irving Street NW. Everything was good to go. Front entrance to the building would probably have to be pried open.

Another damn arrest and search warrant. Hadn't had this many warrants in a row for some time. All that had to be done was to try and get some sleep, because we had another long day ahead of us and my weekend was history.

Celeste had left a couple of messages on my cell. When I got home and before I undressed, I poured myself a nice drink, sat on the sofa and gave her a call.

She answered right away.

"I was worried about you," she said.

Her speech was slow. Sounded high or maybe just had a couple of drinks. I hoped for the latter.

"An officer was shot and killed. It was a tough day. I'm sorry I didn't return your calls, but it was crazy."

"I'm so sorry to hear that."

"Thanks," I said like I cared.

"I miss you. Wish I was snuggled up beside you right now."

"I'd love nothing more. Need to get through tomorrow, though. I know it's my day off again, but we have to work this case through. Hopefully it won't be a long day."

"You can come over here when you're off."

I've said it before. I didn't like the idea of going there, being in the same home as him. Same damn bed, but I wanted to see her. I had to.

"Yeah, that'd work."

"It can be late tomorrow. I don't care."

"I'll know more tomorrow. I do miss you too. Want to get tangled up in your hair."

She laughed delicately.

"I like when you tug at my hair."

"Stop." I smiled to myself. "I need to get some sleep tonight. This kinda talk'll keep me up."

"As long as it's me you're thinking of."

"It would be. Are you having a drink?"

"Yes. Vodka soda."

"I'm having a bit of scotch."

She didn't respond, but I could hear her breathing. It was a turn-on, as if she was doing it on purpose or nodding out.

"You still there?" I asked.

"Yes, darling."

I loved the sound of that. *Darling*. Seemed like it was all happening so fast though. A whirlwind. Was that how it was supposed to be? I mean, with normal people? I don't know. I'd never been in a real relationship. Always been too wrapped up in work. Or scared. Or both.

"I don't mind if you don't talk," I said. "We can just pretend we're sitting beside one another. Snuggling."

"I like that."

It was an odd feeling. Not anything bad—a comfortable silence. No need to say anything. The thought of her being on the other side was enough. I've never experienced that before. I wanted to tell her everything. That I knew what happened. I'd wanted to do that before, and for some reason now more than ever. I wanted her to know that I knew everything and that it would be all right. She was safe with me. I couldn't, though. I knew that it would scare her. It'd be too much. I had to force myself to let go. I needed sleep anyway and was hopeful that I'd find it tonight.

"I'll call you tomorrow. Let you know what time I'm getting off. "

"Okay," she said, almost under her breath.

"Goodnight, sweet thing."

"Goodnight, love."

I disconnected, but it sounded like she was about to say something after that. I felt the need to call back but didn't. I went to my room and got ready for bed.

Hoped for the best.

50

I didn't like waking up to darkness. It always unsettled me. The predawn light wasn't even ready to peek through the blinds. The unpredictable hours associated with my work had to have some kind of negative effect on my mind and body. I could feel it starting to break me down inside and out. I took a hot shower, hoping that would both awaken my body and relax my mind. It did. Sort of.

I dressed in my tactical gear. When I stepped outside, the cold air bit at my face like it was angry. The weather here was always angry. The seasons too. The seasons plagued you with bitter cold, heat, and the worst kind of allergies.

Next stop would have to be 7-Eleven for a large coffee and a couple dozen donuts for the crew.

Cain, Jac, and Kelly and other squad members were already in the office. They wanted to dive into the boxes of donuts. I held them back.

"ERT gets first dibs," I told them.

They reluctantly agreed. Had to make the emergency response team happy first.

Not all the detectives would be going. A few had to stay back to hold up the office in case of another homicide. Marr would not be there either. This was a murder, not narcotics, and our captain, despite all that Marr did, wouldn't allow him in on it. Marr was obviously disappointed. ERT would be making entry on this one because we were going to hit hard, not take any chances when it came to someone like Bull. Kelly told me ERT was already in the briefing room. They would ram the door at six a.m. sharp. Those guys were all about business. Rarely even said a word unless it had to do with something tactical. They'd always send a couple of members to confirm the location on the day or night before. Have everything covered. Once they made entry, they'd secure the location and detain everyone inside. Once that was done, they'd release the scene to us and leave as quickly as they came. Usually no mess. Usually.

Everyone was given their assignments. Kelly and I along with two uniformed officers would secure the exterior front of the building, two other detectives from the office would take the west side, and Caine and Jac the east side. Two other uniformed officers got the rear. ERT would notify us when it was good to go in. Cain, Jac, Kelly, and I were the only ones that would be conducting the search. Two uniformed officers would remain outside the building and the other two in the hall, securing the front entrance to the apartment.

We arrived just before six.

Moved slowly up the block and parked in a line.

Exited quietly and took our posts while ERT ran one behind the other to the front. A short stocky member pried the front door open with one thrust and they entered. They were controlled chaos.

All was quiet. Moments later, even from where we stood, we could hear the door being rammed. Two quick hits and then—

"POLICE! POLICE! SEARCH WARRANT! POLICE!" from an unknown member.

Seconds later Kelly and I heard something like a window being smashed out on the east side of the building where Caine and Jac were.

Then I heard Caine order in a loud voice: "Police, drop the gun! Drop the gun!"

"Stay here," I ordered the uniformed officers.

Kelly and I kept our weapons at a tucked position. We ran to the side of the building. Maybe three seconds.

Bull was standing there, just under a shattered-out second-story window in nothing but his red boxers. His right arm extended, holding a gun.

It was all so fast.

Two shots popped out. I saw that Caine went down.

"Fuck y'all! Fuck y'all!" Bull shouted as he continued to fire.

Jac was firing and so were we. One right after the other and just as fast several more. I don't know how many. I emptied my magazine and instinctively dropped the mag and inserted another. I could tell he was hit several times. Blood covered almost his entire bare body, but he stood defiant, like adrenaline or PCP had taken him over.

He finally dropped, his giant frame going limp like he had finally given in.

"Officer down, officer down," I heard Jac call out over the radio right after.

I stepped closer to Bull's body to secure the weapon. He had fallen on his right side with his back facing me. His handgun was in the yellowed grass, just two feet from his head. I kicked the gun farther from his body. I used my foot to roll him to his stomach. With my handgun steady in my right hand, I pulled his right hand out from under him. He was not moving. I pushed him farther, so he was flat on his stomach, quickly holstered my weapon and removed my cuffs. I grabbed him by the bloodied fingers of his right hand and squeezed hard, stretched it out and cuffed his wrist, and then with my free hand did the same with his left hand. I was thankful to be wearing tactical gloves. I rolled him to his back. Looked like he was hit several times in the chest area and once through the left eye. Blood was flowing out of his chest and legs and streaming down to stain the yellowed grass a shiny dark red.

I secured the weapon and looked toward Jac and Kelly.

"He's secure," I called out to them.

I hoofed it toward them.

Kelly and Jac were leaning over Caine. His eyes were open. His vest was peeled off. Kelly was applying pressure with the palm of her left hand and the right hand over that to his right shoulder area. Caine was wincing in pain. Didn't look like he was hit anywhere else.

"Fuck an ambulance," he said, "just drive me to MedStar."

"You're gonna be fine," Jac said.

"Looks like a through-and-through," Kelly advised.

"Quit fucking pushing so hard," he grunted at Kelly.

"Sorry, buddy, but no."

"Fuck you," he told her, trying to smile.

Jac turned to me and asked, "That was Bull. He alive?"

"I don't think so," I said. "I gotta call it in."

"We're taking you to the hospital, partner," Jac said. "We gotta lift you to a sitting position. You ready?"

"As I'll ever be."

I turned the knob on my radio to the Fourth District channel. I heard Caine huffing with pain as they lifted him.

I called out the address we were at and then said, "We need an ambulance to respond for a man down. Multiple gunshot wounds to the chest area and head."

The dispatcher confirmed what I said and advised that an ambulance was on the way. I also advised the dispatcher that Detectives Kelly and Jacoby were transporting Caine to MedStar and to notify the hospital.

Caine was standing.

"No ambulance," I heard Caine snap. "No fucking ambulance."

I made my way back to Bull.

I removed my left glove and placed two fingers on the carotid area of the right side of his neck. I could not find a pulse.

51

Kelly and Caine were gone. I called Kelly on the cell. She didn't answer so I called Jac.

"Yeah," he answered.

"How is Caine?"

"Being a baby."

"Fuck you," I heard Caine say.

"Fuck you," Jac told him. "You're going on vacation, so you got nothing to cry about."

"I'm not crying."

"How far out are you?" I interrupted.

"Two minutes."

"I'll wait for the ambulance to respond here. ERT is still holding the scene. I'll get there when I can."

"Copy that. Pull Myers and Dex to assist. Keep me notified."

"Keep me notified too," I said, and then disconnected.

I heard the ambulance siren in the near distance getting louder every second. The watch commander from the Fourth was on the scene and talking to LT and the Fourth District commander. As usual, crime scene tape secured the area of the shooting and a portion of the road to prevent onlookers and media from entering.

When the ambulance showed, the EMT uncuffed him and examined him, then pronounced Bull dead. They quickly lifted him onto the gurney and into the ambulance and still transported him to the hospital, where the doctor would make the final determination. Once they were gone, I found Myers and Dex, who had been at the west side of the building earlier. We entered and walked the stairs to the second floor and a short distance along the hallway to the apartment. The two uniforms were at the front door. We badged our way in.

A slender young man, wearing jeans and a big white T-shirt, with his hands cuffed behind his back, was sitting on a sofa without cushions. He looked to be in his early twenties or late teens. ERT had tossed the cushions before sitting him down to make sure it was free of any weapons or other potential evidence. Other than that, the apartment was left as it was found. It was up to us to toss it.

An ERT officer approached us. He was still masked so the kid on the sofa could not identify him. We were on the other side of the room and far enough away from the kid so that he couldn't hear us either. Another ERT officer was standing in front of the kid.

"My sarge just notified me about the shooting. He smashed out the bedroom window and dropped down before we could get to him. How is the detective?"

"Transported to MedStar. He was hit in the shoulder and should be okay."

"Damn. We shoulda got there faster."

"For a big guy, he was fast. It's not on you guys. Appreciate you guys," Myers said.

"Without a doubt," I added.

"You get anything off the young man over there?" I asked.

"Nothing. Just a wallet with a license and some cash and a set of keys."

"Okay."

"All right then. It's all yours. Be safe."

We all thanked him, and they all left.

"You two mind if I talk to the kid?" I asked Dex and Myers.

"No prob," Myers said. "We'll take the bedroom."

I walked over to the kid, pulled the scuffed-up wooden coffee table farther back and sat on the edge of it to face him. His wallet and keys were beside me, a Bic lighter, and a full ashtray with cigarettes smoked to the filter and half a blunt.

"I'm Detective Blum. What's your name?"

"Anthony. Is my uncle all right?"

"He was taken to the hospital."

"I heard gunshots. Was he shot?"

"Yes. He also shot a detective."

"Is he gonna live?"

"I'm not a doctor. This is a one-bedroom. You live here with your uncle?"

"Naw. I just been sleeping on the couch for a couple of days 'cause my girl kicked me out for a bit."

"This your wallet here?"

"Yeah. I ain't done nothin'. I have no part in what my uncle did."

"What do you know about what your uncle did?"

He shot me a slight sunken expression like he suddenly realized what he said.

"I don't know nothin' about what he did. I just meant I have no part in whatever his business might be."

"Not the way it sounded. Sounded like you know what he did and why we're here."

"Naw, man. I don't know shit about nothin'."

I picked up his wallet, opened it and took out his license.

"This is expired."

"Yeah, well, you got me there."

"Sit tight," I told him, and then stood up and walked to the other side of the room.

I turned the volume down on the radio. I gave my name and location.

"I got a ten twenty-nine when you get a chance."

"Go ahead with your information," the dispatcher said.

I provided his name, date of birth, and social.

"Stand by."

Shortly after, she came back with "Nothing current and no wants or warrant on subject Anthony Leonard."

"Copy. Thank you."

I walked back and sat back on the coffee table. I slipped his license back in the wallet.

"I ain't got nothin' on me," he said.

"Yup."

I saw a black shoulder pack on a beat-up brown leather chair.

"That your pack over there?"

"Yeah, just got some clothes and shit in it."

I got back up, stepped over to the pack and unzipped it. Emptied all that was in it—another pair of jeans, couple of T-shirts, white socks, and four boxer shorts. I unzipped the smaller pouches, found a four-pack of Swisher Sweet cigarillos. One was missing. I assumed it was the half a blunt in the ashtray. Nothing else in the pack. I returned it to Anthony.

"All right, we're going to keep you here until we finish up."

"I told you I ain't got nothin' to do with all this here. I just been here for two days."

"I know. Just procedure. You sure you want to stick with you don't know anything? I know your uncle talks to you."

"C'mon, man. He just my uncle. He helping me out by letting me stay for a bit until I work things out with my girl."

"Sit tight," I told him, and stood.

I walked to the door where the officers were standing in the hallway.

"Can one of you come in here and keep an eye on this guy for me?" I asked.

"I'll go," the shorter one said.

"Appreciate it."

He entered and stood to the side of the couch where Anthony was sitting. I headed to the bedroom.

52

The window in the bedroom was busted out with a plastic fold-up chair. There were two handguns, about an ounce of weed, and a couple of large Ziploc bags that contained several smaller green zips of what appeared to be heroin all on a cleared area of the floor. Myers found the revolver under the mattress and the 9mm semi-auto in a winter coat hanging in the closet. Dex recovered the narcotics from the top dresser drawer.

"Got some mail matter too," Dex advised. "Didn't know what you might want to take, so I left it on the dresser."

"Thanks. Just take it all for chain of custody. We'll sort through it back at the office."

"All righty."

"I'm going to try to call Kelly to check on Caine, then I'll search the living room."

I got on my cell, but Kelly didn't answer. She was probably in the OR area and turned her ringer off. I wasn't concerned. She would've called if it turned bad. I went to the living room.

We conducted a thorough search. It would take a couple of days for Firearms to process the weapons and see what they came back to if anything. Hopefully the 9mm will be good for Bobby's shooting, and even better both of them come back to other shootings. After Crime Scene Search processed the scene outside where the shooting occurred, they came up to the apartment to dust the evidence that was recovered for prints and then put everything in an open box for me.

No mail matter or any other information was found that could connect Anthony Leonard to the apartment. After I interviewed him for a few more minutes, confirmed his cell number and the address for his girlfriend, I cut him loose.

The LT was still outside with our sarge. They walked me to my cruiser, where I put the box in the trunk.

"I'd like to go to the hospital to check on Caine and pick up Kelly before I go in and put this on the book and do the write-up."

"I checked in with Jacoby and he advised that Caine was stable, but they wanted to keep him overnight for observation," the LT said.

"That's good news."

"Two officer-related shootings back-to-back. I can't recall the last time that happened. Damn happy that Caine will be okay, though, and you, Kelly, and everyone else came out unscathed."

"But then there's all that paperwork, huh?" I said with a slight smile.

"Go on with that. Get to MedStar and then back to the office. I expect a copy of the write-up on my desk by the end of the day."

"No problem, Lieutenant."

Kelly was standing in the waiting area when I entered. It was crowded. Most of the seats were taken.

"I was just going to call you," she said.

"LT told me he was stable."

"Yeah, doesn't look like any nerve damage either. He'll have some good time off, though."

"Good to hear. He still in emergency?"

"Yes."

"Good. I want to see him before we get on all the shit we have to do."

"I'll take you to the room. You recover anything?"

"Yeah. Couple of guns, drugs, cell phone, and paperwork verifying his address."

"That's good."

"We need to get to it."

"Jac's in the room with him."

I followed her to the double doors that led to the emergency room. Kelly smiled at the receptionist, and I showed my identification and went in.

Caine was propped up in the bed, sipping something out of a Styrofoam cup with a straw. I pulled the curtain shut. Jac and Caine's wife, Tricia, were sitting in chairs beside the bed.

"Hey, Tricia," I said.

"Hello, Alexander."

"You look cozy," I told Caine.

"Ain't all that bad. Gave me some good shit. Feels like I'm floating."

"It's the anesthesia," Jac told us.

"Don't get used to it," Tricia said.

"Oh, I could if allowed." He smiled. "So how did the search go?"

"Thirty-eight, nine millimeter, good amount of heroin, and some weed."

"That officer was shot with a nine," Jac said.

"Yeah. Let's hope for the best. Maybe he was stupid and kept the weapon," I said, and turned to Tricia. "Sorry for the shop talk, Tricia."

"I'm used to it. Not so much this, though."

"I like the stupid ones," Caine said like he didn't hear his wife.

"LT said they'll probably release you tomorrow."

"Yep."

"You going to be able to put up with him for a couple of weeks?" I asked Tricia.

"I have no choice. I took some time off work."

"I'll be a good boy." Caine smiled like the Cheshire cat.

"They going to get you a room for the night or are you stuck here?"

"Bed shortage. I don't know. I'm good here, though."

"Yeah, he gets a lot of attention here," Jac said. "Well, now that your wife is here, I should get to it. Lot of work to do."

"Sorry I can't help, partner."

"Don't worry, you'll make up for it."

"Us too," Kelly said, speaking for me too.

She was my work wife after all.

Jac walked us to our car.

"I'm gonna take the car to the wash to get the interior cleaned up. Bit of blood back there. I'll meet you at the office."

"We'll get the evidence on the book," I told him.

"Leave the guns for me. I'll take them to Firearms in the morning," Jac told us.

"No prob."

"I'll do the write-ups too. You guys have done enough."

"Here to help," Kelly added.

"Thanks, but I got it. You all get home at a normal time."

"See you back at the office," I said.

Wasn't about to argue with that. I wanted to get home in time. Give Celeste a call, maybe have dinner, and more.

When we got back to the office, the LT met us at our cubicles before we could sit down.

"Some good news for you," he said.

I set the box of evidence on my desk.

"The results for Trevor Miles's twenty-two came in from Firearms. I took the liberty of looking at it first. The marks on the recovered crime-scene bullets are a dead match for both of your victims. Excellent job. The folder's in Kelly's box."

Like I didn't know, but was hoping not so soon. So much for having dinner and more with Celeste.

Kelly was ecstatic. I tried to act like I was too.

53

Kelly wrote up the affidavit for the arrest of Trevor while I put the evidence on the book. Jac showed up and took the weapons and did the write-up. Trevor was in jail, but our supervisors wanted this thing wrapped up, so we went through the process again with the on-call AUSA and judge. I was working on nothing but what bit of adrenaline I still had from earlier. Trevor would soon be good to go and we'd pick him up from DC Jail the next day and transport him back to VCU to be processed for the murders. Did I feel guilty? Fuck no.

"I'll notify Artie's girl, Celeste, after we finish with Trevor," I told Kelly like it was nothing.

She looked at me almost suspiciously, with no expression at all, held it for a second or two.

"All right then," she finally said.

"I just figured since I go back with Arthur, and in a way her too, that it'd go easier for me to notify her on the way home. I mean after we finish up tomorrow."

"You don't have to explain."

A woman who was a detective had double the intuition. I was afraid she knew about my relationship with Celeste, but she didn't say anything. Her expression said it all. But how could she know?

By the time I got home it was too late for dinner, but not so late that I couldn't call Celeste.

She definitely sounded high when we spoke. I had no doubt. I was concerned, but afraid to express it for fear of getting a bad reaction from her or making her feel down.

"Can I see you tomorrow after work?" I asked.

"I would love that."

"It's getting late, and you sound tired. Get some sleep."

"I am a bit tired. Please call me tomorrow when you're on your way."

"I will. Goodnight."

"Goodnight, love."

I knew it was bad—I knew I was bad—but I couldn't resist. I had lost whatever willpower I once had. I wanted to drive over there and stay with her, make sure she was okay, but knew seeing her like that would scare me and I was fucking tired. *So, do I have a bit of willpower left after all?*

The next morning, Kelly and I got an order, based on the arrest warrant, to have Trevor taken to a holding cell at DC Jail, where we'd pick him up. I hated going to DC Jail. Last time I was there they had a lockdown, and I was trapped in the tiny interview room with some mope for three hours. I hated when something happened that I could not control. Picking up a prisoner is a bit easier. When it was time, we drove to the tower where the guards opened a large chain-link fence. We drove in and the fence closed. There was another one ahead of us that had to be opened, but first we had to exit and secure our weapons and mags in a lockbox and allow them to search our vehicle. Once that was done, they allowed us entry into a secured parking area.

I grabbed the leg shackles and we stepped out of the car, walked to the double steel doors, and were buzzed in. To the right of us was the holding cell with several prisoners, including Trevor. I looked at him directly. He was obviously confused and looked angry. Thick bulletproof plexiglass surrounded the area where four guards were. Kelly slipped the paperwork through an opening on the metal counter. An overweight female guard took the paperwork and stepped to a computer.

"Be a minute," she said.

When she was done, she slid us our part of the paperwork. I took it, folded it up, and slipped it into my back pants pocket. A guard came around from the other side. We met him at the holding cell. He opened it to let us in.

"Y'all step back," he ordered the prisoners.

They obeyed. In unison.

"You can step up, Trevor," I said.

"What the fuck this about?"

"Over there by the wall," I told him.

He moved to the cement wall away from the other prisoners. The guard stood watching them while we took care of Trevor.

"Face the wall," I said.

"Where you takin' me?"

"You need me to help you?"

"Fuck this."

He turned and faced the wall.

"Hands behind your back."

He reluctantly obeyed. I cuffed him, then kneeled down and cuffed his ankles.

"Let's go."

"My lawyer better be present."

54

I sat in the back behind Kelly, who was at the wheel. Trevor was beside me. He didn't say a word. I was sure he thought he was being brought up for another debriefing and that his lawyer would be present. If he knew the real reason for us picking him up, this short trip would be quite different. He'd be yapping his mouth to no end.

He was looking out the window when we turned into the rear parking lot of our building. Looked like his mind was churning.

He turned to me and asked, "Why we back here?"

"We'll answer all your questions once we get you situated," I told him.

"Where's my lawyer?" he asked.

"You can notify your lawyer once we finish up here," Kelly said.

"Finish up? Finish up what? We already went through all that."

When we got to the office we put him in the same interview room. We didn't bother to sit down because we figured he wouldn't waive his rights and sign another rights card to allow us to ask him questions. Can be tricky, but we've done it in the past when defendants decide they want to talk even though they asked for a lawyer or already have one assigned. Sometimes they just gotta know.

We read him his rights and told him he was being charged with the murders of Arthur Holland and Chris Doyle.

"This is some shit here," he said immediately. "You gotta be kidding me? I didn't have nothin' to do with those murders. What the fuck is this?"

He declined to sign, of course.

"I want my fucking lawyer."

"You'll see her at your arraignment tomorrow," Kelly advised him.

"Fuck that. I want her here now."

"You saying you want to talk to us?"

"Fuck no."

"You can call her when we're done processing you, then."

"What you got on me for those murders? You ain't got shit is what you got. I'm gonna sue your asses and this whole fucking department."

"Do what you gotta do," I said.

"This is some real shit here."

"You keep saying that like it's supposed to make a difference," I told him.

"Tell me what evidence you got!"

"Your lawyer will get everything," Kelly began. "She'll more than likely set up another debriefing with the prosecutor after she sees everything. We'll see you again soon."

"You ain't got shit. You all settin' my ass up."

"By the way, I know how news travels, even in DC Jail. You hear about Bull?" I asked.

"Bull? What? Why would I hear about him? You arrest him too?"

"Didn't have the chance. He got himself killed when we hit his apartment on a search warrant. Got stupid."

"What the...? You all killed Bull?"

"Why'd he murder Officer Bobby?" I asked.

He shook his head with a defiant smirk on his fucking face. I could tell he knew and was probably the one who ordered it.

"You think Officer Bobby was going to give you up for something more than what we originally arrested you on?"

"You know I had nothin' to do with that boy Artie's murder. You had nothin' and so you set my ass up. I ain't gonna take this lightly."

"Is that a threat?"

"It ain't no threat. I got people who gonna look into it, though. You can be sure of that."

"Well, do what you gotta. I'm sure we'll all be talking soon."

"Yeah, we will."

We left his legs shackled and took the cuffs off his wrists, walked out, and locked the door. We watched him from the monitor room for a while as he sat there fidgeting in his wooden chair. Not something that looked to be out of fear. It was anger. No soda or Snickers for him. No need to play nice anymore. I personally knew that there was nothing he could offer. How could he? This was simply about going through the motions, processing his ass, and having him transported back to DC Jail.

"It's weird, but he does seem genuinely confused," Kelly said.

"About what?" I asked, but already knew what she meant.

I admit he didn't have that look they sometimes had when you told a defendant what they were being charged with.

"When we told him he was being charged with two murders he had this look of absolute surprise."

"Yeah, of course. He probably really believed we didn't have anything. They do make mistakes sometimes, even the smart ones."

"I guess you're right."

She didn't seem convinced. That scared me.

We processed him, allowed him to call his lawyer, then had him transported to the cell block. I was getting off on time. I called Celeste and made arrangements to pick her up then head to Toledo Lounge in Adam's Morgan for a burger. Stop by one of the local bars after for a couple of drinks and then back to my place. It was nice to have something to look forward to.

After we ate, I told her that we closed Arthur's murder.

She didn't ask who or how. All she said was "I knew you would." And lit a cigarette.

55

Y 2K was approaching. If the end of the world was soon to come, why not take advantage of everything you could? I certainly took advantage of everything I could with Celeste. We were up most of the night doing things to each other I had never done before. It was something else. Most of the things we did together, to each other, were her idea. I did not realize I had such stamina until that night. I felt like a weight was lifted after Trevor was charged. Felt like I could move on and put that behind me. Behind us.

"Sorry I couldn't get tomorrow off."

"I understand."

I didn't want to look at the time. I already knew it was late. We were still in bed. We shared a cigarette. I wondered why she didn't inquire about Arthur's murder after I told her.

"Why didn't you ask me about his murder?"

She snuffed out her cigarette and turned to her side to face me. She tucked her left hand under her cheek to hold up her head on the pillow.

"Because I don't care. I'm glad he's dead. Does that scare you?"

"No."

"Good."

She rolled to her back, laced her fingers together across her bare belly, and stared at the ceiling. After a few seconds she closed her eyes. I didn't know yet what would come of her living in the house that belonged to him, but I didn't worry about it. I would take care of her, no matter what. I think she knew that.

I rolled on my side to face her and snuggled closer. I wrapped my arm over her breasts, slid her hair back, and tucked my nose into the nape of her neck. Kissed her softly.

We stayed like that until sleep found us.

I drove Celeste home on the way to work. It was obvious a car was staying with me. It was an older model sedan occupied by only the driver. I knew he was following me because I made a couple of turns that took me the long way to Florida Avenue and the car was always there. That's why you use more than one car if you're going to successfully follow someone. But why in the hell was I being followed, and by who?

"Where are you going?" Celeste asked.

"Wasn't thinking and made the wrong turn."

"You must be tired."

"Yeah. Sort of. You wore me out."

"I wish you didn't have to work. We could spend the whole day in bed."

"I wish that too."

I slowed down. Looked in the rearview, hoping the driver would get stupid and creep up on my tail and I could get a better glimpse of whoever was behind the wheel. No such luck. All I could see was that it was a Ford and had a DC temp tag. I couldn't make out the tag, but probably wouldn't matter, because they were more than likely fake and wouldn't come back to anyone. The car slowed down and at the intersection the driver allowed another car to make a left to get in front. Not so stupid after all. I stopped to make a left on 14th. The following vehicle was behind the other car so I still couldn't make out the driver. After a few cars rolled by north and south, I made the turn and hurried to Florida Ave. I looked toward the intersection where the car was. The other car was still in front of it and unable to make the turn because of traffic. I sped up and made a quick right onto Florida, cutting in front of another car. Horn honked angrily at me.

"You're in a hurry."

"Don't want to be late for work." I smiled. "I have court."

I got a couple of blocks out. Looked like I lost the tail but didn't know for sure because there were about four cars behind me. I wanted to make sure and didn't want to be followed to where I was taking Celeste.

"I'm going to take the side roads. Traffic on Florida gets bad and I can't be late."

"Okay."

I made a right on 7th and drove a few blocks and made a left on Q. A bit out of the way, but it would lose the tail. That is, if it was following me. Either way, I'd feel a bit more comfortable.

I made my way to Rhode Island Ave. and to her house. I pulled to the corner and parked illegally. I was getting ready to step out of the car.

"You don't have to walk me, doll."

"I like walking you."

I stepped out of the car and walked her to the front door. We hugged and kissed.

"I'll see you soon," I said.

I unlocked her door and opened it. Before she entered, she turned and gave me a quick peck on the lips, then stepped into the house and closed the door. I heard her lock it.

I drove to the office, last night into the morning still heavy on my mind.

Kelly was at her cubicle as usual. Usually got there before me.

"How's it going?"

"All's good," she said. "Talked to Graves. She told me that Trevor was not interested in debriefing and wanted to go to trial."

"He's an idiot. Sounds like his defense attorney is too."

"Has to listen to her client, even if he is a knucklehead."

"By the way, I'm pretty sure I was being tailed from my apartment on the way here."

"Seriously?"

"Yeah. I took whoever it was for an out-of-the-way ride, and they stayed with me. I did manage to lose the tail way before I got here, though."

"Why would anyone follow you? A PI, maybe?"

"I don't know why. And no, don't think it was a PI. It was the kinda car some mope would drive. Older model Ford sedan, DC temp tags I couldn't make out, heavy tint on the side windows."

"You think one of Trevor's or Bull's people?"

"I don't know, but just want you to be aware, just in case."

"Yeah. You should tell Jac and Marr too."

"I will."

56

At roll call there was another briefing about Y2K and that all leave would be restricted on New Year's Eve, and everyone would be working a double. That sucked. I needed a break. What the hell did they think was going to happen? Would darkness create panic? Yeah, probably. Hell, I just wanted to get through the day. I'd hardly slept at all. I wasn't complaining. The reason for the lack of sleep was all good. Something I would keep with me for some time. At least until after the next time with Celeste.

I got with Jac and advised him about the possible tail on me and gave him a description of the car.

"How's Caine?"

"All good. He's getting released from the hospital today. I'll let him know too."

"Good."

I went to my desk. Kelly was not there. Probably outside having a smoke. I called Marr and told him too. He acted like he welcomed the possibility of an encounter. He was gung-ho that way, though.

Sort of hope it did happen for him. It'd relieve me of having to look over my shoulder.

Kelly, Marr, and I got through the prelim for Trevor. He was held without bond. We figured that would happen. He never made eye contact with me when I took the stand. I did notice the young kid, Anthony, who was at Bull's apartment when we hit it. He was sitting on the second-row bench beside Trevor's grandfather, behind the table where Trevor and his defense attorney were seated. He looked over his shoulder at us before I took the stand. Had no expression at all. Couldn't read him. I figured he just wanted us to know he was there.

"Future Trevor," Marr whispered.

"Your responsibility then," Kelly whispered back.

"And I look forward to it."

"Be sure to get him before he kills somebody, okay?" I said.

"I'll give it my best."

After the prelim, Graves advised us that the grand jury was set. She gave us the date. It was soon and fortunately not on my Friday off.

Friday and the end of the tour couldn't get here soon enough. I requested leave for Sunday with the sarge. He approved it.

I returned to my desk to finish up a bit of paperwork. Had to take a hard piss when I finished.

"Gotta hit the head before I split," I told Kelly.

"All righty then."

I got back to my desk. Kelly was turned in her chair, eyeballing me. It was an uncertain look.

"Your work cell rang while you were gone," she advised me.

"Okay."

"Noticed on the screen that it was Arthur's landline so knew it had to be Celeste."

The way she said it bothered me.

"It dinged with a voice mail."

"Probably just wants an update."

"You should listen in case it's important."

"It's not gonna be important. She shoulda just had your cell in the beginning, not mine. She's a pain in the ass," I said, trying to sound convincing. "But since you sound like you're up in my *ass* about it, I'll listen."

I picked up the cell and listened to the message. Held the phone tight against my ear so Kelly couldn't hear. Hopefully.

It was a message about how much she was looking forward to seeing me. I closed the phone.

"Just like I said. Worried and wants to know about the case."

"You going to call her back?"

"Hell no. I'm going home. My day is done. You can call her if you want."

And after saying that, I hoped I could get to my car to call Celeste back in case Kelly took me up on it.

"I have no interest in calling her, Alex."

I was still going to call her to advise her never to talk to Kelly about us. I couldn't get outta there fast enough. Almost forgot to say goodbye to Kelly 'cause I was so nervous.

"Have a good weekend," she said with an odd smirk. "Don't do anything I wouldn't do."

"Wouldn't dream of it."

I knew her brain was churning, and that worried me even more.

First thing when I got to the car, I called Celeste. She said she understood and not to ever worry. I believed her.

Traffic was a monster, even the side streets. I managed to get home without bursting a blood vessel. I parked, grabbed my pack, and shouldered it. Walked toward the apartment and was surprised when I was approached from behind.

"Gotta talk to you," a soft voice said.

I turned and when I noticed it was Anthony, I instinctively grasped the grip of my holstered Glock. He stepped back.

"Ain't no need for that."

He lifted his coat back and raised his shirt. An effort to show that he was unarmed. He even turned around and back to face me.

"Turn around again," I ordered calmly.

He obeyed. I set my pack on the sidewalk and moved behind him. Using my left hand, I squeezed the front chest area of his coat and then the pockets. I stepped back to a safe distance.

"Can I turn back now?"

"Just keep your hands where I can see them."

He turned to face me. I had to move closer to the curb to let a couple of pedestrians walk by. A few other people were walking on the other side of the street. Didn't notice anything that might alarm me. Obviously, except for him.

"What the fuck you think you're doing here?"

"I'm here to give you a message from Trevor. That's all."

"That's what he's got an attorney for. Have them contact me. You're the one that followed me the other day."

"He just wants this to be between the two of you. No attorneys or nobody else."

"You didn't answer my question. Were you following me the other day?"

"Ain't against the law, is it?"

"I'll charge your ass with harassment if I see you a second time. You might want to be careful with yourself."

"We in a public place. People walkin' all around."

"I catch you following me again, you're going to jail."

"Just need to give you a message."

"Go with what you got to say then, and move the fuck on."

"He wants to meet you one-on-one at the jail. Said you'd know how to set it up."

"Why would I want to meet with him?"

"Said it might be of interest to you."

"I can't without his attorney present. He should know that. I'm not going to fuck up these cases just 'cause he wants to see me for who knows what. That's probably what he's trying to do."

"He told me you might be against it and to tell you it's in your interest to get with him."

"You said that already. Second time sounds like a threat, little man."

"Naw, ain't no threat. Just something real. He said he's got a feeling about you and that girl you been seeing. Artie's girl."

I stepped up to him and grabbed him by his shirt. Pushed him back hard. He stumbled a bit and almost fell to his butt. He was scrawny and I could break him like a twig. I noticed a couple of onlookers so I backed off.

"Dang, no need for that. I'm just the messenger, you know?"

He straightened his coat out.

"You fucking stay away from her. You understand me? I'll fuck you up so you never see the light of day."

He seemed unfazed.

"You should see him. His attorney ain't gonna know about it."

"Get your ass outta here. I won't be this nice if I see you again."

"I'm gonna get my cell outta my pants pocket. Don't go and shoot me."

I gripped my weapon again.

"Just a cell phone," he says.

"I told you to get out of here."

He pulls out his cell phone. Taps in a number. I didn't want to walk away and let him see me enter my building. I figured he might already know, but still, he might not.

"I don't know what the fuck you think you're doing."

"It's me," he said to whoever it was he called.

I had a feeling I knew who it was.

"Trevor wants to talk to you. Said you'd want to hear what he has to say."

He held out the phone for me.

"I have nothing to say to him. Tell him to have his defense attorney get in touch with the prosecutor."

"This ain't got nothin' to do with them. Just talk to him and I'll be on my way."

I don't know what I was thinking, but I took the cell. Curiosity just got the best of me.

"Say what you have to say," I told him.

"I figured you'd refuse comin' here so I thought it best we talk this way."

"You buy yourself time on a dirty CO's cell?"

"You should know you can get whatever you want inside. Hell, it's just like a hotel, but you can't check out until the vacation's over."

"Go on then with what you have to say."

"I know I got set up. I been thinking to myself for a while and when you said at the hearing that you recovered the guns from my room, I figured it was you. I ain't some corner boy you can pull some shit on. You think I'm stupid enough to leave a gun I used on a murder in my bedroom?"

I didn't respond.

"I also figured that you might benefit from Artie being outta the picture because of what you got goin' with that fine bitch of his."

"You're out of your fucking mind. You might want to be real careful about what you say, because it's sounding a lot like threats."

"You tryin' to put me away for life. You think I give a damn about you thinkin' I'm making threats?"

"I think you're playing some game right now and for all I know you're recording this because you think our conversation might work in your favor. You're not as smart as you think."

"Your life is about to change, Detective Five-Oh."

"That would be a threat," I said, and flipped the cell closed and tossed it on the ground at Anthony's feet.

He picked it up and put it in his pocket.

"You might want to be careful, little man. You're playing with big boys here," I told him.

He turned and walked away. I watched him until he disappeared around the corner and was out of sight. I grabbed my pack and shouldered it. Stayed there for a bit just to make sure. I walked back to my car. Celeste would be staying with me now until I could figure out what the fuck to do.

57

I knocked on Celeste's door several times and was starting to worry because I called her on the way and told her I was coming. I knocked louder and finally heard footsteps and the door being unlocked.

She smiled and said, "Sorry, I was in the back and didn't hear."

She opened the door for me.

"It's okay."

She was wearing the same long-sleeved sweatshirt she wore a while back, and tight blue jeans, torn at the knees. I wanted to see her arms, make sure she wasn't shooting up. Don't know why I felt one means was worse than the other. Smoking and shooting were addictive, dangerous. It was just the thought of track marks on her body. I didn't feel comfortable with that.

I stepped in, closed and double-locked the door behind me. We hugged and she kissed me on the lips.

"You should always lock and bolt the door too."

"I do, silly."

"Just sayin'."

"I'm happy you're here. I was thinking we were going to get together later, though."

"Couldn't wait to see you."

"Obviously. You're still in your suit. You come straight from work?"

"Yeah."

She pulled me by the hand into the living room.

"Is it too early to offer you a drink?"

"Never too early for a drink, but I was thinking maybe it'd be nice if you stayed at my apartment for a while. Pack a bag and we could go there for drinks and then out for dinner or something."

"I went to the grocery store for tonight with some of the money you gave me. I wanted to make you dinner here."

My apartment is more secure, but I had my gun and two mags so what the hell.

"Okay, but you come over tomorrow, all right?"

"I'd love that. I'm sorry you don't like staying here."

"It's not really that," I lied.

"Good. You know I can actually cook."

"Never doubted it."

"I'll get us drinks."

She walked into the kitchen. I loved the way her body moved when she walked. Like she didn't have a care in the world. Such a joy. I needed some of what she had, but then I realized it was probably because she smoked a little before I came over. I don't need that in my life, especially with the piss tests at the police and fire clinic the department surprised you with.

I took off my coat but kept my suit jacket on to conceal everything I had attached to my belt. Folded the coat over an armchair and sat on the sofa. She returned with two tumblers of vodka soda with ice. Handed me one and then sat beside me. I slipped my hand across her shoulder and under her hair.

"Why is your jacket on? Get comfortable."

"I'll take it off in a bit."

She tucked herself against my shoulder and sipped her drink. I did too. Mine was strong.

"You trying to get me drunk?"

"Maybe a little. Might take advantage of you too."

"Don't need to be drunk for that to happen."

"I might want to be in control, though."

"Don't need to be drunk for that to happen either. What did you get for dinner?"

"Good ol' simple comfort food. Steaks, a couple of potatoes and asparagus that I'll bake. Bottle of red wine, too."

"Sounds wonderful."

We finished the bottle of wine with dinner. It was nice sitting at the table with her like we were a normal couple. I still didn't feel comfortable in the house for obvious reasons, and even more so the thought of being in the bed Arthur slept in. I was toasty after the wine and a couple of vodka sodas. It made it easier. We took the half-bottle of vodka to bed with us, got naked and drank straight from it. I noticed her left arm. She had what appeared to be new track marks.

"You're shooting up," I said with a bit of anger.

"I was just experimenting." She tried to smile. "I didn't like it, though. It knocked me out."

"Don't fucking do that. Please, Celeste."

"I won't."

"I mean it. I can't be a part of that."

"I won't, I said."

I believed her. Like I said before, heroin was heroin. Didn't think it really mattered how you put it in your body, but the thought of her shooting it made all the difference to me. Felt more like a junkie that way. I left it alone. We drank some more. We had great sex. Shared a smoke after. More great sex. Stayed up into the a.m. until we were overwhelmed with exhaustion and then sleep became easy.

It was almost noon when I woke up. I had never slept that long, that hard. Celeste was still sleeping, her back toward me. I let her sleep. Stayed on my back and stared at the ceiling for I don't know how long. She stirred on her side a bit and turned to me with tired eyes.

"Good morning," she said.

"It's the afternoon."

"It is? I was in a deep sleep. I don't even remember my dreams."

She wrapped her arm over my chest.

"How long have you been up?"

"Not long. I got some good sleep."

I turned on my side and pulled her tight against me. Started getting aroused again.

"My God," she said.

"I might have morning breath," I said.

"I could care less."

We kissed and that led to much more. I was no longer in control. I knew that. She had me.

About an hour later she got out of bed to take a shower. I got dressed and secured everything back on my belt. Picked up the cell from the nightstand and slipped it in my pants pocket. The shower was running. I could hear her moving around like she hadn't stepped in yet. The water just smacking the porcelain tub. I wanted to get to my apartment. Still had that encounter with Anthony heavy on my mind. What in the hell was Trevor thinking? What was he up to? *He doesn't know shit. He was fishing, but I didn't bite so I'm not gonna worry about it anymore.*

When I was walking into the living room I heard a loud thump from the bathroom. The shower was still running. I didn't hear Celeste say anything. I wondered if she slipped. I ran to the bathroom and knocked on the door.

"You okay in there?"

There was no response. Couldn't hear any movement. I didn't hesitate to open the door. There she was, fallen into a slumped position on the tile floor. Her back against the tub and her feet to the side of the toilet. She had a thin elastic band wrapped around her upper arm. A syringe was beside her. A spoon by her legs. I noticed her works kit on the sink counter. I took in all this in no more than a second, then stepped in quickly and got on my knees beside her.

"Celeste? Celeste?"

Whitish foam was spewing from her slightly open mouth. Her eyes were open and glazed. Kept her on her side in case she was going to vomit. Her legs stretched out and started to shake uncontrollably. This was not good.

"Fuck. Celeste. Stay with me."

I checked her carotid for a pulse. Could hardly feel it.

"You'll be okay, sweetheart. I took care of everything for you."

It seemed like she was looking at me with those wide milky eyes. I felt like she would come out of it. Come back.

"I know what happened. I know everything. What Chris Doyle did to you. What you had to do to protect yourself. Arthur told me."

Her chest began expanding and contracting rapidly.

"You're gonna be okay. I love you and I'm here for you."

Her breathing slowed, and for a brief second I thought she was coming back, but then it stopped. I put my ear against her mouth. I couldn't feel her breath. I carefully slipped my left hand under her head and opened her mouth, and with my index finger checked for possible obstructions. I wiped her mouth gently with the palm of my right hand and then carefully moved her so she was on her back.

I grabbed my cell and called 911. Then I began CPR.

58

I was outside the bathroom when an EMT put her on a gurney and rushed her to the ambulance. They couldn't do anything. I still ordered them to take her to the hospital. They knew me from other scenes we'd been on throughout the years, so they didn't argue. When they were out, I stepped in to pick up my cell phone I'd left on the floor. I noticed a ten-pack behind the toilet. It had small green zips inside. It must have fallen somehow. There was also a small empty green zip beside it.

I rushed out, found her keys in the living room, and secured the door on my way out.

Siren was wailing and had already sped off to Howard. I hoofed it to my car. Before I made my way to Howard, I broke down and cried. I couldn't stop. I covered my face with both hands and dropped my head to the steering wheel.

I knew I needed to get to the hospital, so I started the car.

On the way, I called Frank Marr. I don't know why I didn't call Kelly first, but I wanted to see if Marr would recover the drugs.

When he answered, I asked, "Are you working?"

"Yeah. What's up."

"Celeste OD'd," I said, trying not to sound broken up.

"Damn, I'm sorry to hear that. How'd you hear?"

"I was there."

"You were there? How the fuck that happen?"

"Can you meet me at Howard Hospital? I'm on the way there now. I'll explain everything."

"Yeah. On my way."

When I got to Howard, I was advised by the nurse that the doctor pronounced her DOA. She said she notified the police because she didn't know I was involved.

"No problem," I said.

Fortunately, Frank got there first so I could give him my story. He called me and we met in the lobby.

"The on-call detectives are responding. Should be here soon."

"What happened?"

"I got approached by one of Trevor's boys earlier today when I was going to my spot for coffee. Front of my fucking apartment."

"What?"

"He was fishing for information. Said that Trevor was sure that I planted the evidence because of some bullshit that I was having an affair with Arthur's girl Celeste, and wanted Arthur out of the way, and that I planted the evidence to frame him for it."

"Tell me you weren't having an affair."

"Fuck you. Of course not. You think I'm stupid? The kid must have followed me to Celeste's when I went there the other day to notify her about Arthur's death. I went inside, stayed for a bit because she was distraught. I left and went home."

"Okay."

"I told the kid to step the fuck off and he did. That was the end of that. Started to get worried, though, like a Spidey sense. I mean about Arthur's girl. You know what these guys are capable of. I decided to go back to my apartment and get in my suit, so I looked like I'm on the job. Headed over to Celeste's to check on her welfare. I noticed the door was slightly open. I knocked several times, maybe six, and she didn't answer. I opened her door and called out, nothin'. I go in and check the rooms. Found her on the floor in the bathroom, but she was still alive. I called 911 and tried to help her, but she didn't make it."

"Damn."

"Yeah. I found her keys and secured the house. There was a ten-pack in the bathroom. Green zips. Just like Trevor's. I was hoping you would recover the bag of zips, maybe have them dusted for prints and see if anything comes up. Be nice to get Trevor's or that kid's prints off it."

"Yeah, no problem. As long as it's okay with the responding detectives."

"They won't give a shit. Last thing they'll want to do is process drugs on what was an OD. We'll wait for them, though. I'll fill them in and then we can head over there. I'll see if they can follow so I can turn the house keys over to them."

"Got it."

"I need to call Kelly. Let her know everything. And Frank…"

"Yeah, brother."

"If you don't get a hit on those prints, I might need your help with something off the books."

He snickered, like he knew what I meant.

"No problem at all. Love doing off-the-book shit on occasion."

59

I loved her.

I loved her. I loved her so much.

I spoke to Kelly on the phone and told her what I told Frank.

"I don't know what Trevor thinks he's doing, but you should stay alert too. I've never been approached like that before. At court, yes, but never near my home."

"Yeah, we need to let Graves know. And by the way, I do know you liked Celeste, so I'm sorry about her death."

"Liked her? She was Arthur's girl and we go back, but I never knew her that well."

"Alexander. I saw how you looked at her. There was definitely something there. The way you two hugged."

"I—"

"Let me finish. All I'm trying to say is I don't give a shit if there was. Let's leave it at that."

"You think something was going on because I was there when she died?"

"Not just that. Again, I don't really know, and I don't care. I would never say anything if you did. I'm your partner."

"There was nothing between us, Kelly," I told her bluntly.

The lies were getting to be too easy.

"Okay. Okay, Alex."

"Keep alert. The detectives are here so I got to get with them. Have a good weekend."

"See you next week."

I disconnected. I felt empty, even a bit sick to my stomach. Thought I might really vomit.

Detectives Paul Bowman and Sheila Brown showed up. They talked to the doctor and then me. They agreed to go to the house.

"We should see if we can find a cell or info that can lead us to next of kin," Bowman said. "We'll secure the house and put the keys on the book as personal property."

"Appreciate it."

"Yeah, it'll keep us busy for a little bit just in case there's a call to respond to a real homicide. We want to get through this day is all."

"I can relate," I said.

Frank and the two detectives followed me to the house. They couldn't find anything related to next of kin but did take her cell phone. Frank bagged the narcotics, but not her works.

"I'll try to get a rush if we're able to recover any latent prints off the bag or zips," Frank told me.

"Thanks, man."

We all left. Bowman locked up. I thanked everyone again and drove home.

When I got home, I broke down like I never had before. The only thing I could think to do after was pour myself a hefty scotch and try to numb what I was feeling.

She was gone. I didn't believe it, couldn't.

I did not know if they would find next of kin and didn't like the idea of her body being taken to the morgue like she was nothing at all. What could I do. I had to let it play out the way I presented it. There was nothing I could do anymore. The more I drank, the more I wanted to see Trevor dead. That little punk of a kid, too. I knew she got that heroin from them. The heroin I left in the top dresser drawer had clear zips. She went through that so fast. Trevor had green zips. Yes, I'm sure there were several other dealers who also had them, but because of her connection with him through Arthur, I was sure that's where she went. She kept it from me is all. There was a part of me that didn't want Frank to recover any prints off the bag because that's when I'd step over the line with him and do what I really wanted to do.

60

I spoke to Graves from home on Monday and told her about the
encounter with Anthony. She said she would get with the defense attorney so she would advise her client that he was treading
on dangerous ground having an associate of his doing something
like that. I needed to let her know, but I still had my own plans,
that is, depending on if Frank was able to get anything off what he
recovered.

Spent most of that day getting drunk again. Had to stagger to the
local liquor store to restock on some booze. Frank called me when
I got back home.

I knew he could tell I had a little too much to drink when he
asked, "You're not at work, are you?"

"At home. I took leave."

"Getting started a bit early then?"

"That obvious?"

"A bit. Yeah."

"Relaxing at home is all."

"I can relate. I do that kind of relaxing a lot. Listen, they could only get partial prints off the bag and a few of the zips. Most of them were smudged, but all of them not enough to get an ID. Sorry."

"No worries. I appreciate you trying."

"So what did you have in mind?"

"The more I think about it the more I don't want to get you involved."

"I can decide for myself. I'm there for ya."

"Okay. I want to find that kid, Anthony. The one from the search warrant at Bull's and the one that approached me."

"And when you find him?"

"I want to put the fear of God in him, maybe more, but I'm only sayin' the 'maybe more' part because I'm a bit drunk."

"You might want to wait until you sober up then."

"I will be by this evening."

"I'm with you, brother. I'll get an address. I still have his info from the search warrant."

"You sure about this? I can do it ten ninety-nine."

"No. I'm in."

"Okay. He can't come up to us like that. I also know Celeste probably got that shit from him, and it may have been a bad batch on purpose."

"That's assuming a lot, brother. She more than likely just went overboard. Too much. Happens all the time."

"Whatever the case, he made it personal when he came up to me."

"I'm good with that part and I agree. I'll get back to you in a little while when I get his info."

"Thanks, Frankie."

"You got it."

I stopped drinking scotch and switched to coffee.

A couple of hours later, in the early evening, Frank got back to me. Said he got a good address and he'd pick me up. Probably thought I was still drunk. Admittedly, I was still light-headed, but not drunk. I was good to go. I dressed down, dark blue jeans, black half-zip sweatshirt, and an old black winter coat.

When I stepped in the car he said, "It's in Southeast, just off Martin Luther King. Don't know if he'll be there, though."

"I'm betting he will be. Nothing to do on a Monday."

It was an older four-story brick apartment building. The double glass front door was jimmied open.

"I love buildings like this," Frank said.

Anthony's apartment was on the second floor. We took the stairs. There was the usual litter along the way. We passed a young buck on his way down.

"Whoop. Whoop," he called out like a siren.

A warning to whoever might be hanging out in the stairwell above us that the police were in the building. Frank shook his head. It was common and something we were both used to.

We found his unit on the second floor. Frank stood to the left of the door, and I was on the right. I knocked hard three times.

"Who's there?" a female voice questioned.

"Police," I said. "We got a call about a burglary here."

"There was no burglary here. You have the wrong apartment."

"Who is that?" we heard a voice that sounded like Anthony ask.

I stepped to the side more so he couldn't see me through the peephole.

"Ma'am," Frank began. "We need to make sure you're okay. Please open the door."

"There ain't nothin' going on in here," the male voice said.

"We're not going to leave until we know the girl inside is okay. We'll get the fire department here to pry the door open if we have to. Just need to know she's safe."

"Shit. Fucking police."

"Let me see your badge and ID at the peephole," the female said.

"Of course," Frank said.

"Why you ask that? We don't have to open the door."

He got his wallet out and showed the badge with the identification. I noticed his index finger covered part of his name.

"You're getting us worried here. I'll call the fire department then."

I heard the chain lock come off from inside and then the bolt being unlatched.

"Fuck this shit. I'll be in the bedroom."

She opened the door.

She was a rail of a girl, maybe mid-twenties. A little attractive.

"Everything okay in here?" Frank asked. "Does that guy belong here?"

"Yes, he's my boyfriend."

"We got a call for a burglary in progress and happened to be in the area so we took it. We need to notebook your name and your boyfriend and then we'll be on our way."

Frank got out his notebook.

"My name is Tania Freedmont."

Frank wrote it down.

"We'll need to talk to your boyfriend, please."

"That is not necessary. I didn't call the police."

"Just give him a call and we'll be on our way."

She seemed agitated but then called out, "Anthony, come back here please."

"Shit, Tania. What now?"

He came to the door. I pushed my way in.

"What are you doing?" Tania asked like she was afraid.

Anthony tried to run back to the other room, but I grabbed him by the collar.

"You about to get in a lot of trouble, Officer," he said.

Frank entered and closed the door behind him.

"We need a word with your boyfriend, Tania. He got himself into a mess of trouble."

I pushed him toward the living room and sat his ass down on a wooden chair from a small round dining table near the kitchen.

"You sit over there, Tania," Frank told her, directing her to the other wooden chair at the table.

"Call the police, girl."

"I don't think you'll want to do that. Then we'll have to take you in," I told him.

"Where's your warrant?"

"Shut the fuck up. Now it's my turn, little man."

"You can't do this," Tania said.

"You want us to arrest him, or you want to keep quiet?" Frank advised her firmly.

"I know you're the one that sold that shit to Artie's girl."

"I don't know what you're talkin' about."

"You sure as hell do know what I'm talking about. Where do you keep it?"

"You crazy, man. I got rights. I'm gonna call the police and sue your asses."

"Now you sound like your man Trevor. Artie's girl OD'd because of you."

"You sit tight," Frank told the girl. "I'll find his shit."

"Hey, you got no warrant to be searchin' here. You can't do that."

I slapped him hard on the side of his head, almost knocking him out of his chair.

"Fuck your rights. You started this shit when you threatened me. Now I'm gonna finish it. I can go much harder if you want."

He bows his head, shaking it in disbelief.

"And calling the police after we leave—who do you think they're gonna believe? I already told the prosecutor about you coming up to me and following me. But you go ahead if you want. See what the fuck happens."

"Anthony, what's going on here?" his girl asked nervously. "What did you do? You promised me you were out."

"You seem like a good girl, Tania. When we leave you'd do well to kick his sorry ass out of here. He's just going to bring you down with him."

She started to tear up. I was already off the edge. I didn't much care.

He started to get fidgety, moving his hands along his thighs. He was wearing a white T-shirt and blue jeans. Didn't look like he had anything in his waist area or pockets. It didn't take Frank long to return with two large baggies. One full with dime bag zips and the other with what looked like a couple of ounces of coke.

"Bing," he said, smiling.

"Well, what do ya know."

"Damn you, Anthony."

"Shit" was all he said.

"Musta taken you a long time to package these dime bags with heroin," Frank told him.

"You gonna get me killed."

"That's the lifestyle you live," I said back.

I lifted him up by the scruff of the neck and his feet almost left the ground.

"What we're doing here is my message to you, not Trevor. He's already got a lot to worry about."

I pushed him back hard and he toppled over the chair, his head almost hitting the edge of the round table.

"I ever see you again, it'll be a lot more than this here. Understand?"

Didn't say anything, just sat up on the floor.

"You hear me?"

"Yeah, I hear you."

"You mind if I take that CVS bag over there?" Frank asked Tania.

She shook her head.

Frank grabbed a plastic CVS bag off the round table and placed the two large baggies in it.

"I'm done shopping," Frank said.

We walked out, closed the door. We both could hear her screaming at the top of her lungs at Anthony as we walked along the hallway toward the stairs.

61

I snapped. Nothing was the same anymore. I was no different from
Officer Bobby and deserved the same fate. I turned to the other
side, and there was no way back home. *What have I done?* Damn, I
missed Celeste so much. I knew then that she was not good for me,
but I couldn't stop. I was consumed by her. The only thing that consumed me now was the memory of her.

The grand jury indicted Trevor for the murders of Arthur and
Chris Doyle. The trial would be set and that would be the end of
him. I held him responsible for Celeste's death. He peddled death.
I wanted to request being transferred back to Narcotics. I felt that
I would make more of a difference there and get rid of people like
Trevor, Bull, and Anthony. Working with someone like Marr would
be great too. Most of the cases we picked up here were nothing but
drug-related shootings anyway. I could've cared less about everyone
killing each other. Why waste our time on that?

The days passed like nothing. On December 31 all of us, except
for the detectives who were scheduled for daywork, sat around the
office and waited for the clock to turn. We had our CDU riot

gear with us. All the higher-ups seriously expected the lights to go out at the stroke of midnight. For the world to shut down and go dark. Looters would run rampant and tear everything down. Let it happen. Please. Maybe it would bring on the Second Coming and God Himself would clean up the mess. I was certainly hoping and ready for it.

Seemed like an eternity sitting there and waiting, but the new year finally came around. And nothing. We waited and waited, like it was meant to happen, but again, absolutely nothing. Most of us sat there and shook our heads, like we realized how ridiculous this was.

"Can we go home now?" I heard Jac say on the other side of the office.

"I wish," the sarge grumbled, "but we're stuck here for the remainder."

"Bunch of shit," another detective said.

"You're all getting OT," Kelly began. "So stop crying."

"Still a bunch of shit."

I stayed out of it. I had nothing to say. Didn't even want to go home. It would be too depressing.

"I'm hungry," Kelly told me.

"I'm not leaving here."

"No, I have food in the fridge."

She pulled herself out of the chair and walked to the other room. Came back a couple of minutes later with a Tupperware dish that looked like it had lasagna in it. She sat down, grabbed a plastic fork from her drawer.

"You want some? I have more than enough."

"Naw, I'm good. Thanks."

I fell asleep at my desk, head cradled in my crossed arms. I woke up to the sound of the daywork detectives coming in and turning on the lights. Lot of the detectives were sleeping or out of the office at one of their spots sleeping. Lot of grumbles from the ones that were here. The daywork crew would be working a double too. I was damn happy no one got themselves murdered. I was ready to leave and go to my pathetic apartment and sleep the day away.

When I got home, I listened to my mother's scornful messages. There were six of them. It was a bad day for her again. She asked about Richard in every voice mail. I wanted to shoot the damn answering machine. Instead, I stripped down and fell into bed. Didn't find sleep, though, so I got up and drank whiskey until I was spinning. I planted myself on the sofa and must have passed out. When I woke up it was close to dark. I thought about calling someone for company, for sex, but there was no one to call. I hated self-pity, but I was stuck in that state because of how I fell. Every piece of this was entirely my fault.

Later the next morning, I called my mom back.

"Hello," she answered like she was on meds.

"Hi, Mom. How are you today?"

"Not so good, son. I'm so worried about Richard. Did you find anything out?"

"Mom, I have to tell you something and it might be difficult, but you need to know."

"Tell me what?"

"There is no Richard, Mom."

"What do you mean?"

"I mean he's not real."

"Of course he's real."

"No, Mom. He's in your head. It might be the medication or it might be your dementia, but he's not real. I'll talk to the doctor."

"Stop it, Alexander. You're scaring me."

"You need to know. I'm sorry."

"But the nurses know him."

"Sometimes the nurses tell you what you want to hear to make you happy. Please let this go. You'll be okay. Everything will get better if you just let it go. I promise."

"No. It has to be real."

"I'm sorry, Mom. I love you. Okay? You have to move on from this."

She didn't respond. I heard what sounded like sobbing. I felt terrible for having to make all that up, but I had to because her mind was not forgetting. I just prayed this wouldn't set her off into some serious state.

"Mom?"

"I'll be okay, Alexander," she answered like she was resigned to the lie I had to tell. "Tell Abigail to call me soon. I can't remember when we last spoke."

"I will."

Fuck me and how this brain of mine worked. She would soon forget. She would.

Two months passed like a fog over me. The trial date was set. Jury selection was made, and there we were—me, Frankie, Kelly, Caine, and Jac, along with a few other witnesses. Took three days. Don't need to go into it. The jury came back after only a couple of hours. He was found guilty, and the judge set another date for sentencing.

Two days later, I set up an interview with him at DC Jail. I needed to get with him face-to-face, and since he agreed, I knew he wanted to get with me too. Tomorrow would be the day.

62

I walked through the main entrance to DC Jail, secured all my shit in a lockbox with one of the COs, and was escorted to a small interview room. I prayed that they wouldn't have a lockdown and I'd get trapped in there.

The room had two wooden chairs on either side of a shiny rectangular metal table. Trevor was escorted in by a CO. The CO left and locked the heavy door behind him.

Trevor was wearing a white T-shirt, beltless jail-brand orange pants, and slip-on navy blue sneakers. He was also wearing glasses. He sat down on the wooden chair across from me.

"Glasses," I said.

He didn't come back with anything.

After a few seconds of just gritting on me he said, "You finally get up enough courage to meet?"

"Courage? You think you scare me?"

"Yeah, I think you should be scared."

"Make your move, Trev. Let's see how far that gets you."

He smiled like he knew he could get to me if he wanted to.

Didn't worry me, though. I almost wanted him to, because I'd love nothing more than to beat him down. I knew I could.

"I know what you done," he said.

"You were a blessing to me when you came into the picture. I hate people like you, the ones who think they have a kingdom to rule over. You were meant to fall, and I'm happy I could make that happen."

I leaned over the table, closer to him, like I wanted to give him a chance to make a move.

"I hold you responsible for Celeste's death and Arthur's. You're going to get sentenced and then transferred to a federal prison, where you'll eventually die. I do hope you live a long time, though, knowing you'll never be sitting with those girls again, acting like the VIP you think you are."

"We all gonna eventually die. Where it happens don't mean shit to me."

I straightened myself back on my chair.

"You think you're gonna get some kind of satisfaction outta meeting me now?"

"Yeah, it does sort of make me happy. Seeing you sitting there with those silly glasses," I told him.

"You nothin' but a piece of dirty shit, just like that Officer Bobby. Look at where he ended up."

"Ha, I'm way fucking worse."

He stood up straight. For a second I thought he was going to make a move, but he simply walked to the door and knocked. The CO opened it.

"We done here," he told the CO.

The door opened and he walked out.

I waited for a bit until I knew he was not in the hall and then I walked out. I felt nothing. I thought I would after meeting with him, but I was empty. It didn't mean anything to me. Didn't know why I came.

Not even an hour after I got back to work, Kelly and I picked up a
shooting. Just like that. Like God was telling me something because
it was nothing but a corner boy rivalry. Drive by. The passenger
stuck half his body out the window and opened up on five other
corner boys hanging at 9th and O Streets NW. It was a TEC-9. Two
shot, one dead and the other in critical condition. There were two
witnesses. One wouldn't talk. The other did and gave us a name.
Kelly and I responded to Howard, but it didn't look good for the
other kid. The doctor allowed us into his emergency room to try
to obtain information about the shooter. Two witnesses are better
when it comes to writing up an affidavit for an arrest warrant.

The kid was fifteen. I didn't feel sorry for him. He was dead
when he was born.

He took one in the stomach, one to the chest, and one in the
right upper thigh. Shattered his femur. He was doped up and didn't
feel anything, but he did know he would probably not make it and
so he gave us a name.

Deon Duncan.

Good to go.

I drafted the affidavit. It was still early in the day, so we decided
to grab sandwiches from one of our spots on New York Ave. before
going to the Nickel to get the warrant. We parked in the small lot
on the side of the old deli, a cinder block wall separating us from
another building.

I stepped from the driver's side and was about to lock the car
after Kelly when I noticed the tinted-out older Ford pull in slowly.
My Spidey sense tingled. The car was moving toward us a bit too
close for comfort.

The Ford stopped. That's when I saw Anthony sitting on the
passenger side. Window down. Gun drawn. I reached for my own
gun, but it was like I saw him stretch his arm out, gripping a Glock,
both slow and fast.

He fired twice. I felt a sharp pain burn through my left shoulder. I got my gun out. He kept firing, but even at that close range his shots were off. I heard the rounds ring by my left ear. The driver's-side window of our car shattered. I saw Kelly move to take cover by the deli wall and she fired her weapon several times, hitting the middle of the windshield and the driver's side. I don't know how many she fired.

Anthony tucked his head back in and the car sped off across the parking lot. Both Kelly and I opened up on the rear of the vehicle. Our rounds went through the rearview window.

The car suddenly turned to the left and smashed into the cinder block wall just before the exit to New York Avenue. I noticed Kelly drop her magazine and slap in another from her pouch secured to her belt.

The passenger-side door swung open, and Anthony bolted toward the rear of the deli.

"You okay?"

"My left shoulder" was all I said, and I ran after Anthony.

Kelly was just behind me and to my left. My adrenaline was pumping. I felt no pain, just warmth from the blood trailing down my arm.

"Driver's down, driver's down," Kelly shouted. "Looked like a head shot."

I didn't respond. Too amped.

I heard Kelly on the radio: "Man with a gun. Shots fired," and then giving our location and where Anthony was running.

Anthony was hoofing it across New York Avenue, nearly getting himself hit by a couple of honking cars. We pursued him and were also nearly hit.

He made it to the other side and down the block, where he cut left into an alley. He wasn't running fast. Maybe he was injured? Got hit by one of our rounds?

He did.

I saw little puddles of blood along the sidewalk as I ran toward the alley.

When we made our turn into the cut, he was on the right side, running a bit slower. No one else in the alley.

We were gaining on him.

"Stop, Anthony, or we'll shoot." Kelly huffed to get the words out.

He didn't stop.

I heard shots ring out from Kelly's weapon. I immediately fired after. That's when Anthony stopped and turned to face us, something like a showdown. He looked like a pint-sized version of Bull when he faced off with us. The same fearless smirk. He opened fire, but only aiming at me. I fired back and so did Kelly. He buckled a bit but didn't fall. I saw more flashes from his gun. Odd, but I didn't hear the gunshots. I suddenly felt intense pressure, like my chest caved in on me, and sharp, burning pain in my left upper thigh. I was hit. Several times, like he made every one of his shots count that time.

Anthony fell to his side against a chain-link fence, at a distance where he was becoming blurred.

My legs gave out under me. Lost all muscle control and went down hard. The fall felt like a lifetime.

It was difficult to breathe.

Kelly was there over me. Didn't know what she was saying. She was mouthing something, but her lips just moving with no words that I could hear. I felt the pressure of one of her hands on my chest, but no pain.

Losing my breath. So damn hard. Even harder to stay conscious. I fought it as best as I could, but then realized what was happening, and it was like I resigned myself to the inevitable. I felt both clear and already long gone.

"I'm sorry." Barely came out of my mouth for some reason, but probably more like a gurgle.

"I know." I finally heard her, whispered back. I knew she understood what I said. Her voice was soft and comforting. It was like she knew everything at that point. Then she removed her hand from me, got back on the radio, and called out—

It was cold. And then, a comforting deep darkness, like a heavy blanket that fell over me.

It was sudden.

David Swinson is a retired police detective from the Metropolitan Police Department in Washington, DC, having been assigned to Major Crimes. Swinson is the author of the critically acclaimed Frank Marr Trilogy—*The Second Girl, Crime Song,* and *Trigger,* and the standalone *City on the Edge.* He lives in upstate New York.